I0779150

HENRY J. PARKS
THE CRYSTAL BLADES

BOOK ONE

KYLLINGMARK

CHAPTER 1

Henry bolted upright in bed, drenched in cold sweat. Sitting frozen for a moment, he fought to get the thoughts out of his head as feelings of dread flooded his mind. Images of death and the people he loved being torn apart by some invisible force rammed into his thoughts. Darkness closed in upon him, and shadowy grey figures approached from the corners of his room.

Suddenly, the alarm went off on the clock on his dresser. It read 3 AM, and flashed brightly as he hit it, and reached over to open his bedroom window. But even the warm summer air billowing out his curtains couldn't stop his shivering.

He dressed quickly, and went downstairs to meet his dad before the morning chores. Yet the dark feelings from the nightmares left a tension in his stomach he couldn't shake. It had stolen his appetite, and he couldn't even touch the toast covered with strawberry jam his dad had waiting for him. Instead he grabbed the coffee pot, filled his thermos, and slipped quietly out the door, heading for the field.

A skinny fifteen year old country boy with dirty blonde hair and dark green eyes, there was nothing special about Henry Parks. Yet, to his credit, he never complained of the daily grind. Working with his dad taught him the importance of hard work, and he realized the success of the farm depended a great deal on him. They were not a big operation, and everyone pitched in to help.

"What's up with Max?" Henry thought as he crossed the fence and started into the field.

His Blue Heeler was acting very strange this morning. "He never barks that much to get them moving."

Suddenly, he felt a searing heat on the back of his neck.

Turning towards the woods, he was shocked to see a blinding fireball shoot across the dark, early-morning sky, illuminating the field before crashing through the trees. It hit with a loud thud, shaking the ground, and sending the cows scattering. He ran to the edge of the field to find a line of scorched branches and smoldering grass. Climbing through the barbed wire fence, he stomped out small grass fires as he moved towards the object. It was half-buried in the dirt, but the heat was so intense he couldn't get within fifty feet. Max barked incessantly as Henry did his best to calm him. He made sure there was no further danger of fire before heading back.

Max returned to work rounding up the frightened animals, but it wasn't easy, and Henry could tell his dog was still upset.

They were about a half-hour late when he shut the barn door.

"Henry Jacob Parks!" his father shouted as he donned his milking apron. "Where were you? I've done half your work this morning!"

"Sorry, Dad; something spooked the cows. I think it was a fox or something," he lied.

It wasn't like Henry to hide things from his parents, but for some reason he didn't want anyone to know of his discovery--at least not yet. Fortunately, the milking went well and his father couldn't stay mad at him for long anyway. He knew his son worked hard.

After the morning chores, Henry ran back to investigate the strange object. The sun was just rising above the tree line as he made his way through the fields still wet with morning dew. Whatever it was it would be easier to see in the daylight, and should have cooled enough by now to get a closer look. He followed the blackened trees and broken limbs leading to a deep trench. The grass was burned in a wide circle around a still-smoldering center. Henry squatted to examine the brightly glowing object, about twice the size of a basketball, embedded in the ground. Grabbing a broken branch, he pried the hot globe from the dirt. He removed his leather work coat, wrapped it in the thick leather shell, and headed across the field for the barn. It was heavy and awkward to carry and the heat radiating from the globe was penetrating. He had to switch arms twice.

His father was in the calf barn washing down the stalls when Henry came quietly through the sliding door. He set the object on the cold concrete floor of the milking parlor, and carefully rolled it out of his coat. An eerie orange glow emanated from the object, reflecting off the small, single-pane windows lining the parlor.

Henry was excited for his find, but decided to keep it to himself for the moment. He grabbed a hay fork leaning against the stall, scooped it up, and deposited it behind a pile of rocks and broken concrete in the yard behind the barn. His coat was still warm, and the leather stiff when he put it back on and headed for the house.

Hopefully his mom wouldn't notice the circular burn across his back. He didn't want to explain the events of the morning.

He had difficulty holding down his enthusiasm as he rushed upstairs. He loved astronomy, and finding something like this was the most exciting thing ever. His sister Kirsten was just coming out of her room as he came up the stairs.

"Good morning," she said sleepily. "What did you do to your coat?"

Kirsten was two years younger, but she was already tall, with long blonde hair. Henry trusted his sister, and there were few things they didn't share.

"Is mom taking us to school this morning?" he asked, ignoring her question as he opened his bedroom door.

"Yes! I have band practice after school, and that way I won't have to carry my saxophone on the bus."

"Ok, but hurry and get ready! I have something to show you before we go."

"I think it's a meteorite," Henry said as he led the way behind the barn. "I can't believe one landed on our property. This is awesome."

"Did you tell Mom and Dad about it?"

"Not exactly," Henry replied a little sheepishly. "Dad was upset about the cows, so I told him an animal spooked them."

Kirsten's eyes narrowed as she shot Henry an accusing glance before returning to examining the stone. But it was still too hot to touch, so they decided to leave it until after school.

His school day went better than he ever thought it could, even though it was a big test day. Henry was an average student who studied hard and tried out for sports. He wasn't much good at either, and math was his worst subject. They had been studying Trigonometry for nearly two months, but he had yet to grasp the concepts, let alone remember the formulas. But today he breezed right through.

When they got home from school that evening, they found their dad in an especially good mood. He said the day's milking had set a new record. But, in spite of the festive mood, Henry couldn't keep his mind off the meteorite.

"I have some studying to do," he said after wolfing down his dinner. "I'll come down later if you and Dad are still up."

"Me too," Kirsten said, following her brother's lead. "I need to practice my sax."

"Alright," his mother replied. "Your father is tired anyway."

"That's right, kids," his father answered. "It was a big day for us, and hopefully tomorrow will be just as productive. This is a good sign that things are looking up! You go on and get some rest. We'll see you in the morning."

"Thanks, Dad," Henry replied, running in front of his sister up the creaky staircase.

"What are you planning?" Kirsten whispered. She grabbed him by his shirttail just as they reached the top.

"I'll bring it to my bedroom where we can see it better. It must be cool enough by now."

Henry used his bedroom window like some people use a door. He often jumped to a nearby maple tree, and headed for his favorite fishing hole. But tonight his destination was different. He quietly worked his way around the house towards the barn.

The sound of his mother washing dishes, and Kirsten practicing her saxophone in the background drifted across the yard. The cool night air felt good against his face as he rounded the corner past the calf stall. The herd was somewhere in the field for the night. His dad let them graze on summer nights to feed on the fresh grass. There were no dangerous animals around in their area, and the cows seemed to give more milk this way.

The orange glow was gone when he arrived. He poked it with a stick, making sure it was safe to touch. Rolling it into an old shirt he had brought along, he held it out away from his body by the tail of the shirt as he headed back for the house.

It was heavier than it looked though, so he tucked it under his arm like a football, and began running for his room. He didn't think of it at the time, but running those hundred yards or so took surprisingly little effort. He climbed the tree, and jumped onto the roof below his bedroom window without even breaking a sweat.

Kirsten heard him coming, and met him at his dresser. The light from the desk lamp revealed a hardened crust of mud and clay that had baked on when it hit.

"I'll get a brush and bucket from the bathroom," she said.

Unfortunately, after some hard scrubbing, it was apparent this was not a pretty rock.

"Bummer," Henry said disappointedly.

He was hoping it would be something they could sell. But instead of being shiny, it was dark in color with a crusty and hard blackened shell. He turned towards his bed for just a moment, but when he did, it rolled off his dresser. The sound echoed through the house as they both held their breath.

"Are you guys ok up there?" Mom asked from the bottom of the stairs.

"We're ok, Mom," Kirsten replied as she stuck her head out his door. "Henry just dropped his dumbbell."

"Alright," she replied, "but tell your brother to be more careful. I don't want him knocking the plaster down."

Henry picked up the rock, and secured it with a rolled up t-shirt. Kirsten looked down, and a piece about the size of a marble had broken off. It was clear, and warm to the touch as she picked it up.

"What do you think this is?" she asked, putting it under the light. "It glows a little and is such a pretty blue color."

"I've never seen anything like it," he replied, taking the fragment from her as he plopped onto his bed, "but it looks really cool, doesn't it? Maybe it's valuable after all, or maybe we can make something out of it."

Kirsten agreed before leaving for her bedroom. It was getting late, and she needed to practice her sax a little more before turning in. Henry, however, was feeling more encouraged now. He just couldn't believe their good fortune. He admired the piece a little longer before reaching up and slipping the blue crystal object into the pocket of his work shirt hanging on the bedpost.

So many good things had happened. First, he found the meteorite, and then he got an A in math. Two things that had never happened before. It had been a really good day.

"Henry," his Dad said quietly as he opened his bedroom door. "Are you going to sleep all day?"

Henry shook himself awake. It was already ten minutes after three, and he had slept through his alarm. Jumping out of bed and into his work clothes, he rushed down into the warm kitchen light. As usual, Dad had a piece of toast with some butter and jam waiting for him, along with a hot cup of coffee. This was their regular routine, and it worked well because Dad liked to let Mother sleep if he could.

He knew that she and Kirsten would be up later, making breakfast and getting lunches together for the day.

Henry was hungry, and wolfed down the toast before quietly slipping out the door behind his father, making sure the screen door didn't bang behind them. Henry and his dog Max worked as a team. He whistled directions, and Max worked the stray cows towards the barn.

He felt especially good that morning. It was his first good night's sleep in a long time, and the early morning air felt refreshing as he took a deep breath. Then he spotted one of the cows wandering towards the creek bed.

"New heifers just don't get with the program," he groaned.

Even worse, Max was working the far side of the field, so Henry had to chase this one himself. He jogged several hundred yards along the fence line bordering the creek where he could get into position to cut it off. His sudden presence startled the young cow, and it made a beeline for the herd and the barn just as planned.

He started following when he heard a sound. The moon was almost full as it lit the field just enough to see a dark shape moving through the brush along the bank on the other side of the creek.

"Another stray," Henry thought to himself as he climbed through the fence. "Dad's not going to like this if I'm late two days in a row. I wonder how it got over there anyway. I hope the fence isn't down somewhere, or I'll be chasing these all morning."

He was just about to cross the shallow creek when he heard a deep growl.

"Oh no!" he thought, instantly freezing in his tracks. "That's no stray!"

The broad head and thick neck of a strange looking animal pushed through the tall grass. It was heavy and muscular, with silvery hair. Henry froze, hoping he hadn't been spotted. The moonlight glistened off the beast's long claws, three on each paw, as it stood on its hind legs and looked around.

He knew he was in trouble as it turned towards him, opening its lips in a wicked smile, revealing rows of razor sharp teeth. Henry swallowed hard, knowing his only defense was the stick he carried to encourage the cows. It seemed of little use now. The creature dropped down, and moved to the edge of the water directly towards Henry. Its eyes glowed a dark red as it squared its shoulders and crouched, its muscles rippling in the moonlight.

It would be on him in a matter of seconds. His heart raced as he considered his chances. He could run for the barn, but he was no athlete, and there was little chance he would even make the fence, let alone outrun this beast.

His moment of decision ended quickly. Even if he had wanted to run, it was too late as the beast made its move. The dark silhouette of a powerful animal leapt high into the air, and spread out its limbs to engulf Henry's slender figure with ripping fury. Instinctively, Henry raised his arms to protect himself, even though it was a useless response.

The beast was mere inches from his throat when his spindly arms collided with the animal's thick muscular chest. But instead of Henry's being shredded into little pieces, the impact sent the creature careening over his head, tearing through the barbed wire fence before it rolled to a stop in the middle of the field.

The beast jumped to its feet with a growl, and shook its head as if in disbelief. Blood oozed from its ripped flesh where the barbed wire had done its damage. Henry leapt the creek, and started running, hoping to make it to the barn for help. The animal pursued, swiping at his legs and back as he ran.

It was nearly on top of him as he approached the edge of their property. There the creek spilled into a deep gully, ultimately joining a river that ran through the wilderness. He was quickly running out of real-estate when he noticed the old tire swing his dad hung from the limb of a large oak tree.

The hot breath of the beast smelled of death as Henry jumped with all his might, grabbing the rope, and swinging high into the air. The animal couldn't stop its momentum as it sailed over the edge of the gully, still grasping at Henry with its sharp claws. In the moonlight, he could see its body disappear into the darkness below, followed by several loud crashes.

Henry landed running as fast as he could, afraid to even look over his shoulder, thinking the beast could pounce on him any second but it was over…for now.

"Wow!" he thought as he joined Max at the barn. "What just happened? Did I really just outrun that thing? I've never seen anything like it. It wasn't a bear or lion. It was definitely something more."

Standing in the cool morning air, he felt a pulsation coming from his shirt pocket. Reaching in, he pulled out the blue, marble-sized piece of meteorite he had put there the night before. It still glowed slightly, and felt warm to the touch. Then it began to dawn on him. What if this wasn't just a piece of space rock? What if it had special powers?

"Did this thing just save my life?" he wondered excitedly. "I've never had that kind of strength before, or been able to run like that. I need to find out what else it does."

He found the morning chores unusually easy. He cleaned and scraped the barn, and was done in less than half the time, but stayed in the barn anyway so as not to raise suspicions until it was time to come in for breakfast. He was still not ready to let anyone in on his secret.

"In here, quick," he whispered to his sister as he caught her coming up the stairs. "You're never going to believe what happened this morning."

She sat beside him on the bed as he opened a large ornate old book he had found in the family library. When they were little, their dad used to read to them from this very book. A book filled with pictures of strange, mythical beasts, and stories of harrowing battles.

"See this picture," he said, pointing to a drawing of a large beast with three claws and red eyes. "You may think I'm crazy, but I saw one of these this morning. It attacked me in the field."

"Come on," Kirsten said, quickly becoming annoyed. "You can't fool me with your stories anymore. I'm thirteen; not eight."

"I'm not kidding," he said seriously. "I really saw this thing."

She looked at him closely.

"Are you sure it wasn't a big dog or something?"

"I know what I saw, and it wasn't a dog or something. It was this creature!" he insisted, pointing to the picture.

"Zender," She said, leaning over and reading the caption under the drawing. "But it's a fictional creature. It's not real! Dad read that story to us--remember, when we spent the weekend visiting Uncle James and Aunt Lori, when we were all hanging around the campfire?"

"Oh yeah, I remember that," Henry replied, closing the book. "But he never finished telling us the story because we were too freaked out."

"I think you should tell Dad," Kirsten said. "If something like this really exists, he would know what to do."

"I can't tell him. He won't believe me any more than you did. But I need to do something, or I'm never going out in that field again. I know--I'll tell him people have been seeing bears around here. Then he'll let me carry my pistol when I bring the cows in."

Kirsten wasn't sure hiding things from their parents was a good idea, but she trusted her big brother. She agreed to keep the Zender story between them, even though it did seem fantastic. If he said he saw a Zender, she believed him.

"What are you doing with this?" Kirsten asked as she kicked the bag the meteorite was stashed in.

"I'm going to take it out to Dad's workshop tonight. He isn't doing any projects there right now, and I know he won't mind my using it. But just to be safe, I'll wait until later tonight. I want to see if I can make something out of it. Maybe I'll even try making you a necklace or something."

Kirsten laughed as she left his room, and headed downstairs. It was time for school, and she wanted to be on time.

Dad was genuinely concerned about the bear story Henry brought home from school that evening. He called several neighbors to see if they had seen anything, or had any problems. That worried Henry some, but to his relief, one neighbor confirmed a sighting of a large animal running through their field towards the mountain. That was enough for Mr. Parks. They were going on a weekend hunting trip.

CHAPTER 2

Henry's dad made arrangements with some friends to take over milking for the weekend. He also kept Henry and Kirsten home from school that Friday to join him on the hunting trip. Though bears were not usually seen this low, he found some unusual tracks along the edge of his field that made him suspicious. However, they were unlike regular bear tracks. They were larger, with only three toes, and the evidence of long claws. He guessed it could be a bear that was wounded or maybe deformed somehow. Either way, it would be necessary to track the animal and destroy it before it got any of their cows.

"Have you packed the supplies yet?" Dad asked.
"I made enough to last a week," Mom answered. "But you had better be back by Sunday morning. Kirsten has a recital Sunday night. Maybe she should stay home."

"Mom," Kirsten protested, a little perturbed with her mother. "Dad said it was ok. We'll be back in time."

Kirsten was as much an outdoor person as her brother, and they both loved hunting and fishing. This time they were heading up Grace Mountain. It was the tallest in a long mountain range bordering the East side, running behind the city and along the edge of the wilderness. There were no defined paths or roads, so they loaded up two pack horses, and saddled three more. Kirsten hopped onto Poke-a-dot while Henry and his father mounted two sturdy trail horses. Poke-a-dot was Kirsten's favorite horse. She was white with yellow spots and a long flowing mane.

The mountain began several pastures over from their property, and that's where Mr. Parks picked up the trail. He was good at tracking, and taught his kids how to follow signs. They wound their way along over rough ground and past large boulders. The Zender's tracks were not easy to spot, but Mr. Parks managed to find enough to follow. They led to a large clearing on a bluff high above the valley divided by a large stream.

"This is a good place to set up camp," he said getting off his horse. "Henry, you water the horses while Kirsten and I unpack."

Kirsten pulled the food pack, and began setting up for dinner. Henry took the horses, two at a time, to the bank of the creek to water them. Poke-a-dot was last. She drank heartily as he patted her on the neck. Suddenly, her head came up from the water, and she backed up several steps.

"What's the matter girl?" he said, surveying the woods on the other side.

Henry held tight to Poke-a-dot's reigns as the brush rustled on the opposite side. A dark shape moved behind the tall grass. He froze, every muscle in his body tightening into a knot.

"Zender," he thought. He tried to yell for help, but nothing came out.

Then the grass parted, and a white-tailed doe came down to the water's edge to drink.

"Whew!" he exhaled. "You scared the crap out of me."

He rode to the campsite. Mr. Parks had driven stakes into the hard ground to hold the large tent they brought, and a few more for picketing the horses. Kirsten had made a fire. . It was moving towards evening now, with the sun dropping in the distance beyond the wilderness. A cool breeze blew down from the snow-covered peak as they set up some chairs, and relaxed to their mother's lasagna heated over an open fire.

"I think we should follow the creek up the mountain because the ground is so rocky here, and it's difficult to find tracks," Henry suggested. "Besides, the bear is likely to stay close to the water, and hunt game coming there to drink. I just saw a deer over there."

"Good thinking, son!" Dad replied. "What do you think, Kirsten?"

"I think we should be careful," she answered glancing at Henry. "Maybe it's not a bear. Maybe it's something worse."

"What could be worse than an ornery old bear?" Dad asked. "We just need to stay together, and keep our wits about us. Besides, you have a fine sidearm there that could stop a bull if need be."

Kirsten smiled weakly. She knew she needed to be brave, but Henry's Zender story was bothering her.

"We'll be alright!" Henry assured her as he threw another log on the fire. "Dad and I have hunted here before. You'll be safe with us."

Darkness settled in around their campsite as the bright orange flames flickered, lighting their faces and casting long shadows into the darkness. The horses had been fed, and were settled for the night. It was getting late, and they would need to start at first light.

Dad set the battery-powered light on a hook in the center of their tent before climbing into his sleeping bag. Kirsten and Henry unrolled theirs, and slid in too. Kirsten slept between her father and brother, where she felt the safest. An owl hooted in the distance as one of the horses snorted. It was a peaceful place to camp, and in a few minutes they were asleep.

Long sharp claws reached through the darkness, catching Henry by the ankle and pulling him through the side of the tent. He tried to scream, but couldn't as it attacked. Feebly, he struck at the large creature with his fists over and over again, but to no avail. The large paw clamped down tightly on his neck, dragging him helplessly along. He felt the ground for a weapon, and his hand landed on something hard and sharp. He plunged it into the beast's side. It instantly dropped him, and disappeared into the blackness.

"Henry, wake up!" his father said pushing against his shoulder. "You're having a bad dream. Man, you're making such a ruckus, I'm surprised you haven't woken your sister."

"Sorry, Dad," he whispered feeling queasy and sweaty.

"Go back to sleep and try to have a quiet dream could you?"

Henry rolled onto his side facing the tent. There was little chance of sleeping now.

"What if that thing is after me?" he thought. "Nobody has ever seen one until now. Why would it want me?"

He lay there for hours, listening to Mr. Parks' snoring and Kirsten's soft breathing before he finally dropped off to sleep again.

"Get up sleepy head!" Mr. Parks said stepping into the tent. "It's time for breakfast."

Kirsten had a campfire burning brightly and a pot of coffee brewing on the propane stovetop when Henry stumbled out of the tent. He helped his dad saddle the horses, and they all sat down to enjoy some breakfast.

"Food tastes better out here," Mr. Parks commented as she served up some scrambled eggs. "It's like you've never eaten breakfast before. I don't mean to say your mom's not a great cook, but your food is perfect."

Henry nodded between gulps as he shoveled another piece of bacon into his mouth.

"Thanks, Dad," she said, pouring herself some coffee.

There was a lot to do today, so breakfast would have to hold them for quite some time. Mr. Parks decided it would be best to leave the camp set up where they had it rather than move it up the mountain. After all, they had only one day to bag the animal, and he hadn't forgotten that Kirsten needed to be home the following morning.

They left the pack horses at the campsite, and headed up the mountain. Mr. Parks planned to make a wood frame from tree limbs tied together with rope once they got the bear. It would serve as a skid to drag it down to their camp. Any one of the horses they brought along could easily handle that.

As they were tracking, Henry kept thinking he should tell his dad about the beast, especially seeing how nervous Kirsten looked. He told himself that it didn't really matter if his dad knew what he was tracking wasn't a real bear. The result should be the same. Each of them carried powerful, long-range rifles as well as their side-arms. He had even made a blade from the meteorite the day before, and was keeping it in a leather sheath he wore on his belt. Not that he would need it, but he still kept thinking about the nightmare.

A shiver went up Henry's spine at the thought as they followed the creek towards a cascading waterfall. The roar increased as they approached.

"This is really pretty!" Kirsten exclaimed as Poke-a-dot dipped her head in the large pool of water for a drink. "We should come back with Mom next time."

"We'll have to leave the horses here for now," Mr. Parks said as he dismounted. "It's too hard to take them now, but we can come back for them when we get the bear."

They slung their weapons over their shoulders, and began the climb alongside the roaring waterfall, with Mr. Parks leading the way. It was slippery going. Finally after about thirty minutes, they crested a ridge surrounded by sheer rock cliffs ascending high above. The creek followed through the mountain and then disappeared around a bend several hundred yards away.

"Let's take a break for a minute," Mr. Parks said, sitting down on a large rock to catch his breath. "This feels more like work than fun."

But Henry was feeling especially energetic.

"I'll scout up ahead, and see if there are any fresh tracks."

"I'll go with him!" Kirsten exclaimed.

"Alright," their dad replied, "but don't go too far. I just need a few minutes, and then I'll be right behind you."

They made their way over fallen trees and boulders while Henry looked for tracks in the gravelly creek bank. Once they arrived at a turn in the creek, they both hopped up on a large rock to wave back to their father.

"Where'd he go?" Henry said. "I don't see him anywhere."

"I can't see him either," Kirsten replied anxiously stretching up on her tippy toes. "Let's go back and make sure he's ok."

"Alright, but I'm sure he's fine. He's probably just looking around."

They were almost half way back when a shot rang out. It was followed a few seconds later by another.

"Dad must have seen something," Henry exclaimed as he broke into a run.

In seconds, he was at the last spot they had seen their father with Kirsten close on his heels.

"Dad! Dad!" Kirsten shouted over the roaring water.

"You wait here," Henry said, spotting where their father had entered the heavy brush.

"I will not," she answered defiantly. "I'm going with you."

"Ok, but you had better keep up."

Once into the brush, it became apparent there was a well-defined game trail leading towards the steep granite mountain side. They moved rapidly, ducking under branches and over stumps, when suddenly the trail opened into a small clearing bordered by the rocky face.

"Over here!" Mr. Parks said in a low voice.

He was hunkered down behind a log, facing what appeared to be the entrance to a cave.

"Did you hit it?" Henry asked when they joined him.

"I think so, but I'm not sure we're dealing with a bear."

"What do you mean?" Henry said innocently.

"That thing didn't move like any bear I've seen," he answered, pointing back towards the creek. "You two had no sooner left when I heard some noise coming from the brush. I circled around where I could get a look at what it was. It was pacing you both as you were following the creek. I saw it come into a small opening and took my shot. I hit it in the back. It reared, and bolted towards that cave. I got off one more shot before it entered. I'm sure I hit it again, but it didn't even slow down. That animal is like nothing I've ever seen."

"What should we do?" Kirsten asked.

"I say we go in and get it!" Henry said boldly. "It's probably wounded, and we can take it down."

"That's the problem," Dad replied. "A wounded animal is way more deadly, and following it in there could be dangerous. But it's wrong to leave it suffer, so you two wait here, and I'll go in and finish it off."

"No way, Dad," they said in unison, "we're going with you."

Mr. Parks looked at his two children for a moment, realizing how much they'd grown. He didn't like the idea, but he saw a confidence he hadn't seen before.

"Ok, but you two stay close behind me. Turn on your flashlights, and have your pistols ready. I don't know what kind of an animal we're dealing with, but it's likely going to be scared and unpredictable, especially if it's wounded."

They entered through a single tunnel, taking several turns and proceeding slowly, freezing at the slightest sound. The light from their flashlights created eerie shadows as they inched their way along. Dad raised his hand, stopping them just as they rounded the final bend that opened into a large cavern. Kirsten and Henry joined their father, shining their lights in every direction. They spotted several other holes on the far side of the cavern.

"It's not in here," Mr. Parks said quietly. "It must have gone deeper. I'll take a look inside one of those while you two wait here."

"Dad," Henry protested, "I think we should go with you."

"No!" he replied firmly. "You wait here in case it gets past me, or comes out a different hole. They could be connected, and it should give you a good shot. Just get down behind those rocks over there, and wait."

Neither of them liked the idea of separating, but Mr. Parks was usually right about these things. He moved across the wide cavern, and disappeared into the hole farthest to the right, his flashlight illuminating the walls as he moved inside. Henry headed towards the large rock with Kirsten tight on his heels. They stepped around behind it to take up their position, when suddenly a section of the cave gave way, and Henry disappeared down a hole. Kirsten screamed, as she managed to grab a sharp outcropping, barely escaping her brother's fate.

About ten feet down, Henry dislodged a large rock that was precariously balanced on one side. It launched him deeper yet down the shaft, and blocked his return as it tipped over. He skidded to a stop as his flashlight tumbled past and rolled to the far side of what appeared to be another cavern. He crawled across the rocky surface, retrieved it, and began scanning the area for a way out.

"Are you alright?" Kirsten yelled down the hole.

"I think so!" he hollered back.

But he wasn't alright. His flashlight revealed bones scattered across the floor, and what looked like a place to bed down. His heart jumped into his throat as he realized he was in the Zender's lair. He looked around for another way out, but there wasn't one. Just then, the light from his flashlight flickered and went out, plunging him into total darkness. He banged it against his leg several times, relieved as it came back to life. But it revealed a stark fact: he wasn't alone. The dark red eyes of the beast looked down on him from a perch above. As he watched, it gave a low, guttural growl that sent shivers up his spine. He reached for the pistol strapped to his leg, only to discover it had been lost in the fall. He thought wildly of racing for the shaft and climbing up, but he knew it was only a panic move. There was no escape.

The Zender dropped to the floor with a heavy thud. Up above, Mr. Parks joined Kirsten, and together they shouted down the shaft. They called to Henry, but he couldn't answer.

His throat squeezed tight, making it difficult to even breathe. The animal's long claws clicked against the rock-covered floor as it approached. Henry braced himself for what surely would be his last moments. Memories of family and friends raced through his mind as the massive beast stood on its rear legs with its front legs out wide, revealing the three wicked looking claws on each huge paw. The beast had fresh scars from their encounter at the barbed wire fence. They were illuminated by Henry's flashlight, which he gripped tightly.

Suddenly his fear left, and a surge of power rose from deep inside his being. The beast lunged, claws ripping through his leather coat like butter. Henry grabbed it by the neck with both hands, and shoved the massive animal away. It tumbled to the ground, but immediately jumped back up and circled to Henry's left, snarling.

Mr. Parks had climbed down to the rock blocking the shaft, but it was too tight, and he couldn't get past. Above him, Kirsten sobbed uncontrollably.

Henry didn't hear them. He didn't feel the deep cuts across his shoulders, or the blood running down his arms. His focus was on a creature so evil it felt like darkness itself. Its red eyes penetrated his mind as it came around for what was likely the final assault.

Henry's pencil-thin body would be no match if it came at him again in full fury. As he stood there helplessly, he felt the handle of the blade he had made from the blue crystal snug in the leather sheath against his leg. He pulled it free just as the beast leapt.

The blade entered just above its broad left shoulder, penetrating deep into its neck. The animal froze in midair, its mouth full of sharp teeth stuck open. But instead of engulfing him, its sinister red eyes flowed into Henry's chest as its body changed from solid to a dark gaseous cloud, dissipating in the dim flashlight.

"What the…" Henry exclaimed, falling back into the cavern's wall.

He shook his head as he picked up the flashlight, and scanned the cavern. The creature was gone, but he didn't understand how. It was nowhere to be seen, but he still felt something was wrong. Something strange had happened to him. Something dark and powerful.

His mind returned to reality as he heard Mr. Parks calling from above. Stumbling over to the opening, he climbed several feet to where he could just make out his father's outline through the narrow opening in the rocks.

"Are you alright, son?" his distraught father shouted.
"I'm ok," Henry responded. "But the animal we were chasing is gone."

"Don't worry about that now! We need to get you out of there."

The rock was too big to move by hand, so his father ran outside to find something he could use for leverage. Kirsten climbed down where she could see part of her brother's face.

"Do you have a rope or anything?" he asked, "maybe I could climb up and help move the rock."

"All I have is the silver cord we found when we were helping Mom in the greenhouse." she said as she took off the cord she used as a belt from around her waist. "But I don't think it'll reach you. It's too short."

She lay flat against the rock, and dropped the silver cord down through the narrow opening towards Henry. Though he was nearly ten feet down, somehow it kept stretching and stretching until he could grab it.

"Pull!" he shouted, "I've got it!"

Henry wasn't that heavy, but still the thought of pulling him up seemed ridiculous. She tried anyway, and to their amazement, she began pulling him up through the shaft. The boulder still blocked his escape, but he passed through the rock like it was nothing more than soft butter. In seconds, he had emerged past the obstruction, and she helped him into the dimly lit cavern.

"What just happened?" she asked, hugging her brother's neck.

"I have no idea," he answered, returning the hug.

He realized he was still holding the crystal blade.

"Henry! You're bleeding!" she exclaimed. "We need to get out and find Dad."

They met him at the mouth of the cave, lugging a large piece of wood he had found to pry his son free with.

"Henry!" he shouted, dropping the limb and grabbing his son. "You're out! How'd you get free?"

"I am skinnier than you think. Kirsten pulled me through."

"I don't know how you managed that," he said, glancing towards his daughter. "I could barely get my hand through there. Hey, are you sure you're ok, son?"

"Dad, he's bleeding!" Kirsten said earnestly.

Henry collapsed as his father eased him down onto the ground. They carefully removed his coat to reveal six deep gashes across his shoulders and down both arms. Kirsten pulled out anything she could find in their first-aid kit to stop the bleeding. Mr. Parks took off his shirt, ripping it into strips to tie around Henry's arms. Even that was barely enough. Blood began to seep through the makeshift bandaging.

Henry felt a rush of adrenaline flowing in his veins. Or was it something else? He glanced back at the dark cave as they left.

The situation was desperate, and they knew it as they worked feverishly to get Henry safely back to their campsite. Mr. Parks built the skid intended for the "bear," and they carefully laid him on it.

Kirsten called her mother on the walkie-talkie to let her know what had just happened. It was dark when she met them at the door as Mr. Parks carried Henry's limp body in. Mrs. Parks fought to control her emotions at the sight of her wounded son. In a matter of minutes, he was on his way to the hospital.

CHAPTER 3

Henry squinted at the bright lights overhead as he opened his eyes for the first time in several days. His mother was sitting peacefully next to his bed reading a book when he lifted his head.

"Mom," he said quietly.

"Henry!" she nearly shouted as she jumped to her feet. "You gave us quite the scare."

"Why am I here?" He asked, looking around at the room full of medical devices and the tubes running into his arms.

"You were attacked by a bear," she replied. "Don't you remember?"

"A bear, you mean the Zen..." Henry stopped quickly, realizing only he and Kirsten knew what they were really after.

"What did you say, Son?"

"Things are still a little fuzzy," he answered weakly. "You just lie back and relax," his mother said with a smile. "You're going to be just fine, but I'll get the nurse in here to make sure."

Mr. Parks and Kirsten were just coming back with some coffee when Mrs. Parks burst from his room.

"Is everything ok Pearl?" Mr. Parks asked anxiously.

"Henry's awake. He's awake! I'm getting the nurse."

They quickly stepped into his room, followed by the nurse and his mom. The nurse made a thorough examination, and then led Mr. and Mrs. Parks into the hall outside his room.

"He's going to be ok," she assured them, "but I've never seen injuries that deep heal so fast. However, I recommend he stay here a few more days just to be sure there's no infection."

"That won't be a problem," Mrs. Parks replied.

Meanwhile, Kirsten slid a chair up close to Henry's bed.

"When are you going to tell dad what really happened?" She asked as she leaned in close.

"I don't know, maybe never. I'm not sure I believe it myself, and you don't even know the half of it."

Just then his father and mother returned with the nurse's good news.

"You'll just need to rest here a little longer," his mom said encouragingly. "We'll take you home in a few days."

"Why don't you and Kirsten go down to the dining hall," Mr. Parks said to his wife. "Henry needs his rest, but I just want to speak with him alone for a moment. I'll join you in a few minutes."

They agreed, as no one had eaten much of late anyway.
"You really had us worried," his father said after they had left. "We were afraid you might not make it and it felt like forever bringing you off that mountain. I just want you to know I would do anything for you."

"Thanks for saving me," Henry said, reaching over and grabbing his father's hand. "I know you would have traded places with me if you could have."

His dad hugged him gently, and then got up to join Kirsten and his mother.

"Just a minute Dad," Henry said before his dad could leave. "There's something I haven't told you about all this. Remember the other morning when I told you a fox spooked the cows. Well, it wasn't. I lied about that. And the same is true about the bear you thought we were chasing. It wasn't a bear either. "Remember when you took Kirsten and me to Uncle James and Aunt Lori's orchard a long time ago with that old book you keep in the library, the one with all those scary stories in it? Well, you read us one of those stories that day about a large creature with three long claws. That's what I saw in the field and in the cave. The book called it a Zender."

"A Zender!" His father exclaimed. "Son, those are just stories about mythical beasts. They aren't real. Look, you've been through quite an ordeal. Maybe your mind played a trick on you?"

"I know what I saw," Henry protested. "This is why I didn't tell you the truth before. I was afraid you wouldn't believe what really happened and what I saw. It attacked me in the field, and again in the cave."

"But they're just ancient stories," Mr. Parks said as he sat back down, "stories that have been told from generation to generation. No one takes them seriously. They're only myths."

"But, Dad, it was real!" Henry said, trying to sit up.

Mr. Parks took his arm, and gently pushed him back down.

"I know it is, son," he said comfortingly. "Kirsten told me all about it this morning, but I wasn't sure I was ready to believe it until I heard it from you. There's more to these stories than you know."

"So tell me now, Dad. I want to know," Henry said.

"It's the story of the Darkness," he said slowly, taking a deep breath. "It goes back generations. I don't know how many. It's an old story about dark times that began with what is called "the day of the beast." The creature you described appeared, threatening the people and killing livestock, but no one knew what to do. So they joined together to try and trap or kill the animal, but they couldn't. It was too powerful. They even tried offering sacrifices in hopes it would go away. But it didn't, and its presence seemed to bring out the worst in people as they started blaming each other for the damage it was responsible for."

Mr. Parks leaned forward, and looked intently into Henry's eyes.

"Son, the version I'm about to tell you is not in any book I've read to you," he said seriously. "The beast is the forerunner of something even worse. My father called it the sea of red and the coming Dark Matter. He didn't know what that meant because over the years, details have been lost. But he said it in such a way that I believed him, and it scares me even to this day. Now I'm beginning to see my fears realized, and I see that this is much more than just a story."

"But I killed it, Dad," Henry said excitedly. "It attacked me, and I killed it. It can't hurt us or anybody any more. The story is over."

"You killed it? How?"

"It came for me, and I stabbed it. Then it just vanished."

"I hope that's true, but things aren't always what they seem. I'm going to meet with the City Fathers and tell them of our adventure. They'll know what to do."

He squeezed his son's hand affectionately.

"There's one more thing you should know," Henry said quietly, looking up at his father.
"You mean the meteorite and the things you've made from it?"

"Yes! You know about that too?"

"Your sister told me about it as we were taking you off the mountain. I also found the blade you made in your belt. You did a great job carving it."

"I'm sorry for not telling you sooner, Dad."

"Don't worry about it. We've all had our little secrets growing up, but I'm glad you told me, son. It means a lot to me. Get some rest, and we'll take you home in a few days."

He left for dinner with his wife and Kirsten, and to give Henry time to rest, but the City Fathers needed to know about the Zender sighting right away. Mr. Parks couldn't wait long, and headed into town right after dinner. He went straight to Rich Lindberg's office, the leader of the City Fathers.

"Hi, Philip," Rich said warmly as Mr. Parks walked in. "I heard about your son, and I'm glad he's going to be alright. I'll send some candy to his room. I'm sure he'll like that."

Rich was a tall, heavy-set man with a long, friendly face. His office overlooked the business district, and he was the most successful engineer the city had ever known. He designed and installed its power system from a discovery he made. He found a substance which, when certain chemicals were added, created incredible heat. The heat turned water to steam, and powered the city's generators. Also, because the substance never ran out, it made energy affordable for all. The city, in effect, had perpetual power.

"Thank you." Mr. Parks replied. "I just left the hospital, and everything looks good. We haven't seen each other in quite some time, and we need to talk."

"Sure! You sounded quite serious on the phone. Is everything ok? How about we ask my secretary to get us some coffee, and move into the inner office."

"I'm not sure where to start," Mr. Parks said as they sat in Rich's plush office. "But my son has seen something, something unbelievable. Something none of us could ever imagine as real. He has faced a Zender."

Rich straightened up, and nearly dropped his coffee cup at the mention of the name.

"That's impossible! They're only a legend. They're fictional."

"I know. We've all been told the same ancient tale by our parents, and passed it on to our kids, believing it was just a great fantasy. What else would we believe? We kept the tradition alive, and it seemed harmless enough. But now the old tale seems more than fictional. It appears to be coming true."

Rich sat back, and folded his hands under his chin.

"If what you say is true, then this is just the beginning. As the story goes, there's peace for a thousand years, and then the Zender arrives. It precedes the darkness, and once the darkness comes, everything is destroyed."

"My father told us the same thing, but he also said fighting the darkness is what destroyed them. I never really understood that. How can you fight to be free, but if you do, you're destroyed? It doesn't make any sense."

Mr. Lindberg got up and stood at the window for a moment, watching the traffic pass below.

"The story your father told you is the same as mine, right?" he said, turning back to Mr. Parks. "The Zender comes to start the suffering. Then, people get angry and hateful at its presence. Once their anger mounts, the sea of red comes and sweeps them away."

"Yes. That's about it."

"Well, I'm going to tell you something my father told me that no one else got. There comes a day when the darkness ends, and the cycle is forever broken. I'm not sure why my father believed that, but he did. It made me feel better as a child, so I thought that's why he said it. Otherwise the story is very hopeless. But what if he was right? What if there is a way to end the cycle, and stop the story?"

Philip sat there quietly, considering the weight of what was said.

"I agree with you there. I never liked the story because it was so depressing. There was no hope of a future - everybody dies. Did your father say how to defeat the darkness?"

"No. He never said how; he just believed it was possible." What if someone actually killed the Zender?" Mr. Parks asked suddenly. "Does that mean the story is over?"

"What are you saying, Phillip? Who killed the beast?"

"I have reason to believe Henry killed it in a cave when we were up on Grace Mountain. I know it's hard to believe, but he has wounds on his body that didn't come from any animal I've ever seen. If he said he faced the Zender, I believe him."

"That could change everything," Rich replied, leaning back against the edge of his desk. "That may be what my father was referring to. But he had no specifics. He never said someone would defeat the Zender, or anything else for that matter. The breaking of the cycle could have meant anything."

"So what do we do?"

"I'm going to call for a full council meeting tonight, and I think you should be there. They'll need to know everything. Remember, the legend always ends the same. Every city that fought back was destroyed, so if this is real and starting to happen, we'll have to come up with a plan, and hope what my father believed was true. Maybe the story ends with us."

"I'll be there," Mr. Parks said, as he shook Rich's hand and left.

CHAPTER 4

It didn't take long for Henry to recover from his injuries, but as he grew older, he did notice significant changes in his body. His muscles became more defined, and his mother noted he seemed to be getting taller every time she turned around. Growing and becoming strong is a natural progression for boys, except Henry was changing in other ways too. Some of those ways were not so normal or acceptable. He wasn't the even-tempered kid his parents raised anymore.

One day, he came home from school after being invited to play baseball with some of his high school friends. He asked his father if Kirsten could do his chores for him, but Mr. Parks said she needed to practice her saxophone for a band recital that evening.

Henry stormed out of the house, and headed for the barn. He grabbed the handle to the large sliding door on the side of the barn, and shoved it angrily open. The door was nearly eighteen feet tall and twenty feet long, riding on a large overhead track. The heavy wooden door whizzed open, snapping off the heavy steel stop on the end as it flew off the track and out into the field.

Henry stood there for a moment, not believing what he had just done. Fortunately, Mr. Parks had not yet come out of the house. Henry ran into the field, picked up the door, and put it back on the track. He was amazed at how easy it was to handle this huge door, but the fact that he could get angry so easily was troubling.

Then he felt a pulsing coming from his shirt pocket. It was the piece of blue crystal that had chipped off the meteorite on the day he first met the Zender. When he took it out of his pocket, it glowed brightly, and was warm to the touch. Just holding it in his hand calmed him down, and quieted the anger boiling in his belly.

"What's happening to me?" Henry asked himself as he squatted down in the tall grass. "I'm acting like an idiot. If it wasn't for this crystal, I may have hurt someone."

He finished his chores, and made it to the game on time. But that night, he took the piece of crystal to his father's shop, and made it into a ring. He decided to wear it every day, and hoped it would help him control the anger.

He kept the meteorite in his room in a duffel bag, but often took it out to the workshop. He was getting better at creating objects from it, and even made his sister a beautiful necklace for her birthday. She wore it every day.

But what he enjoyed most was making blades. Some were long like swords, and others were shorter. He carved ornate wooden handles for each one from some curly maple his dad had. They were beautiful. One strange thing he noticed was that no matter how many things he made from it, it always stayed about the same size.

One afternoon after school, Henry began practicing throwing the blades he had made. He went behind the barn, and nailed a plywood target to the back of the barn. On his first throw, he hit the bulls-eye dead center. But the amazing part was that it went into his target clear up to the handle.

"I didn't throw it that hard," he said as he walked to the target. He pulled the blade out, but there was no mark on the plywood.

"What the heck!" he exclaimed as he examined the surface.

He heard the sound of water running behind the wall, and went in through a side door to check it out. He was met by a spray of water. One of the pipes used to water the calves was cut neatly in two. Henry quickly found the shut-off valve, and then made a close examination. The pipe was directly behind his target.

"I don't get it," Henry muttered. "My blade leaves no mark on the target, but slices through iron water pipes behind it. This is really weird."

He took his target down, and leaned it against some large sheets of thick steel his father had stored for a future project. His next throw was just as accurate. He expected the blade to either shatter or bounce off the hard metal, but instead the blade passed through the wood, and was stopped again by its wooden handle. The crystal blade had cut through the steel plate, but left no mark on the plywood.

In time, Henry learned there was nothing the crystal blades couldn't pass through, but they wouldn't leave a mark on the surface of the intended target. The possibilities were endless, but his father warned him to be careful. There were people who would want to take advantage of him, or try to steal the crystal if they knew about it, so he was careful not to say anything to anyone about his find.

High school went better than his parents could have hoped for their children. Kirsten had a natural ability with math, and Henry excelled in athletics. They both managed to hold a four-point grade average, which was outstanding. In his senior year, his friends started calling him Parks, and the name stuck. One afternoon, the school counselor invited him into his office.

"Henry," his counselor said, "have you thought about what you want to do with your life? When you finish high school, I mean."

"Yes, sir!" he replied. "I've been thinking about it a lot."

"Great!" the bearded man exclaimed. "But you have to make a plan, and work your plan. I've watched your progress through school, and I've seen your potential. You could go places if you want."

The counselor handed him several booklets.

"These are some of the best colleges the city has to offer," he continued, pointing to the top one in Henry's hand. "With your grade average, there is no doubt in my mind you would be accepted. I think you would be eligible for scholarships, and find it paid for."

"Wow!" Henry replied flipping through. "I never really thought about places like this."

"Think about it," the counselor said. "This could really unlock some doors for you."

"Would it help if I wanted to enter law enforcement?"

"Law Enforcement," the man replied leaning back and folding his hands behind his head. "You're interested in law enforcement?"

"I really am," Henry answered. "My parents and I have talked about it, and Dad thinks it would be perfect for me since I like the idea of helping people. We toured the Citadel last week, and it's fantastic. They're responsible for the protection of the city, you know."

"Sure they are," the man said a little disappointedly, "but wouldn't you like to do more? I've heard from some colleges regarding your sports potential. They scouted you when you took our football team to the championship this year. It seems a waste to not take advantage of what you've been given."

"Thank you for thinking so highly of me," he answered, setting the brochures on the desk. "But my sister is the one who likes this kind of stuff. I have my heart set on becoming a Cadet."

"Well, if you change your mind, please let me know," the counselor said with a smile. "They'll be getting one fine enforcement officer!"

"I have to get to class now," Henry said getting up from the chair. "Thank you again!"

His counselor shook his head, and put the brochures back in his desk with a sigh.

Once Parks graduated from high school, he worked on the farm until it was sold. His dad kept a parcel of the land to build a house and barn, but get out of the daily grind of farming. Parks studied for the academy and helped his father build. Kirsten graduated just as they put the finishing touches on their new home and were ready to move in. Mrs. Parks was happy with the change. Selling the farm meant they would have more time.

Kirsten had a full scholarship to one of the most prestigious colleges as a math major, while Parks applied to the Academy, and was quickly accepted. Starting out as a cadet, he quickly rose through the ranks. He was a natural--smart and strong. His commanders saw his potential for leadership early on. Before long, Henry J. Parks was encouraging other younger Cadets to think for themselves, lead by example, and treat others with respect, the way they would want to be treated.

The days of the Zender seemed a distant memory now, as nearly five years had passed since that fateful day on Grace Mountain. He was twenty years old, and enjoying success at every turn.

Parks met his sweetheart, Della, in their senior year of high school. She was a natural beauty with an infectious laugh, and they quickly hit it off. When she asked him to a Tolo dance, they became inseparable. After several years of dating, they married, and rented a small apartment in the city close to the college where Della was busy working towards her medical degree.

His parents were comfortable in their retirement home, and Kirsten worked on her bachelor's degree in math. They had grown even closer as a family, and Kirsten and Della were much like sisters. Beyond their family success, life in the city was at an all-time high, and people enjoyed peace and prosperity. Life was great, and it was truly a beautiful time until the dreaded day *they* came.

Parks was training new Cadets in the exercise yard at the Citadel when the ground began to vibrate. At first they thought it was a small earthquake tremor, but then the city emergency alarm began to howl. Parks grabbed several Cadets, jumped into one of the security vehicles, and headed for the city wall.

"What do you think it could be?" one of the Cadets asked.

"It could be nothing," Parks replied. "Maybe there's a fault in the system, or something triggered by the tremor. Either way, we need to check it out."

They crested the top of the hill overlooking the city wall, and he slammed on the brakes, skidding sideways to a stop.

"What the…" Parks exclaimed as he climbed out, and ran to the edge.

Below him, a dark red horde spilled into the valley just outside the city walls from the west. The vibration they felt came from strange chanting, and the force of thousands of feet marching in perfect time. In front of this massive army were various armored vehicles, some with open tops, from which commanding officers directed the army. They were short, in bright red armored suits, and brandished a variety of sharp weapons.

The city walls were massive, built over many centuries. They stretched the full length of the city, and were closed on each end by vertical rock walls carved out of the mountains. Entry could be gained only through huge iron gates that were built to withstand the heaviest assault.

"Who are they, and what do they want?" one of the Cadets asked nervously as he joined Parks.

"I've never seen the likes of them before, but it doesn't look like they're here to make friends."

Several hours later, the last of the great red horde had assembled in front of the wall. They stood silently, in countless neat rows. Parks estimated there had to be thousands of them.

People from the city had gathered along the ridge to get a look, and Parks realized something had to be done before panic broke out. He hopped back into his vehicle, and headed for the Citadel. Men and vehicles were already being dispatched to defensive positions along the wall as he pulled in.

"You're to meet with Rich Lindberg right now," his commander said as he stepped in.

"What's this all about?" Parks asked.

"We don't know who they are, but we have to assume they have bad intentions," his commander replied grimly. "The City Fathers are gathered at City Hall, and Mr. Lindberg called for you. I have no idea why, so don't even ask. We have been instructed to muster as many able-bodied people as possible just in case this turns ugly."

Parks was quickly ushered into the meeting room by the secretary when he arrived. Twelve men sat in a semicircle against the back wall. They were distracted, talking anxiously amongst themselves as he came in. Rich saw him, and waved him over to a plush chair in the middle.

"Henry!" Rich said. "I'm glad you came."

"What's going on?" he asked quickly. "Who are those people gathered outside the city?"

"We don't know for sure but we think they belong to a very old organization," Mr. Lindberg replied. "Your experience in the cave when you were a teenager has brought up many questions and concerns regarding the reality of our folklore," Rich continued, motioning towards Parks' Dad sitting among the City Fathers.

"Before that, we all thought the stories were fiction. However, there is nothing in the ancient writings about the death of the Zender, so we are really confused about what this is all about. It may have nothing to do with the story, but it does seem you are central to this event, and we need you."

"I'm ready for whatever you require," Parks replied as he looked at his father.

"Thank you for that," Mr. Lindberg continued. "Your dad said we could count on you. We need you to mount a defense long enough to allow us to prepare for surrender."

"Prepare for surrender? They haven't even attacked yet, and you're planning to surrender? I don't get this at all."

"We understand your confusion," Mr. Lindberg said.

He walked around from behind the long bar, and stepped in front of Parks.

"Look, we're not cowards, but the lives of our citizens--and the city itself--is at stake. I assure you we will all be destroyed if we fight. Every man, woman, and child will be killed, and our city leveled to the ground. You have to believe me when I say this is the only way. You have to trust us."

Parks could barely believe his ears, but the serious looks on the men's faces told him it was true. His Dad had said many times he could trust Rich Lindberg and the City Fathers, but this was stretching his faith. There had to be more to this. Surely these men had a plan.

"Let me talk to him for a moment," Mr. Parks said.

He came around the bar, and took his son by the arm. Father and son left the conference room together.

"I know this isn't what you want to hear, but we have to do this," Mr. Parks said quietly as they exited. "You know I would never ask you to do something I didn't believe was right for us."

Parks looked deeply into his father's eyes for a moment, and then walked back inside.

"I'll do what you ask," he told the City Fathers.

"Good! Just keep the city safe and secure as long as you can," Mr. Lindberg replied. "We'll need about two weeks to prepare."

Parks walked out into the bright sunlight, still confused, but he wasted no time in organizing the Cadets. The invaders did not seem anxious to attack, and spent the next two days just standing outside the walls without making a sound, or even moving. It was eerie, and their sheer numbers drove terror into the hearts of the people. Maybe that was the goal.

On the third day, they began their assault. The small red men beat tirelessly against the face of the wall, chipping off small pieces of stone with each blow from their sharp axes. The guards shot at them from above, but the bullets just bounced off their armor.

Finally after days of constant pounding, they breached the city wall on the South side. The red armored creatures, followed by men driving powerful armored vehicles, poured into the city. Everyone they met was cut down with razor-sharp blades, and they systematically took out vital communications and power lines. Parks led the city forces in a defense, and momentarily halted their advancement, but there was chaos everywhere.

The hospital was soon overwhelmed with casualties. Parks did his best to hold off the invaders, and managed to stop many of them with his crystal blades. The city's forces were armed with automatic weapons and the powerful Nullifier, which inflicted serious damage on the small red attackers, but the tide of destruction was unstoppable. They greatly outnumbered the Cadets, and killed without mercy everywhere they went.

The ancient folktale seemed to have become reality.

In a little over two weeks, the city was beginning to crumble. Children and adults ran from place to place, trying to hide. Panic-stricken parents looked for lost children. Many people were wounded, some were dead, but most were never found. Everyone did their best to avoid the sharp weapons of the Testers, as they became known.

All seemed hopeless and lost until the City Fathers, led by Mr. Lindberg, walked down the center street of the city. They headed into the heart of attackers by the main city gate, carrying a large white flag on the end of a long pole. Strangely, the red horde stopped their bloody assault, came to attention, and seemed almost hypnotized by the sight.

The twelve men walked through the gate to a large black tent pitched just outside the city walls. Parks, and those able to see, watched in amazement as the City Fathers entered the tent. Several anxious moments passed before they came out, followed by six well-dressed men. Men who looked more like business owners than ruthless attackers. The City Fathers led the six men through the city to the main square, where Mr. Lindberg climbed the steps to City Hall, and addressed the people.

"My beloved friends and family," he began, "it's time to lay down your arms, and surrender. I have signed a good faith-agreement with these gentlemen. It establishes peace in exchange for our cooperation. They are going to control our city, but we'll be able to live in peace, and our lives returned to normal. Please do not continue to resist, and all will be well."

And that was it. The city was handed over to the invaders. But, not everybody was in favor of giving up so easily. It was difficult to watch the foreigners assume control. In the end, however, most chose to go along. What should have been a fight to the bitter end turned into a secret resistance instead.

Parks helped establish the new regime in spite of his feelings. His father told him to work within the system until an opportunity came to change things for the better. With that guidance, he joined the conquerors, and became a leader among their ranks. He made the best of it, although sometimes he found himself too much a part of them. The new controlling force, called Management, had a way of enticing people into its web of thought, and causing them to do things they would later regret.

From the day of surrender, everything changed. Even though Parks and Della were married, they decided to keep their relationship secret from anybody they didn't know and trust. Many others did similar things, keeping their private lives as quiet as possible. Their city, once light and energetic, was now filled with uncertainty. People spoke in hushed tones, careful over what they said, and the easy smiles were gone.

Hearts were heavy with loss of family and friends, and the people's minds were filled with fear. The conquerors went about methodically setting up their regime, and taking control of every important function in the city. Management was in control now, and making its presence felt.

CHAPTER 5

"It's really beautiful here, isn't it?" Parks said, stretching back against the log.

"I love it!" Della responded as she snuggled into his chest. "But I can't believe you have to go out again. Is there no end to this madness?"

He hugged her tightly as the evening sun began its lonely descent beyond the wilderness. She shivered as he covered her small frame with his coat.

"I have to go, you know that," he said softly. "If I don't, people will get hurt, maybe even die. The Testers are being massed together for an all-out blitz tonight. I must do what I can."

She rolled up tighter against him.

"I just wish it was over," she said disappointedly. "I wish these strangers had never come. They've ruined our city, hurt our friends and you're even helping them. When is it going to end? I've hardly seen you since this started."

"I know," he replied softly, stroking her face and looking into her sad brown eyes. "I hate it too, but if all goes well, this may be the last night."

Wrapping her arms around his neck, she pulled close to his face.

"I want that more than anything," she said warmly, kissing his cheek. "Do everything you can to make tonight the last one."

Just then, the whistle sounded from the military base positioned outside the city wall, piercing the evening quiet. It was time for Parks to go.

"Tomorrow," he said returning the kiss. "Tomorrow will be ours. No more pursuits. No more secretive nights. It's the dawn of a new beginning for all of us!"

"Promise?" she asked as he got up.

He just smiled as he picked up his gear.

Parks was taking lead in what was supposed to be the final sweep to locate anyone still resisting the new regime. The short, muscular creatures in dark red armor were well-equipped for the task with their deadly instruments. The camp was full of Testers as Parks strolled in.

"You're ten seconds late," Barron chided. "How are we going to get this thing done if you're always late?"

"Shut up," Parks replied, shooting a cold look at Barron. "I have my orders and you're bringing up the rear, as usual."

Barron laughed, knowing he got under Parks' skin. He liked being in the rear, especially if there was any chance Parks could be eliminated by being out front.

Parks began jogging down the path as the Testers clambered clumsily along behind. He ran faster than they could, gaining nearly a half mile on them, when he spotted a burned-out barn just as he crossed over a small creek.

Management had determined it was more cost-effective to kill rather than capture, but Parks refused to follow that directive. He believed it was wrong to kill people just to save resources. So he returned night after night with people he captured, delivering them to the charge of the guards. It felt horrible, and those he captured hated him for it, but there was little choice. The City Fathers said cooperation was the only way, and Management promised fair treatment for those captured, even if they would have preferred them dead.

He set his nullifier to 'stun,' and blew a hole through the wall. Stepping through, he scanned for inhabitants. Suddenly, he was launched forward from a blow to the back of his head. Fortunately, the thick collar of his heavy leather coat absorbed most of the impact. Turning instantly, Parks caught his attacker by the throat, lifting him off his feet, and pulling him close.

He pressed the nullifier to his assailant's chest.

The young boy's face turned red, his eyes watering, as he flailed about, trying desperately to hit Parks again. Parks nearly pulled the trigger before realizing it was just a boy. Instead, he knocked the stick from the boy's hand, and shoved him to the ground. Just then, several more kids rushed from the shadows to their friend's aid. One had a broken piece of concrete and another had his fists up, ready to fight. They took a defensive stance around their fallen friend.

"Easy now," Parks said lowering his nullifier, "I'm not going to hurt you. Just relax."

He quickly scanned the group: eight of them total, and two appeared injured.

"What's your name?" he asked the boy that attacked him as he dropped onto one knee.

The boy, still rubbing his throat, glowered at Parks. He postured for an opportunity to do something, anything, but he was helpless against the powerful Parks.

"What's your name, son?" he asked again a little more gently. "We need to get your comrades some help. My name is Parks, and it would be easier if I could call you by yours."

The young man stood to his feet still shaking.

"You want to help us?" he asked suspiciously. "Why would you want to do that? You wear their uniform. You're one of them."

Parks looked the kids over carefully before returning the nullifier to his holster.

"We're here because we don't want to be taken," the boy said defiantly. "We're fighters fighting to be free and you're not going to take us. We would rather die first!"

"Dying is the easy part!" Parks snapped. "Living to save your friends is not. "What's your name?" he asked again. The young man looked over to his friends for direction. They nodded in agreement.

"My name is David and these are my friends. That's Troy, Joshua, Aaron, Kenzie, Isaac, Burke, and Normand," he said as he pointed to each of the children. "Joshua and Aaron are hurt the worst. They were out in the open when the bombs came. I saw Aaron thrown into a tree, and Joshua was hit in the back with a broken rock. We carried them in here to keep them warm and patch them up. Kenzie understands first-aid. She helped with our burns and cuts. But don't think we'll go peaceably."

Parks was amazed at the resolve of these children. They couldn't have been more than thirteen at best, and some were younger. For a moment, he questioned his agreement with the city's decision to surrender. He should have been standing with them instead of against them. In that moment, watching them care for each other, unafraid at what danger might await them, he decided not to deliver them over to Management. These kids deserved something more, and he needed to get them to safety--fast.

"Ok, David. I'm not going to hand you over to anyone, but you'll need to hurry," Parks said. "The Testers will be here any minute. If you can't carry your wounded friends, you'll have to leave them behind."

"We all go or we all stay," David said boldly. "Come on, guys. We can do this."

David and Kenzie quickly grabbed some planks lying nearby. Ripping some burlap bags into strips, they strapped their two friends to the boards. Several other boys took off their coats, laying them on the rough planks to use as cushions and blankets.

They quickly made ready, and followed Parks through the opening and over a pile of rubble. David and Troy had Aaron's plank since he was the heaviest, and they were the biggest. David was nearly five feet tall, and Troy was six months younger, but equal in size. Isaac and Burke took Joshua's make shift stretcher, with Kenzie and Normand close on their heels.

Once outside, Parks led them down a narrow path into a swampy area. It was cold but the moon provided just enough light to see where they were going as they stepped into the marsh. They sloshed their way along, doing their best to keep up with Parks as he plowed through cattails and under low hanging branches. Parks was keeping a quick pace, but he soon realized the kids would never keep up.

"Look, guys," Parks said sternly, stopping for a moment, "we don't have much time. Once it's light out, we'll be easy to spot, and if I'm caught with you, I'll have to turn you in."

The seriousness in his voice sent a shiver down David's spine.

"Don't worry about us," he said confidently, "we'll keep up."

Parks turned, and led the way out of the marsh and into some fields, leading to rocky ground. He slowed some, allowing them to stay close. David was amazed how easily Parks moved through such rough terrain without making any noise. They struggled on without stopping or saying a word.

After another half mile or so, a large set of double wooden doors set in an ancient rock wall came into view. Behind the door stood a rugged rock cliff face that rose high above the valley floor. The sun, just peering over the top, illumined the valley floor below as it started its daily climb. Parks knew it would be only a matter of moments before the cover of darkness was broken.

The doors were impressive, outfitted with large metal hinges and steel strapping. They towered over the huddled group. They seemed like they belonged to an old castle. Parks took a small blue crystal from a pouch around his waist, and placed it against the keyhole in the center.

The blue crystal began to glow slightly, and a mist started forming, slowly engulfing Parks' figure. Then the mist completely hid his form as the kids strained to see what was happening. Just then a light breeze picked up and blew the mist away, revealing Parks was gone. The young resisters instinctively dropped to the ground, nearly dumping their two wounded comrades.

Everyone stared at the massive doors.

David set Aaron's plank down, and rushed to the great doors. He strained against the cold, wet wood, but they didn't budge.

"What's going on?" he shouted as he pounded on the door. "You can't just leave us here."

The rest of the children struggled to their feet, anxiety and fear streaking across their faces.

But then the doors slowly began to open as their hinges creaked in protest. David stepped back as Parks emerged through the morning mist.

"Come in!" Parks said encouragingly. "But we must hurry. We don't have much time." They followed him along a winding path as the doors groaned, and swung shut behind them. No one said a word as they glanced back and forth, but they were all thinking the same thing.

Who is this guy?

The narrow path was overgrown with brambles and bushes, and led up a small hill. The group marched single file until a dark glass structure came into sight. It was an old greenhouse, covered with slimy moss and wet leaves. The glass doors hung slightly off their hinges as Parks pushed past.

It was just as cold and damp inside as it was outside, and the children huddled up as they came to a halt in the center of the plant-filled room. Their eyes adjusted quickly to the dim light streaming through the glass ceiling panels. The room revealed a long-abandoned growing facility, with wild-looking plants popping out of containers, and growing totally out of control.

"Where are we?" David asked nervously.

"A place long since abandoned," Parks replied matter-of-factly as he remembered his youth. "It used to belong to my family, and I came here often when I was a kid. My mother loved growing exotic herbs and medicinal plants to sell in the local markets. This was a special place for us when we were kids."

David's shoulders relaxed as relief spread over his face.

"Look," Parks said crisply to David, "you're not out of danger yet. You and your friends are going to die unless you do exactly what I tell you. There's a way out that will take us above the rim of this valley to a spot within the Citadel where you can get the medical care you need."

"What," David said, anger rising in his voice, "the Citadel? You're turning us in?! You've tricked us."

"No! I didn't trick you but you'll have to find a way to trust me," Parks answered. He grabbed David by the shoulders, and looked directly into his eyes. "Resistors are not going to win this conflict right now, as much as you might want them to. Management is too strong. But you have a better chance to win the future by living to fight another day. Look, there will be somebody up there waiting to help you, wanting to save you and your friends. I don't have time to explain it all now, but if you want to live, you'll have to trust me! The way back only leads to certain death."

David looked dismayed as he turned to his friends. The concern on their faces was obvious, but what to do?

Kenzie stood up, and faced the group.

"Everybody listen! This is a choice we need to make together," she said clearly, "and I vote we trust him. Our families are lost, or worse, dead. He's the only one who has given us any hope we can get out of this alive."

"Raise your hands if you agree with Kenzie," David said.

One by one, each one raised his hand in agreement.

"I don't know you or where you came from," David said, raising his hand too, "but we will do as you say."

Parks turned, and headed through the vines littering the inside of the greenhouse to the back, and went through another set of heavy glass doors covered in dark green slime. They exited into a narrow walkway between the building and the rocky cliff. The path led slightly away from the building, but ended at the corner. Pausing for a moment, he waited as the group crowded around. The puzzled looks on their faces spoke volumes, but no one dared ask why he had led them to a dead end.

He reached into the wide sash around his waist, and pulled out a slender leather bag. Untying the leather cord, he removed a slim, bluish-colored object. Stepping back quickly from the wall, he turned to address the group.

"I need a volunteer," he said looking the children over like a sergeant intending to send a solder on a suicide mission. "Someone who's not afraid to be last. Who among you is brave enough?"

The kids looked at each other briefly and stepped forward as a group. Parks laughed, and smiled.

"So, you are all equally brave." he said, seeing the confidence in their eyes. "Well, I don't need all of you, just one."

David immediately demanded to be last, but from the end of the line came a high-pitched voice.

"I'll be last," said a small fellow with soft blue eyes and a puff of red hair shooting out from under his cap.

It was Normand. Normand was the youngest of the group, only nine years old and barely four feet tall.

"David, you're too important," he continued. "You need to help carry Aaron. I'm too small to do that."

Parks looked him over carefully despite the others' protests.

"You're my man," Parks said firmly. He opened his leather coat, revealing a silver cord wrapped around his waist. "My sister found this many years ago in this very place. It was hidden behind a carving in the rock on the other side of the wall, and it has a very special quality."

As he slowly unrolled the silky thin silver cord, it glistened in the dim morning light that spilled down over the cliffs above. Squatting down, he motioned to Normand, who walked up boldly, shoulders back, and his narrow little chest puffed out. Parks handed the end of the cord to Normand, and looked intently into the little boy's eyes.

"What's your name again son?"

"Normand," came the bold reply.

"Ok Normand, here's what you do," Parks said, as he tied one end of the cord around his own waist. "As I move forward it will be your responsibility to wind the cord around your friends. If the cord is not connected to each of them when the light turns orange, they'll be trapped here. The two being carried will not need the cord because they're connected through their carriers. However, if anyone stumbles or trips and loses the connection, I cannot say what will happen. Can you handle that?"

"I can handle it," Normand said with a high squeaky reply.

Parks shot a glance to David, who shrugged his shoulders before nodding his approval.

"The last thing you must do is tie the cord to your waist," he instructed firmly. "It cannot just be around you. It must be tied! If you don't get the cord tied in time, you and your friends will not make it."

"I can do it," Normand affirmed, deepening his voice as he looked straight into Parks' eyes. "I can do it, Mr. Parks, I can do it!"

He put his hand on the small boy's shoulder and squeezed gently.

"Ok, son," he said rising to his feet. "Let's do this."

With that, Parks turned towards the solid rock face with the bluish crystal in his hand. A beam of white light emanated from it into the rock wall as it began to glow a brilliant orange. Hot molten rock started running down into a fissure along the base, and back up the other side, following a barely visible crack. The lines connected, forming an outline the size of a man.

The boys flinched.

"Stay firm, and be ready to move," Parks shouted, holding tight to the crystal.

He stepped forward as the glow intensified.

Normand was small enough to wrap the cord around David, and dip under the plank holding Aaron to wrap around Troy. He quickly weaved in and around his friends, and finally he tied the end of the cord around his own waist.

"Is everybody ready?" Parks asked.

"All ready," came Normand's reply.

"Let's go," Parks commanded stepping into the glowing mass of molten rock.

The looks on their faces told it all, terrified and awestruck all at the same time.

The cord stretched tight as Parks pulled the line of children forward.

"Come on!" Parks shouted. "You can't break the cord, but you must walk with me!"

The light from the crystal penetrated the stone, creating a translucent path through solid rock. The wall felt thick, like warm butter, as they forged through. Each one stepped into the wall in single file, staying tight to the next. Normand was the final one in, and as soon as the last part of his body was inside, the rock behind him turned solid again. The sides were orange, lit up by light emanating from the crystal. The path wound around, and became a steep uphill climb.

David's arms and shoulders ached from Aaron's weight, and his legs felt like they were on fire, but he couldn't show weakness; his friends were counting on him.

Normand worked hard to keep up, and kept his head low as he pushed along. Parks' body created a wake in the soft rock that closed quickly behind him, since he was last in line. He could feel the pressure of rocks solidifying behind his every step. It hurt his heels, but he forced himself to push ahead. The crushing pressure, like being deep under the sea wore on everyone. Fatigue set in as they plodded through.

At last the path leveled, out and the pressure eased momentarily.

Normand became distracted as he watched the flickering light along the sides of the tunnel while they moved through. Suddenly, he saw Kenzie's outline disappear in front of him as the walls began to darken.

"Oh no!" he thought, panicking. "Parks' light went out,"

Frozen with fear, his heart pounding in his ears, Normand felt the rocks squeezing in as they slowly began to solidify around him. Despair gripped his heart, but then a hand reached in and pulled him forward. The next thing he knew he was standing in bright sunlight.

"Are you ok?" Parks asked softly kneeling down to look him over.

Normand jumped into his arms, squeezing Parks' neck.

"You're going to be fine," Parks said gently, hugging the small child for a moment. He untied the rope from around Normand's waist before turning to address the group.

"Take deep breaths," Parks said. "Breathe!"

It was then they realized they had been holding their breath the whole time they were inside the mountain. Amazingly, they didn't need oxygen while passing through. They all started talking at once as the realization of what had just happened swept over them.

"Where are we?" David asked looking around at the unfamiliar surroundings.

"You're in the Citadel," Parks replied as he returned the crystal blade to his sash, and wrapped the silver cord around his waist.

Everyone became very still, and a solemn look fell over their faces as they realized the gravity of their situation.

"It is very important that you do exactly as I say. This place is safe for the moment. The large wall in front of us is the back side of the infirmary. I have a friend here who will tend to your wounds, and provide you the necessary help you require. Wait here for a moment, and I'll be right back."

Parks turned, and headed towards a dark door several paces down the narrow alley, and disappeared inside. The children set down their make-shift stretchers, and David was the first to speak.

"How are you guys doing?" He asked his two injured friends as Kenzie joined him.

"I'm ok," Aaron said raising himself up on his elbows. "My left leg has stopped throbbing."

Joshua was lying still, but managed to muster a thumbs-up. David moved closer to Joshua as Kenzie put her hand on his shoulder.

"You saved us, Joshua," David said looking into the eyes of his friend. "If you hadn't heard the whistling of those bombs coming in, we'd all be dead today. We owe our lives to you. But I need to know if you want to stay here, or could you move if we have to make a break for it?"

"Don't worry about me," Joshua said grabbing David's arm, "I can take care of myself. You do what you have to. Anybody who tries to get me will have this to deal with," he said defiantly, as he lifted his arm to reveal a knife hidden under his shirt.

"Joshua," Kenzie said, glancing up at David. "We're not going to leave you here by yourself. Right, David?"

"We have to be ready to move if things go bad," David said reluctantly. "I'll stay here with Joshua and Aaron, but the rest of you find places to hide out until we get this worked out. There's no point in all of us being captured. You'll have a much better chance on your own. This Parks guy is really powerful, but we're inside the Citadel. Who knows what could happen next."

"No!" Normand said pushing through. "We're not leaving. I believe in him. I know he's not going to hurt us. We need to wait here until he gets back just like he told us to."

The children looked at Normand for a moment. He was just a kid, but the confidence in his eyes somehow worked to dispel their fears. They looked at each other, realizing he was right.

"We'll stay together and wait for Parks," David said, putting his arm around Normand. "I trust him too."

A door near them opened suddenly. Joshua slid his hand around the handle of his knife as David's back stiffened. They quickly prepared themselves for the worst.

"Relax," Parks said. "I've someone here to meet you."

He stepped aside as the silhouette of a small young woman appeared from within.

"This is Nurse Della Larson." He continued. "She's the chief nurse for this facility, and she is here to help, but you must do exactly what she says!"

Miss Larson quickly assessed their needs with the help of Kenzie, who explained their injuries in great detail. The more seriously injured boys would need proper stretchers, and the rest physical examinations. Despite their pain and exhaustion, everyone felt better instantly.

Miss Larson, as she and Parks agreed she should be called even though they were married, was warm and confident. She gave them hope things were going to be alright after all.

"Before you go inside," Parks said addressing the group one final time, "you need to understand what's about to happen. I realize you've lost your families and friends, but Nurse Della has agreed to bring you in and care for you until she can get you some new families. Please don't resist her, as there are people left in the city that will help you and take care of you. But if any of your loved ones are still in the city, I'll find them for you, and make sure you're reunited."

Parks dropped down on one knee, and reached into his pocket. He pulled out a leather pouch, and poured seven blue crystals into his palm.

"These are for you," he said," handing a crystal to all but

Normand. "Keep them with you always, and never lose them. They will remind you of today, and of the family and friends you lost. This is the day your lives started over, and one day, you will help lead the city back. However, right now you need to grow up, and the power in these stones will help you. You don't understand it all right now, but you've witnessed enough to know how powerful they can be."

He took a leather cord from around his neck, and removed a heavy golden ring with a dark blue crystal in the center from his pinkie.

"Normand," Parks said, "this is for you. I made it with a special thought in mind, I just didn't realize you would be that thought. One day, this ring will fit." He slid the cord through the ring, and put it over Normand's head. "When that day comes, wear it proudly--you've earned it."

Parks was slowly beginning to understand why he had found the meteorite on that warm July morning. It wasn't for him alone. It was for those worthy of its power. These eight kids showed deep resolve. They were bound to each other by a pact of friendship made from determination, yet until he had found them, it had been a determination without hope. Now they had a new future and a promise.

With that, Parks headed back to rejoin his mission, confident the children were in the best of hands--Della's hands.

CHAPTER 6

Parks walked briskly through the city's main gate, well ahead of Barron and the Testers. Efforts were underway to refurbish and remake the Citadel in honor of its new tenants, making it the cornerstone of a new order. The banners lining the city streets waved in the warm afternoon breeze, welcoming a new beginning, but this beginning was not the one people had hoped for. Management's grip on the city was complete, as he even assisted in securing their control out of respect for the City Fathers, who had insisted there be no resistance.

Parks felt they were wrong, but his father stood with them, and he wasn't about to go against him. He supposed they had good reason, such as limiting the number of casualties, but he didn't like not being able to fight back. Some continued to try, and it was those he had to stop. This was not the time for rebellion.

Long nights of pursuit had taken their toll, however.

He picked up the pace a little more as he headed towards the Citadel, and a welcome shower. Stowing his gear in his locker, Parks headed upstairs to report. He was looking forward to change and a new position now the final sweep was over.

"The conquering hero," General Olliver said, smiling as Parks walked in.

Olliver's greeting hid an underlying contempt for Parks. He had little use for converted city dwellers, but Parks was necessary, at least for the time being.

"They'll be coming in soon," Parks replied flatly, showing no emotion. "It is the last of the last. There shouldn't be any more now."

"What makes you so sure?" the general enquired, leaning back, and putting his hands behind his head.

"We swept through the final quadrant." Parks answered, holding his voice steady. "The Testers were able to collect about a hundred or so. I worked the area thoroughly, and I believe that's it. We searched every nook and cranny."

"So, you're not planning another mission tonight?" Olliver asked, digging a little deeper.

"No!" Parks replied sharply, unable to hide his anger any longer. "I'm done. You can send Barron out with the Testers if you want, but I'm not going."

"Shouldn't that be up to me to decide?" the General snapped.

Parks neck turned red. He was through chasing his city family for these outsiders, but he couldn't let Olliver see too much of his true feelings. He had to remain calm.

"I'm telling you, it's a waste of time," Parks replied as he steadied himself. "If you really want me to take another jog through the wilderness with your team, fine. But I'm telling you they're exhausted, and we're not going to find anything."

Olliver stared at Parks for a few moments as he sized him up.

"Alright," the general said finally. "We'll call it good for now. But if I get more sightings, you'll be going out again. In the meantime, get your butt out of here, but report back Monday-early! There's a lot to be done if this city is ever going to be worth anything."

Parks exited, his mind burning with Olliver's words.

"Worth anything," Parks thought to himself as he passed the first wave of Testers returning from the night's work. "Worth anything? If we had no value, why spend all the effort taking the city over? Olliver is such a dope. He wouldn't know value if it hit him in the face."

The afternoon faded to early evening as Parks' mind turned to better things. He had a special place to be tonight and was looking forward to it, but in the meantime, he needed to see how Kirsten was doing.

"Hi sis," he said quietly as he opened the door to her office.

"Henry," she replied, spinning around in her chair. "What are you doing here?"

Kirsten was busy helping out with the wounded. Several years ago while in college, she had worked as a nursing assistant, and she hadn't forgotten a thing. Her skills were a big help to Della, and a blessing to the people she cared for.

"Just checking to see how you're doing. Did you get the kids placed yet?

"Not yet. It's going to take some time, but there seem to be plenty of interested people. A lot of families have lost friends and loved ones, and are willing to do anything they can to help."

"That's great, but I don't want just any families for these kids."

"What do you mean?" Kirsten replied scooting back a bit.

"Only that they are special, and need to go to families we know. I know there are a lot of good people around, but make sure you clear each one with Della before you ok their release."

"That's fine with me," Kirsten replied, "but what about you? Are you feeling alright?"

"I'm ok. Not much to say. Hey, is Della around somewhere?" Parks said, quickly changing the subject.

"She was, but there have been a lot of important visitors here today. I haven't seen her for several hours. You probably should get going if you don't want to get spotted hanging around."

Parks did just that as he quickly exited the building, and headed towards her apartment. She lived in one of the many complexes built years before to satisfy a growing professional middle class. They were two-story single-family dwellings with many nice amenities. Clean neighborhoods, and low crime rates drew people to the comfortable surroundings. He liked coming here, but was careful not to be seen. Their relationship was still a closely-guarded secret.

A gentle breeze blew through the small trees lining the path to her front door, but Parks hopped the fence to the backyard instead, making sure he wasn't followed. Picking the spare key from under a porcelain frog in the flower box, he let himself in, and stretched out on the couch to wait.

"Hi, sweetie," a soft voice said as he shook himself awake.

"Della!" Parks replied sleepily, looking into her smiling eyes. "You're home!"

She bent down, and kissed him gently.

"Are you doing ok?" Della asked, squeezing onto the couch next to him.

"It's finally over," he replied, stroking her dark brown hair. "I told General Olliver I'm through chasing people. He might not like it, but I'm not going out again."

"Is it really over?" she asked somewhat distantly. "I'm not so sure."

"What do you mean?" Parks asked, rising up on his elbows. "Of course it's over!"

Della looked away for a moment before replying.

"I was called up to the Citadel this afternoon," she answered quietly. "The new head of medical resources for the city, Susan Thomas, wanted to see me. You know I completed medical school shortly before the invasion but didn't get a chance to finish my residency. However, helping the wounded pretty much completed my training. Anyway, she wants me to accept my doctorate, and is offering to build me my own medical facility. It's like a dream come true!"

"That's wonderful," Parks said, hugging her tightly. "Things are getting better by the second."

Della pulled away, got up, and headed into the kitchen. Parks hopped off the couch behind her.

"Is there something you're not telling me?" he asked as he checked the fridge for a snack.

"It's all wrong," Della said, leaning against the kitchen sink.

"Wrong? Nothing's wrong," Parks replied, taking a bite from an apple. "It sounds to me like everything's perfect. Better than we had even hoped."

"It's not, Parks!" she said, turning towards the kitchen window. Tears streamed down her cheeks. "It's not."

"What do you mean?" Parks asked as he spun her around.

"It's us, Parks," Della said as she buried her head in his chest. "You don't understand. You can't."

"Us?" Parks asked anxiously. "What do you mean, us?"

Della trembled as she hugged Parks tight. The city around them was changing, and she felt helpless to stop it. They'd been apart for years, and had agreed to wait to live together until she was through with her studies. Parks had secretly supported her during the time she was in college. He had a good job in law enforcement that enabled him to pay for her apartment and his too, as well as helping with tuition and books. Not a typical arrangement, but it worked.

Taking Parks by the hand, she led him back to the couch.

"Important people came through the medical facility, and I heard things," Della said. "Things that could hurt us."

"In what way?" Parks asked, his curiosity engaging.

"Your name came up, and they said some weird things about you," Della continued. "People think you're dangerous. The way you act, and those weapons you carry make them nervous. They think you're too powerful."

"So what," Parks said defensively, his voice rising. "People think what they want, you know that! I'll never be trusted by them, but that won't stop us. We can live above what people think."

"Important people would react differently if they found out about us," Della continued with a sad look. "We've worked hard for what we have, and I don't want to lose us. These people I'm talking about have power, power to stop my promotion, and power to hurt you if they find out."

"Come on, Della!" he said angrily, getting up from the couch. "How are they going to find out? Besides, we agreed to wait for a while, and then get back to living together the way we should. Forget about them. This is our chance. It's our time."

"It's not what I want, but things are changing," Della answered softly, knowing how important this was to them both. "You have your work, and I have this opportunity. It could be really good for the city, and for us. I just think we may have to wait a little longer before we go public."

"Just a little longer," Parks said feeling a little bitter at the thought. "How much longer?"

"Not too long, I hope," Della answered tenderly, melting into his embrace. "In the meantime, we can still be us just like we have been. Nobody has to know."

Parks lifted the small woman into his arms, hugging her tightly. They both understood how unpredictable things were, but what they had between them would have to be enough. They'd played this secretive game for a long time, and a little longer shouldn't hurt, but they would have to be even more careful now.

Della's new position would bring her into a whole new social realm where she would be more public and visible. Parks, on the other hand, needed to become less visible, and limit the use of his weapons, and make sure not to draw unwanted attention. That was never easy with him.

The less Management knows of crystal power, the better! Parks thought as he settled into the couch with Della. *I once believed I could be a positive influence, and maybe even change some attitudes. Now I'm not so sure.*

He reached up, and turned off the lamp on the table next to the couch. Their future seemed less certain, but he didn't care as long as they had each other.

CHAPTER 7

Now that he was finished chasing resisters, Parks settled into his position as a cadet trainer, hoping things would go well. But just two weeks in, reports began to surface of people trying to escape the city. Management was in no mood to tolerate resisters. They made it clear that anyone who was caught faced imprisonment and harsh punishment. The majority of people wanted nothing to do with resistance, as they were more interested in finding their lives again, and getting along under the new authority. But there were still some who couldn't tolerate the change, and wanted out no matter what.

"You assured me we were done with this!" General Olliver snarled as Parks stepped into his office. "Now I hear people are trying to leave, and to do what? Come back and attack us? Don't take me for a fool."

Parks sat down quietly, and endured the general's rant. He had hoped people would follow his example, and flow into the new order, so he wouldn't need to arrest anyone else. But it seemed that he would soon be chasing resisters again. "I understand, Sir." Parks replied after Olliver finished. "I had no way of knowing people still wanted to get away. I've been telling everybody I know they just have to give it time, and adjust."

Olliver leaned back, crossed his legs, and picked up a report from his desk. He scanned it for a few moments before answering.

"I'm sending Barron with you to find two resisters," the general said, as he handed the report to Parks. "They were spotted several times outside the city walls, but no one has been able to identify them, or get a lead on where they're hiding. Don't come back until you've dealt with them."

Parks exited the general's office, dreading the thought of working with Barron.

Barron was a large, muscular man with sharp facial features, and a sinister glare. General Olliver loved pairing the two of them as much as possible. Parks believed he did that just to annoy him, knowing how much he hated Barron's arrogant attitude. But he had no choice, so he grabbed Barron, and headed out.

The two resisters proved to be more of a challenge than expected. He and Barron spent several weeks tracking their movements through the outlying wilderness area, but without success.

One day, Parks spotted the two men as they left a treed area, and headed towards the river. He sprinted through the tall grass, and leapt on the larger man from behind, pulling him down on the bank of the river. The man was strong, and threw Parks off. Parks pulled his Nullifier, and ended the struggle with a shot in the back, as the man turned to run. He slumped to the ground, and Parks began immediately scanning for the second.

The other resister saw Parks take down his friend, and made a break for the trees. He was about to escape, when Barron fired.

Barron had been watching from the safety of a nearby ridge waiting for his opportunity, and he got it. He made the perfect shot just before the resister could re-enter the safety of the woods, hitting him squarely in the side of the head. The resister dropped like a rock.

"I could have stopped him, you heartless jerk," Parks said as he ran up. He crouched down by the body. "What's the matter with you? You know our procedure. I'm the one to call the shot, not you. You didn't have to kill him. It's not what we do."

Barron dropped next to Parks, shoving the body over. The shot had crushed the side of the man's head, and one eye bulged grotesquely. Barron smiled with satisfaction at his accuracy.

"You and your BOJ Order morality," Barron said with disdain. "You have to admit that was a great shot. Besides, I can take these resisters any way I want, and it saves our having to pack him out for trial. The animals will take care of the problem for us, and we have one less to deal with."

Parks checked the man's pulse, more out of habit than expectation. This felt so needless. Finding these men should have ended in a clean capture, not a fatality. But there was no way he could stop Barron. He just shook his head as he got up to retrieve the resister left by the river. At least one of them was still alive.

Parks was angry as he jogged the hundred or so yards back.

When he arrived at the river bank, he was shocked to find the man had mysteriously vanished. The blast from Parks's nullifier should have put him down for longer than a few minutes. He checked for signs, but there were none. The sand and rocky shore along the river revealed their tracks, and the large indentation where they went down together, but that was it.

"Maybe he jumped back onto one of these rocks," Parks mused, looking at the ridge above the river. "It's about ten feet, but it's still possible. But that still doesn't explain why we didn't see him. He would have had to pass by us if he was making a break for it."

Barron came up as Parks was carefully examining the area.

"Way to go, big guy," Barron said with satisfaction. "So you lost one, eh? It seems like I chose the correct method after all."

"Come on, man, look around you." Parks shot back. "You saw him go down. Do you see any way he could get out of here without being spotted? The river might hide some noise, but he couldn't fly. He should be right here."

"Alright, you work that side," Barron replied, realizing the truth in Parks's statement, "and I'll work this side. If we crisscross the area, we'll find him. He couldn't have gotten that far."

Parks nodded, heading into the thick brush on the right, as Barron went left.

Parks had gone only a few dozen yards through the tall grass and brush when he spotted a black object wedged into the crux of a small tree. Thinking it could be evidence of the resister's escape, he waded through the heavy reed grass and scrub brush to find out. Reaching through the branches, he retrieved the mysterious object. It was a small black book with a worn leather cover. A piece of heavy string wrapped around held it together. He slipped it into his pocket for later examination, and continued the search.

Meanwhile, Barron was busy working his way through the thickets, small trees, and brush, back towards the tree line where they had started.

"Barron, you're such a noisy thug," Parks muttered to himself. "No matter how much I work with you, you never get it. You might as well have bells on."

They made their way along, and met at the edge of the woods after combing through the heavy grass with no results. But when they returned, they were shocked to find the body of the man Barron had killed a few moments earlier was gone.

"What the?" Barron said in disbelief.

Parks and Barron quickly scanned the area, looking for signs of movement. There was nothing. Not a sound or movement anywhere nearby.

"This is weird," Parks said as he knelt down, examining the area the man had been just moments before. "He couldn't have walked away after the damage you did!"

Parks felt along the ground. It was slightly warm to the touch, confirming a body had been there. The blood from the side of the victim's head left a dark red stain, doubly confirming the obvious. But where was the body?

Parks stayed down, pondering the scene and looking for clues, while Barron ran thrashing about and hollering in hopes of scaring up something. He stood up just as Barron returned from his search.

"What is going on here?" Barron asked, catching himself as he slipped on the wet grass. "I got that guy good. Somebody must have taken the body while we were down at the river."

"Doesn't look like your methods work any better than mine," Parks replied sarcastically. "But you're right about one thing: Your shot killed him. There's no doubt about that."

"This is like nothing I've ever seen," Barron replied, still breathing hard. "It's as if they were never here. But that's not possible. We tracked those guys for two weeks. You know it, and I know it."

Barron continued to scan the area, trying to keep an appearance of calm. Parks could tell that despite his best efforts, Barron was starting to lose it. Nervously, he unbuttoned the strap on his Nullifier, and slid his hand around the handle.

"I have no idea," Parks replied evenly, "but I think we may want to keep this to ourselves, at least for now. I doubt General Olliver would be pleased to find we had two resisters in hand, and lost them both."

"How about we tell him we left them both dead?" Barron volunteered. "We can say it was too much work to haul them back, so we left them for the animals to eat. He wouldn't care, as long as he believed we killed them."

"Alright," Parks answered in agreement, "it's all we've got anyway."

"There's nothing more we can do here," Barron said uneasily as he glanced towards the woods. "We might as well head back to the city."

They made their report, and covered for the incident as agreed. The General was angry they didn't return with the bodies, but Barron convinced him it was the right move.

Parks settled into his routine, putting the whole thing behind him. He was trying to get his life back to normal, but it wasn't happening. Just like years before when he was a child, the nightmares returned. Vivid images of death and destruction plagued him night after night, leaving him drenched in sweat. He tried everything, including staying up all night, but nothing seemed to work. Even when he became so exhausted he couldn't stay awake, they would come anyway.

One morning he got up early after hours of fitful sleep, and stumbled into the kitchen to put on some coffee. The lack of sleep was getting to him, and he was feeling miserable, but hoped a stiff cup would snap him out of it before work. He dropped onto the couch with his toast and coffee, when he suddenly remembered the book he'd found in the tree.

He had forgotten all about it, but the nightmare from the previous night had a similar book in it. He thought for a moment about where he might have placed it when he noticed a bulge in his heavy leather coat hanging by the door. Jumping off the couch, driven by a sudden surge of curiosity, he retrieved it from the zippered pouch. Settling back onto the couch, Parks examined the book.

It was obviously old, bound in black leather, and worn. It was only kept together with a leather cord. He carefully untied the leather string, and opened it. Some of the pages were stuck together, and were very thin, so he was careful not to rip them as he flipped through. However, the writing appeared clouded and fuzzy.

Probably from being exposed to the elements, he thought, as he reached into a drawer for his magnifying glass. *Who knows how long it was in that tree.*

He studied each page carefully, trying to make something out, but it seemed hopeless. The book was obviously ruined. Disappointed, he closed it, and flipped it toward the trash can next to the door. He missed, and hit the wall instead. It bounced onto one of his small sectional couches, and flipped open.

A small slip of yellowed parchment slid out, and fell to the floor.

What's that? Parks wondered as he walked over and picked up the strange paper.

It was at least as old as the book, and had been carefully folded, but it was different, made from something that felt more like animal skin than paper. He unfolded it, hoping to find something of interest, but it seemed just as useless as the book.

It was blank at first, but as he put it up into the warm lamplight to get a better look, a faded symbol began to emerge in one corner. It was faint at first, but as he held it closer to the light, more of the image began to appear. It was a crude drawing of a man holding a candle in front of a door. The door was dull in appearance, with no handle on the outside, only hinges. Picking up his magnifying glass again, Parks noted an inscription above the door.

"YOU MUST SEEK THE SIX TO FIND THE TRUTH."

"Find the truth?" Parks puzzled, "What truth? Whose truth?"

He continued to examine the sheet, warming it with the bulb, and as he did, the picture of the man by the door began to fill with horrible scenes. There were images of death and violence, and nightmarish creatures.

"This is insane!" Parks exclaimed, looking away for a moment. "These images are just like what I see in my dreams."

A dark feeling of dread inched up his spine, and he shivered suddenly, as if a cold winter wind had whipped through his apartment. Then he saw a familiar shape.

An image of the Zender appeared in the corner of the page.

Parks dropped the parchment like it was on fire, but it only fluttered harmlessly to the floor. He was sweating, and breathing hard as he reached down to pick it up. Returning it to the light, he strained to focus. Suddenly the image sharpened, and the man with the candle facing the door moved. Parks looked up for a moment, and rubbed his eyes.

I'm not getting enough sleep. I'm starting to see things, he thought to himself.

When he looked again, the man on the paper turned, and his face became visible.

It was Parks!

His knees buckled slightly as he stared at the parchment in disbelief. He wondered for a moment if he were losing his mind.

Parks was spiritual in some respects, but never truly considered there could be much more than what his senses told him. How could something so old, found in the crux of a tree, and hardly readable have his image on it? It just wasn't possible, and yet here it was, in his apartment.

"Ok," Parks said pulling his thoughts together, "are my nightmares related in some crazy way? I might be overtired, but there's more to this than I ever imagined; way more! This book and parchment are like the meteor I found, or which perhaps found me. I've never thought of it that way before. Are these things seeking me out, and if so, why? What possible reason could there be? I'm nothing special. Why would I be on this parchment, or involved with an old book?"

He had more questions than answers as he opened the book again, intending to return the parchment. He paused, parchment in hand, as the title of the first chapter suddenly appeared.

"Six Marks of Red".

Parks leaned back into his couch, perplexed by the words. It was warm in his apartment, so he hadn't bothered to put a shirt on yet.

"What could "Marks of Red" mean?" he thought as he glanced at the three long, deep scars on his right shoulder from the Zender attack.

His mind returned to that frightful day, and he remembered when his father pulled off his bloody coat, and how he thought the gashes looked like three big red stripes on each shoulder.

"Six bloody stripes," he said, running his fingers along his shoulders. "Six Marks of Red; it couldn't mean these, could it?."

Parks was becoming more curious by the second. Could something outside his realm of existence be communicating with him? Staring into the book again, he was amazed as each sentence followed by the next emerged on the pages. He was actually able to read the first chapter, and that was all it took to get his mind working overtime. It described the significance of the crystal blades he possessed, with dire warnings for those who misused them. But the final sentence left him deeply disturbed.

"Many will stand against the dark, but one must fall to save them all."

He returned the parchment, closed the book, and stowed it in the trunk under his bed. He returned to it many times in his search for answers. With each sentence came a new revelation. He was beginning to see things, and they were not always things he wanted to know. Some of the things he read spoke of an internal dark energy. It was the power of the beast, the Zender.

He was growing in knowledge, but there were significant events coming; events the book didn't explain. Events that would forever alter his life and the lives of those he cared about most.

CHAPTER 8

The Citadel, a looming structure surrounded by high walls topped with rows of razor wire, was rebuilt by Management. It intimidated everyone, even those who worked there. The gates were heavy steel, and controlled from a fortified booth just outside the main entrance.

Why put so much effort into security for this place? Parks thought as he pulled up and identified himself to the guard. *Are they trying to keep people out or in? It looks more like a prison than a center provided to protect the city's citizens. We're here to provide security for the people, but it looks like we're the ones being protected.*

The crisp morning air welcomed him as he pulled into his parking spot. Swiping his card at the turnstile, Parks walked in slowly, glancing at the tall concrete walls, and saluting the city flag flying above. It was the last remaining symbol of better days, days when the city danced with joy, and people lived in peace. There was a peace of sorts, but it was more of a restrained dissention.

Today was going to be different, however, and if Parks had known how different, he might have chosen to stay home. Young cadets were milling about along the side of the large auditorium as he walked in. Barron immediately spotted him coming through the open double doors, and headed his way.

Parks was the ranking member of a very elite group, The Band Of Justice, or the BOJ Order as they were commonly called. Only twenty five candidates had successfully completed the grueling process. It was a commitment unlike any other. Candidates were stretched to the breaking point both physically and mentally. The goal was to break past mental barriers taking each one to a deeper place inside. He was a diligent teacher; watching, and making sure their training was fair. Many cadets washed out in spite of his efforts, but it still remained the goal of every young cadet to join the Order, and the accomplishment of a lifetime for those who succeeded. Parks glanced over towards the cadets as Barron approached.

"Yeah, I see them too," Barron said in a gruff voice. "We're certainly lowering the standard for the Citadel. Most of those guys are going to wash out the first week. No way can they keep up with me. They don't have a chance."

"Barron, you're a poor judge of ability," Parks replied, still looking the cadets over. "I bet I can take most of these men through standard training, and some may even qualify for advancement. From what I've heard, at least two of them are standouts, and I give them an even shot to qualify for the Order. There are good men here–we just need to lead them along."

"Again with the Order," Barron retorted, sneering at Parks. "You guys think you're so special. Give me a break."

"What do you know about it?" Parks asked sharply. "At least they know how to control their emotions. You should try it sometime."

"I'll do a lot more than that!" Barron said threateningly. "Just push me and you'll see."

Parks knew how Barron felt. He was a good athlete, but the order was not just physical. Barron was smart enough, but he lacked patience, and often acted impetuously. That was the main difference between Barron and the Order. He preferred the easy road, and liked his bully position, and the authority it gave. He could push people around rather than working with them.

Park's musings were interrupted as General Olliver strolled into the room. Olliver was tall, broad shoulded, with a hawkish nose. He moved through the auditorium towards the front like a big gorilla heading to the only banana tree. As he moved, he gazed around the room. Any Cadet who accidentally made eye contact quickly looked down, or away. Olliver's reputation for violence and intimidation preceded him. He often bragged of his abilities, and he enjoyed tricking his subordinates into challenging him. The few who were foolish enough to do it were lucky to escape with their lives. He enjoyed injuring people, and that's why Harry liked him.

Harry Allison was the manager of the Citadel, and responsible for security, and law enforcement throughout the city and outlying rural areas. Harry answered to no one but the President. Olliver served Harry well. He did many things for him, including certain jobs that had to be done behind the scenes.

The General stepped to the podium, setting his papers down, and glaring over the crowd for a moment. The cadets quickly sat down.

"Gentlemen," the General said in a low voice. "I need you to pay strict attention as I am only going to say this once. This department is not meeting its goals and expectations. You're lagging behind, putting up a poor showing, and I'm not happy about it."

Olliver glared over where Parks was leaning against the back wall.

"I'm speaking to all of you," General Olliver continued. "Not just you Cadets. Some of you think you're doing your part, your fair share. Well, you're not! I want more from all of you!"

Parks could feel heat rising under his collar. He knew the General well. Olliver had never liked him from the moment they first met. Parks enjoyed being in the field and working with new cadets, and the cadets loved and respected him, but that made the General feel threatened. He didn't like the fact that some of upper Management appreciated Parks' attitude, believing him to be promotable. Parks was patient, and good at what he did, so Olliver's hands were tied, but that didn't stop the general from trying his best to get rid of Parks.

"Look, men," General Olliver continued, "from now on things are going to be different. It seems there are some who think you Cadets need more training before making the step up to the level of the Order. But Management has decided to enact a new standard, an attainable standard, where Cadets can grow at a faster, more efficient rate!"

Olliver slammed his fist on the podium for emphasis.

Olliver lowered his voice and shot a dark glare in Parks's direction,

"Of course Management appreciates the Order, but it's too exclusive in its current form. We need more Cadets processed, and on a faster timeline. Our citizens must see how quickly you progress. The city needs to feel we're interested in the future, and it will help improve morale.

"People like seeing cadets with the Silver Star on their vests. It makes them feel safe, like they have friends in Management. So the idea that you Cadets are not capable of serving in the Order is over. The BOJ is an outdated concept, and the time has come for change. We need all our Cadets and leaders bonding together as a team, not separated by arbitrary, artificial rankings.

"If a Cadet is weak at some task or function, I expect you leaders to step up and help them. Likewise, you Cadets need to assist where you see a need, and follow your leaders. Management wants everyone on the same level working together, no excuses. And we start today by promoting each and every Cadet in this auditorium to the full rank of BOJ."

Parks couldn't believe what he was hearing. The Order was not about appointing; it was about achieving, and proving your worth. Now Management was effectively eliminating it by making it entry-level. Something anybody could do.

"This is crazy," Parks murmured, working hard to contain his anger.

He wanted to take Olliver outside, and show him how powerful he really was, but this was not the time or place. Yet the urge pushed hard, so he stepped into the hall out of sight, and slammed his fist into the wall. Fortunately, the crowd inside couldn't hear the sound as he punched through the concrete blocks.

"How is this going to work?" Parks asked under his breath as he stepped back into the auditorium, not feeling any better. "I gave my heart and mind to discover the power, and now a simple announcement is going to make these guys equal to the task? Not a chance. Leadership comes from experience and effective training, not something you're given. Even if I help them, I can't make them become something they must find on their own. That's the secret of the Order."

Barron pushed his way through to the front, glancing up at Olliver, who nodded his approval.

"Gentlemen, this is a great day," Barron said, turning to face the crowd, and raising his voice for effect. "The General is right! You must all become part of the Order today. You are needed."

The Cadets leaned forward in their seats. He had their full attention.

"The resisters are becoming bolder," he said. "Recently, we were chasing them through the wilderness. Even though the daylight was well upon us, they still broke into the open. Their boldness to escape during the day is evidence of their disdain for law and order. They have also found new methods to elude us.

They couldn't escape us, however. We tracked them, found them, and had to kill them before they killed us. We need more help if there is any chance of getting control of the situation. The Order is opening to all, so let's use our new-found position to get things moving. To put a stop to those who resist. With your participation and help, the resistance will be over. Welcome to the Band of Justice."

Barron raised both hands in victory as a cheer rose from the crowd.

"To the Order, to the Order, to the Order," The Cadets chanted.

The General stepped back to the podium, and enjoyed the praise for a moment before raising his hand to quiet the crowd.

"Management has spoken," he declared. "Now let the transformation begin!"

The crowd went wild as the General stepped down, and made his way to the rear exit.

"And, there it is," Parks growled to himself, watching the chaos from the rear. "Things are changing alright, but not for the better."

General Olliver's dislike for Parks was evident as he looked with satisfaction at the frown on his enemy's face. Olliver knew he was effectively eliminating the famous Parks by watering down his precious Order. It would take a little more planning, but with the new Cadets yearning for exposure and attention, it wouldn't be long before the Order was nothing more than a name. Still, he wouldn't be completely satisfied until Parks was gone forever.

Parks stayed in the back and waited for Barron as the jubilant crowd of Cadets filed past. But Barron stayed close to Olliver, smiling and shaking hands with the Cadets as if he were a celebrity. He wanted to be the head man, and would do anything to get it.

"Barron," Parks said, catching him in the hall as he walked out. "What's this all about? You know we have to keep close tabs on the cadets, or their mistakes could be costly."

"Come on, Parks," Barron replied coldly, trying not to make eye contact. "We have to change with the times. The General is right. We have to do things differently around here if we're going to stop the resisters. So what if a few cadets get hurt in the process."

Barron's attitude was not surprising. But this had little to do with stopping resisters, and everything to do with destroying Parks. Olliver was looking for a weakness, and now it was clear he had succeeded. Barron's support for the watering down of the Order added substance to his plan. It wouldn't be long before Parks was out.

Things were moving in a dangerous direction, and would soon get out of control. Parks could feel it coming, like the East wind pushing in a winter storm. He wasn't ready to quit just yet, however. He would play along, at least for now, and hope he could find a way to influence things for the better. But it wasn't looking good.

CHAPTER 9

Bruce Clawson was an engineer and middle manager working in the Central Power Processor for the city. He married his college sweetheart, Mary, and they had a twenty-six-year-old adopted son named David, who was one of the children Parks and Della rescued. His life had changed little since the city surrender. The first couple of years had been a little uncomfortable as Management implemented their controls, but life had improved as trust in the new government increased.

They were financially secure, and his four-day work week allowed for more family time. David was nearly through with his Master's degree, and Mary was looking forward to having him around the house again, at least until he got a job.

Their best friends were Kevin Knobbs and his wife Kari. Kevin and Bruce worked in the same office complex, often spending time talking about their weekend plans, and sharing the daily gossip. Mary and Kari were equally close, meeting several times a week for coffee. It was a good life, filled with fun and fellowship.

Eight weeks ago, something changed. Kevin wasn't a secretive man, but he'd become distant, not dropping by Bruce's office or their house anymore. This wasn't like him, and Bruce was worried that he may have done something to offend Kevin, though he couldn't imagine what. Mary thought it more likely that Kevin and Kari were having marital problems, and needed time to work things out. She suggested Kevin might be too embarrassed to talk about it.

One afternoon, Kevin came rushing into his office.

"Bruce!" Kevin said in a hushed voice as he shut the door behind him. "I need to talk to you."

"Sure," Bruce replied, relieved his friend was finally talking again. "Sit down. I've got some time before I need to go out on the line."

"Not here!" Kevin said anxiously, glancing around the room. "Meet me in the parking lot after work tonight, but be sure you're alone."

Bruce agreed, and Kevin left quickly without even saying goodbye. It was a confusing moment, generating numerous questions in his mind. He wondered if Kevin had done something stupid, like cheat on Kari. But that just wasn't like him, so he would just have to wait a few more hours to get some answers.

Bruce walked to his car that night, but he didn't see Kevin anywhere. It occurred to him that Kevin, who loved a good practical joke, might have been pulling his leg earlier. He arrived at his car, hit the door lock, and threw his briefcase into the back seat before settling in behind the wheel. Backing out of his parking slot, he was about to take off when Kevin suddenly appeared, pounding on the side window with his fist.

"Open up!" Kevin yelled, slamming his hand against the glass.

Bruce hit the door lock, and Kevin dove in.

"What's going on?" Bruce asked, totally confused by his friend's strange antics.

"Just drive," Kevin answered. "I'll tell you about it on the way."

He looked his friend over for an instant before deciding he was serious.

"Look," Bruce said as he drove out of the lot and onto the city street. "If you're having problems at home, Mary and I are here for you guys."

"Problems at home," Kevin answered, somewhat bewildered. "This has nothing to do with my home life."

"Then what is it?" Bruce pressed. "You've been acting plenty strange lately. And what about last week, when you started spouting off in our weekly meeting? I thought you were joking when you said if Management got any more involved in our lives, they would be telling us what color shorts to wear. It was kind of funny, but did seem a little out of place."

"Exactly," Kevin replied. "I'm out of place. Look, Bruce, you're a good friend, but there are things going on you don't know anything about."

"Things? What kind of things?"

"Dangerous--no, deadly things--things that keep me up at night. Things we're not supposed to know."

"What are you saying, Kevin? What's wrong?"

"I can't tell you much yet," Kevin answered bleakly, staring out the window as Bruce drove along. "But you need to come to a meeting with me and Kari this weekend. Maybe then things will start making sense to you just as they have to me."

"What kind of meeting?"

"I've seen things, Bruce, things you wouldn't believe if I told you. But you have to trust me. Things are not as they appear."

"You're scaring me!" Bruce replied, gripping the wheel tightly. "I hope you haven't gotten involved in anything illegal. You know we're not like that."

"It may be too late already, man!" Kevin said, nearly shouting as he hit his fist on the dash. "We're all in trouble. Just drop me off at the next stop. I'll get home on my own."

Bruce was really worried, and didn't want to leave him alone, but he was adamant. He dropped Kevin off after agreeing to go with them to the meeting that coming weekend. That seemed to calm Kevin a bit.

That weekend, Kevin and Kari picked up Bruce and Mary, and headed to the outskirts of the city. Kevin kept to the back roads, constantly checking his rear view mirror, and Bruce pretended not to notice as he kept up a steady stream of small talk. Eventually they turned down a long gravel drive that ended at a large barn. There were already hundreds of cars parked by it.

"Wow!" Bruce exclaimed. "You really have a crowd here."

The meeting lasted about an hour, and was dominated by a central speaker who stayed behind a screen, and used voice distorting equipment. It didn't sit well with Bruce who didn't understand all the secrecy. But Kevin assured him he would be in danger if Management found out who he was. That was hard enough to swallow, but when he went on about conspiracies, disappearances, and even deaths, Bruce had heard enough. He told Kevin it was time to leave.

The ride back was quiet until Bruce finally spoke.

"Why are you interested in stuff like that? Management has done nothing but help us since they took over. We have good jobs, and plenty to eat. Why listen to some lunatic talk about weird stuff? You guys were never like this before."

"I know it must seem strange to you," Kevin replied, leaning forward on the steering wheel, "and I know you probably think we're crazy, but I've seen things, things going on at work, and other places. They're not what they pretend to be."

"So, where's your proof? Show me something--anything."

"Kari and I were hiking on Grace Mountain several months ago when I slipped, and fell down a hole into a cave. I wasn't hurt, but I found this small cavern with markings on the wall. I also found an object inside, and it was really cool looking, and interesting. But then I discovered there was more to it than I could ever have imagined. I can't say any more about it now. It's too dangerous for you to know too much. You'll just have to wait."

Bruce wasn't satisfied with Kevin's explanation, and pressed for more details, but he wouldn't say any more. However, Bruce had always trusted Kevin's judgment, so he let it go. But over the following weeks, unexplainable things began to happen.

"Things have really changed since we went with Kevin and Kari," Bruce said while Mary laid out his clothes. "It's been a little over two months, and nothing is right anymore, and that blasted meeting keeps coming to my mind. Can they really be secretly euthanizing people? Anybody thought to be a resister? And now both he and Kari are missing. It has been nearly a week with no word. Could they really be gone? Taken by someone, somewhere? This is way too crazy."

"I know!" Mary sighed. "I'm really worried about them too. I've been calling their house for two days straight, but they're not answering. Yesterday, I drove over to see if I could catch her at home, but the house was locked up tight. I checked their mailbox, and it doesn't look like anyone has picked it up in a while. I let myself in with the spare key they keep under the mat, and put the mail on their table. It definitely felt weird. Dirty dishes were stacked on the counter, and the laundry hadn't been folded. That's just not like her."

Closing the bedroom door, Bruce sat on the small couch at the end of the bed to put his socks on as Mary sat next to him. He leaned back, and looked at her. They both knew the day had come.

Mary squeezed Bruce's hand as she looked deep into his blue eyes.

"Are you sure, Bruce? Our life was just starting to feel normal again."

"I know," he said, looking away. "But you know how tight it's getting at work. Every week it's something new, but this thing with Kevin is the final straw. Did I tell you Harry Allison came down to see him? They came out of Kevin's office together, and Kevin shot a glance at me I've never seen before. I swear, his eyes were full of fear. They left together, and that was the last time I saw him. The next day, this new guy arrived, and took over his office. I've been quietly asking around, but nobody knows anything."

Bruce fumbled nervously as he tied his shoe laces.

"Then Harry calls us up to his office," Bruce continued. "To end the rumors, I guess. But all he would tell us is Kevin has been reassigned. You and I both know that's not true. They would have come over and said goodbye before they left. They would have given us their new address. I asked how to reach him so I could send him a card, but Harry just brushed me off, saying he was unavailable right now. When I pressed a little more, he closed the meeting, and sent us back to our offices. I tell you, Mary, it was unnerving. I could see fear on the faces of some of my fellow supervisors. Even worse, Harry's been milling around the offices more of late. That's not like him to come around "the help." I do my best to play dumb until he gets bored, and leaves."

"Be careful today, Bruce," Mary interjected.

"We need to stick to our plan. Have you arranged things with David?"

"You said not to use the phone, so I sent David a letter letting him know where we're heading. I wrote that things were not good, and he needed to be careful. But, he knows where to find us."

Mary slipped her arm around Bruce's neck, hugging him hard.

"This has to be our final day then," Bruce continued. "We'll head out of the city, and go to your mom's until we figure out what to do. Her house is big, and well-secluded in the country. I've been very careful not to say anything to anyone, so no one knows what we're doing."

"I'll be ready when you get home. I have everything we need in the special case under the bed. It has taken me nearly three days to gather the necessary supplies, but I believe I have most everything. All we need is a few more bottles of water, and I think I can borrow them from our neighbor, Jackie Cantrell. I told her last week you were working out again, and our allotment was nearly out. She always takes the full amount, but can never drink it all. She said I could have whatever extra she has. She likes you anyway."

"I had better get going," Bruce said getting up, grabbing his lunch, and heading towards the front door. "I don't want to be late today!"

Mary took Bruce's arm gently as they walked through the living room. Stopping at the door, Bruce gave Mary a long kiss and big hug before heading down the stairs. She locked the door, and pushed the curtain aside to watch him leave.

The traffic was heavy as he headed into the city. Normally, Bruce would call Mary on his cell, and chitchat about their day, and what they were planning for dinner that night. But the clicking noise Bruce had noticed the last couple of weeks had made him suspicious.

"Was somebody listening in on our conversations?" Bruce thought, as he replayed recent events in his mind.

Several weeks earlier he decided to test his theory, so he interjected the phrase, "going outside the bubble," into one of the conversations involving their son, David. Bruce was surprised when that very afternoon, Harry dropped in unannounced. Harry asked how things were going, and how Mary was doing. It all seemed a bit surreal. He stayed a long while, conversing about different things. Bruce provided vague answers, trying not to say anything that would be suspicious.

"And how is David doing?" Harry finally asked unexpectedly. "Is he getting along ok in his studies? I've heard you say such good things about him, and would love to meet him. Why don't you bring him by the office soon--maybe next week? I'm sure he's a chip off the old block and would fit in here nicely."

Bruce swallowed hard, and tried not to appear nervous.

"Sure, I think David would like that," Bruce answered calmly. "I'll give him a call, and see if he can make it. I think his finals week is coming up soon, so he may not be free, but I'll call him just to be sure."

Harry checked his watch.

"Oh, one other thing I forgot to mention," Harry said stopping at the door. "Your name came up for promotional review. You're smart, and a good supervisor. I'm thinking you could make a good addition to my team."

Bruce stood up, stumbling for words.

"Wow," Bruce said, more nervous than excited. "I've been working hard, but never thought anybody noticed. It would make Mary very happy to see me progressing."

"And don't forget the raise associated with an appointment." Harry said encouragingly. "I'm sure you could afford to move up from that little house you're in on the outskirts, and find a nice apartment here in the city. Think about it, and we'll talk some more, maybe at dinner some night."

Harry provided one of his plastic smiles as he left.

Bruce's thoughts returned to the present as he pulled into his parking spot.

"A good addition to the team," Bruce laughed to himself, turning off his car, and depositing the keys in his pocket. "They've never shown interest in me before, so why now? Putting me on their supposed list for appointment is a joke. I run a tight ship, and get the job done, but I don't brown-nose, and they like people who slobber after them, and hang on their every whim. The only reason to tempt me with appointment is to watch me. I really need to find Kevin."

Bruce buried his head in his hands, feeling the pressure of the day.

He just wanted to get the day over with, so he could get home, and they could leave. The man from the meeting had said Management would do anything to control their lives, including making people disappear. Bruce hadn't really believed him at the time, but given the last few weeks, it no longer seemed ridiculous.

Bruce was starting to feel ill as he walked up the steps to his office. Settling in for the day, he leaned forward in his chair, and tried to concentrate. Doubts filled his mind as he fumbled through production reports from the previous nightshift.

"We've been hearing unusual things, and we're just curious people, that's all," Bruce assured himself. "Management has been good to us, providing our daily needs, supplying food, medical services, power for our home, everything we need.

"But then they came out with their public announcement, condemning resisters as radical. But we're not resisters. Going to that meeting seems like a bad dream, and because of it, today we're changing our lives forever…"

Bruce's thoughts returned to the day at hand as he realized the shift had started. He needed to get down to the line.

"Come on, man!" Bruce said to himself, as he grabbed his hardhat off the rack. "Pull yourself together. Things are going to work out fine."

He usually enjoyed walking through operations and talking with his operators, but not today. He stopped by each control room to review the night shift reports, and check the stability of the system. Things were normal as he reviewed printouts, and talked briefly with his team leaders, reminding them to be safety-minded. Bruce walked out of the central area, and headed towards the outer area, where raw materials and dross containers were kept. His morning round was going well, and he wanted to be sure everything was in order. Today was not the day for problems. He hoped to get out early if possible.

He could hear the Blue unit working, and every few minutes a large, heavy transporter would lumber by, headed to or from the main units. Taking out his portable scanner, he began a quick material inventory. The cavernous outer ring would take several hours to walk, so Bruce hopped on a small electric cart he kept charged for just such occasions.

He was about half way through the morning inspection weaving in and around the stacks of materials when he noticed smoke rising from one of the dross containers. Dross was a byproduct of the power generator, but it was also recyclable, and fed back into the main processor.

Curious, Bruce, pulled up next to the hot container, stood on the running boards, and peered over the side. The smoke was black, with a curious, sickening smell. Safety rules required no foreign substances be thrown into these containers, as it could cause an explosion. It was a serious safety violation, and Bruce was plenty mad.

"I just can't believe people can be so careless," he said, parking his cart, and hopping off to walk around the back side of the huge container.

Pulling his note pad from his pocket, he recorded the dross container number, seven, and noted its location and condition before returning the pad to his pocket. Each container had welded numbers on the sides for inventory purposes, but they worked just as well for tracking situations like this. Somebody was responsible for this container, whether they put the trash in it or not, and it was Bruce's job to get to the bottom of it.

It was hot, and in spite of his fire retardant clothing, standing close to the container was uncomfortable. But, he needed a closer look, and more evidence if he was going to nail the person responsible. He had once watched a careless operator dump garbage in one, and the explosion had nearly killed him and a passerby.

It was impossible to tell if the substance was thrown in number seven before or after it was filled, but whatever it was, it was large and heavy. Heavy enough to stay nearly submerged in the molten material.

"If I can figure out what's in there," Bruce mumbled, shielding his face from the heat with one hand, "somebody's going to pay."

It was apparent Bruce needed more protection as he stepped away from the container to put on his respirator, gloves, and face shield. He looked around until he found a long piece of wood. The smoldering material was in the middle of the container, so he poked at it, trying to shove it closer to one side. The surface of the dross was beginning to solidify as it cooled.

He shoved hard into the dross, breaking through as the end of his stick caught fire. Shoving hard, the sweat rolling down his face, he finally hooked something. He lifted up to see what appeared to be a blackened stick with a rounded end. Try as he might, he could not coax the stick close enough to the side to get ahold of it. It was attached to some larger object under the surface. The heat was getting more intense, so Bruce pulled away, throwing the burning stick to the floor. Staring intently at the oddly-shaped object protruding from the superheated material, he couldn't quite think what it reminded him of.

Suddenly, the horrifying realization dawn on him: it was a human femur bone.

Bruce stood there, trying to wrap his mind around the sight. Flames licked up the side of the blackened bone as it slowly slid back under the surface.

"I'll need to get help down here, and cordon off the area," he thought. "Security will need to investigate. Something terrible has happened here."

He had taken only a few steps towards his electric cart when a dross container truck came whipping around the concrete barrier. The truck operator, hidden by dust and smoke, slammed into container number seven, spinning it around, and sending a wave of white-hot dross over the side, and onto Bruce.

The pain was incredible. His fire-resistant clothing barely slowed the superheated dross as it lit him on fire. Worse, Bruce had taken off his gloves a few seconds earlier, and a reflex action caused him to lift his unprotected left hand to shield his face. Instantly, the material burned through layers of skin. Bruce dived behind a second container, avoiding being engulfed entirely as the dross spilled onto the concrete surface, spewing smoke, and throwing ash into the air.

The driver paused for a moment, apparently looking for Bruce, and then pulled back, and sped away. Bruce stumbled to his feet, holding his left arm as he heard the transporter roaring into the distance.

The ground around him was smoking, and he coughed heavily, his eyes burning. Flames shot up the sides of the hard rubber tires on his electric cart as hot liquid ran across the concrete. Bruce worked his way along, skirting the widening pool of burning floor, until he was in front of the cart. He climbed over the handle bars onto the seat, and floored it. The cart bolted forward, tires flaming, as he pulled onto the main roadway.

Bruce was in so much pain, he could barely think. But years of training paid off as he instinctively pulled the emergency package specially designed to help burn victims from the compartment on the back of the cart. His left arm hung limply at his side, unable to assist as he ripped open the package with his teeth, and pulled out the burn cloth.

It was his first look at the damage to his hand. Two fingers were covered with a hardened, silvery substance, and the rest, including his palm, was black as coal. Bruce knew he was in trouble as he wrapped his hand with the gauze soaked in a special burn solution. It was designed to protect from further injury, provide pain relief, and keep the patient comfortable until they could be transported, but shock was setting in as he forced himself to remain conscious.

Using his right hand, Bruce tried to secure his arm to his body with the gauze. However, things were becoming foggy as he leaned forward on the cart handles. Bruce put it in gear and headed in the direction of the aid station. He tried to call for help, but the radio was fried to a crisp. His situation was dire, and his vision blurred as he wheeled around the outer area through the causeway. He was fading in and out, and struggling to maintain consciousness as he weaved his way along.

"Keep going!" Bruce said to himself as the cart glanced off a concrete post. "You can do it."

The pain from the burns on the back of his neck drew his attention away from driving as the effects of the adrenaline rush were wearing off, and the pain was becoming unbearable. His condition was quickly worsening, with no help in sight as waves of nausea overwhelmed him. He lost consciousness, and slumped over the wheel just as he entered the area below the control center. His cart coasted to a stop against the side of a concrete pillar, and he fell out onto the hard, cold concrete.

CHAPTER 10

George had just returned from his coffee break when he spotted Bruce from the control room window. Leaping to his feet, he ran down the stairs and across the vast building, heading for his injured friend.

"Dead, dead in number seven," Bruce mumbled as George assessed his condition.

"You'll be ok," George said as he radioed in the emergency call, fearing the worst.

Bruce had become unresponsive, which frightened him even more.

"I've got a seriously injured man on the lower level below the control room." George shouted into his radio. "He has burns on hands, arm, and I think under his shirt. I can't tell for sure, but it looks bad."

"I'll send the ambulance to your location," the radio crackled back at George. "Use a burn kit if you have one."

In a few minutes, the rescue vehicle pulled up, and two medical personnel dressed in white jumped out. One assessed his vitals as the other offloaded the gurney. George was a powerful man with a barrel chest, and he helped lift Bruce into the ambulance. He hopped in as they headed for the hospital. The EMT covered Bruce with a sheet designed to transmit electronic stimulus and help stabilize him. It was connected to a machine that monitored bodily functions.

The ride was quick–before he knew it, they had pulled into the emergency room at the hospital. The EMT asked George questions regarding the incident along the way, questions he couldn't answer. He had no idea how Bruce had gotten hurt. All he could provide was his name, and some general information. Fortunately, all workers at the plant were required to wear special tags containing personal and medical information, so they were able to access Bruce's medical records.

"Thank you for your help," one of the EMTs said before wheeling Bruce onto the elevator. "But you can't come in here. This is for medical staff only."

George walked past the tech's outstretched arm, and onto the elevator.

"I'm staying with him," George asserted. "He's my friend, and I'm not leaving his side."

The tech quickly weighed his options as George took his place alongside the gurney. He reached past him, and pushed the up button.

The door opened on the third floor where an emergency team led by Dr. Della Larson waited. Quickly inserting needles into Bruce's right arm, they began a flow of rehydrating fluids. Aides took over wheeling the gurney to the intensive care unit, and heavy glass doors opened automatically as they approached.

George was right on their heels when the doctor stepped in front.

"Sorry, sir," Dr. Larson said, "you'll need to stay out here. We'll take care of your friend now. The next couple of hours are critical. I'll let you know as soon as possible how he's doing. There's a waiting room, and some fresh coffee just down the hall."

Dr. Larson was quite attractive, and George was equally unattractive, with a large, bulbish nose bent slightly to one side from one of the many bar fights he enjoyed. However, she was not to be trifled with, and even a bruiser like George knew better than to question her.

"You be sure and let me know how he's doing, ok?" He said, stopping short of Dr. Larson's outstretched hand. "Here's my number," George continued as he wrote it on a piece of scrap paper from his pocket. "I need to go back to the plant, and see if I can figure out what happened. They'll want to start a safety investigation right away."

"You do that, and don't worry; he's in good hands now," she assured him as she headed into the ER.

Dr. Larson's selfless service to wounded civilians and soldiers during the struggle had made her reputation. Even though it had only lasted a few weeks, she had dealt with countless dead and injured.

Once the initial conflict ended, Management was eager to bring her on board, and even built the hospital according to her specific needs before making her the chief administrator. She could be of use, they reasoned; a popular figure, bringing people together under the new order---the perfect public relations score. But as much as she was needed to run the place, she was also the city's best surgeon and general practitioner. Cases of this magnitude required her personal attention.

She followed the gurney into the chamber designed specifically for burn victims, and quickly assessed Bruce's condition. Hooked to life support, she applied a silver ointment to his wounds. His skin felt cool and clammy to the touch, and those were clear signs of shock. He was in serious trouble, but there was little more to do than wait. It was up to Bruce now, and the best they could do was to keep him comfortable, and wait for the drugs to kick in.

Meanwhile, George called the incident in to the main office. Serious injuries at the Central Power Processor unit had to be reported to the Citadel, which was responsible for all emergency services. Barron was available for duty when the call came through, but he hated spending time with the "lessers," as he called them, so Parks was dispatched instead to inform Mary Clawson of her husband's condition.

Mary was busy in the kitchen packing their carryalls when the knock came. She quickly slid the bags behind the pantry door, and went to see who it was.

"Did Bruce get off early, and forget his house key?" She wondered as she headed for the door.

"Hi, Mary," Parks said as she opened the door, "may I come in?"

"Parks?! What are you doing here?" she said nervously, as he stepped into the entry. "I mean, how are you doing? It's been a while since I saw you last. Wasn't it at the office several years ago when Bruce was promoted? What brings you way out here?"

Mary's mind was racing. She thought their plan was safe, but had Parks found out somehow? It was then she realized the case she had been packing was sitting on the bed, and visible through the reflection in the living room mirror. Struggling to keep her composure, she took Parks's right arm, strategically turning him from the living room into the kitchen.

"Come in and sit awhile," Mary said, pulling mugs from the cupboard. "It's so great to see you. I'll make some fresh coffee."

"Thanks, Mary, but no," Parks replied as he sat down, "This is not a social call. Please sit for a minute. I have something important to tell you."

She sat across from him, feeling the weight of their decision as he looked compassionately into her eyes.

"Bruce was injured today at the facility," he said quietly, taking her hand. "I don't know all the details, but I'm sure he'll be ok."

Mary froze. She was both relieved and mortified at the same time.

"Bruce is hurt?" she stammered, her voice cracking slightly.

Parks gently squeezed Mary's hand.

"There was an accident," he said calmly. "That's all I know. But Bruce is in the best of hands. Why don't you ride in with me and see for yourself?"

Mary leaned back against the chair, visibly shaken.

"Ok," she replied, "just give me a minute to get ready." She headed into the bedroom while Parks stepped outside.

Mary shut the door, and quickly slid the lead-lined case under their bed. Bruce designed it to keep prying eyes out of their most personal secrets. He had filled it with things they would need once they left, including several illegal weapons. Security forces did random neighborhood scanning, looking for things Management technically considered the scans illegal, but they made no effort to stop them either. But the scans couldn't see through lead.

She grabbed her coat and wrap, and met him on the porch.
On the way, Parks made light conversation to keep her mind off the accident. There was no reason to speculate on the seriousness of Bruce's injury, and Mary struggled to keep her composure as they worked their way through the city. She jumped out of the vehicle as he pulled up to the main entrance, and bolted for the hospital, nearly running into the heavy glass doors before they could open. Stopping momentarily at the main desk, she frantically asked where Bruce Clawson was.

Parks stepped up alongside, and leaned over the counter. The receptionist was busy checking her files for Bruce's information.

Finally, she got on the phone.

Mary was in a state of shock, and impatiently tapping her fingers on the counter. She was working hard to keep it together.

"Somebody will be down in a moment," the receptionist said, putting the phone down, and pointing in the direction of the crowded waiting area. "You can take a seat over there."

Parks followed Mary as they found a couple of seats.

"He's going to be fine," Parks said comfortingly. "You'll see."

Mary looked a little pale as she wrung her hands nervously.

"Bruce has become quite influential, and I hear nothing but good things," Parks said trying to keep Mary distracted. "He talks about you and David all the time when I do get to see him. He mentioned David is getting close to graduation, and has a 3.9 GPA. You must be very proud."

"We are," she replied just as she spotted Dr. Larson approaching. She jumped up, and hurried out of the waiting area to meet her.

"Hi, Mary," Dr. Larson said, taking her hand warmly. "I'm sure you have a lot of questions. Please come into my office. You come too," she said, glancing up at Parks.

They walked together down the hall past many overflowing rooms. The facility was built to handle a certain number of patients, but it was not enough to truly meet the needs of the city. It was just big enough to look good, like everything else Management provided.

Dr. Larson's office sat at the end of the corridor, and she held the door for both Mary and Parks. Her office was modestly furnished with a large desk, several comfortable lounge chairs, and a couch positioned next to some windows. The walls were lined with cabinets filled with patient charts and medical books and the large glass windows behind her desk, which overlooked the main entrance to the center. She liked seeing her patients walk out healed, and it also gave her a bird's eye view of incoming casualties. Her life was committed to the well-being of people, and she loved her work.

"Please, sit down," she said gently, waving towards the two overstuffed chairs as she sat behind her desk.

Folding her hands, she looked compassionately into Mary's worried face.

"Mary, I won't kid you," she said. "Your husband has endured a severe accident, but I want you to know we're doing everything possible. His hand suffered most, but there are also burns across his neck and back. He's a smart man, though, and by using the first-aid burn kit, he reduced the damage. The wrap is designed to stay in place until the wound heals, and then it softens. Unfortunately, he couldn't reach his back, where there was a large burn. I've had him put into the burn tank. He's submerged in an even more potent balm than the one used in the wraps. It'll help stop further damage and aid his recovery."

Dr. Larson paused to give Mary a chance to absorb what she had said.

"Are you ok?" Dr. Larson asked gently.

"I'm ok," Mary answered weakly.

Parks reached over and gave Mary a reassuring hug.

"However, there's more to this accident than I understand, and that is why you're here, and not with your husband," Dr. Larson continued, her eyes darting between Mary and Parks. "Your husband's condition is primary, and I'll take you to him in just a few moments, but I need to tell you a story first."

"A story," Mary replied, somewhat confused.

"Please bear with me, and it'll all make sense." Dr. Larson said, coming around and leaning against the front of her desk.

"Two weeks ago, a patient of mine came in unexpectedly. He was upset, and claimed his life was in danger. At first I just listened, thinking he was overworked, or maybe having problems at home. I see that a lot nowadays with the pressure people are under. I treat at least ten cases a week, so it's not unusual.

"Anyway, I asked him why he felt someone wanted to hurt him, and he said it had to do with something he found, but he claimed he couldn't say too much, or it might get me into trouble too. That's when he got up, half-apologized for taking up my time, assured me it was all just a mistake, and apologized for coming.

"I told him I could prescribe something to help him sleep. Sleep deprivation can cause all kinds of mental issues and serious mental health problems, but he didn't want any drugs. I suggested he make a follow-up appointment in a week or so. He assured me he would do just that, and quickly left."

"What does this have to do with Bruce?" Parks interrupted. "I don't get it."

"Just give me one more minute, please!" Dr. Larson said, as she shot Parks a hard look. "You need to hear this."

Parks nodded, seeing how important this was to Della.

"Then an emergency call went out late one evening last week. I was told the victim had been beaten severely and stabbed, but when they brought him in, I couldn't find an entry wound. The only reason I believed it was a stabbing is that the men with him saw it happen, and swore up and down he was stabbed in the chest with some strange, clear-looking knife. A bruise on his chest confirmed something happened, and when I opened him up, I found severe damage consistent with a knife attack. However, his wound was cauterized, like someone had stabbed him with a hot poker. Fortunately, they missed his heart."

Parks leaned back in his chair with a far-away look.

"You can imagine my surprise when I found out it was the same patient who had been in my office the previous week." Dr. Larson continued, glancing over towards Parks, who stiffened a bit. "I did everything I could for him, even putting him in our special care unit on the second floor, and set the treatment protocol. I believed he had a solid chance, even though his injuries were severe.

"The point is, he told me something like this could happen to him, and it did. Well, it could have been coincidence, but this just didn't feel right."

Mary shifted nervously in her seat as Dr. Larson continued.

"That first night, one of my new nurses was making her rounds, doing her normal bed check. She went into his room, making sure everything was ok, and he was comfortable. I was holding him in a deep sleep with a sedative, and an analgesia drip combination to give his body the best chance possible. She made her check, charting his condition, and double-checked everything before leaving for the next room. I had him on a twenty-minute bed check, and the nurse was right on schedule. But when she returned on her following round, she found his IV had come out. She quickly checked, and found his pulse was negligible, and his breathing shallow. She immediately called for emergency help, and two other nurses arrived to assist, but they couldn't get his blood pressure stabilized, so they decided to move him up to Intensive Care on the third floor."

Dr. Larson walked to the window, and gazed outside for a moment before turning back.

"I know you're both wondering what this has to do with Bruce, but this is where the story takes a turn I can't explain, and it could have everything to do with him. Two orderlies suddenly appeared in his room, and prepared him for the move. My nurses were surprised and pleased, as you usually have to find those guys that late at night. They're either on break, or sleeping somewhere. Anyway, my second-floor head nurse instructed them to take him up, and report to ICU immediately. They pushed his gurney out of the room and down the hall to the elevator while she went for the phone to alert ICU.

"After making the call, my head nurse pulled the new nurse into her office to examine her regarding the IV incident. The new nurse assured her there was no way the IV came loose. She started crying, insisting it's impossible as the connection requires two hands to secure, and it was secured when she left the room. Both her chart notes and the ID on the IV bag confirmed she didn't change it, so there was no reason it should have come loose. While they were still talking, the phone rang from ICU. They wanted to know what the delay was."

Dr. Larson took a deep breath.

"He never made it to ICU."

"He never made it?" Parks said curiously.

"No, and I see by Bruce's tag that he works at the Central Power Processor as a supervisor. Coincidently, my missing patient also worked there in the same position. Do you know a Kevin Knobbs?"

"Kevin Knobbs?" Mary said, her voice quivering slightly. "Kevin is Bruce's best friend. We've been really worried about him, and haven't seen him or his wife, Kari, for quite a while. You mean he was here, he's the man you're talking about?"

"Yes, and all I can say is he disappeared, and I don't know why," Dr. Larson replied. "It's only when I realized they worked together that I thought it best to meet with you personally, and bring this to your attention. Just a minute, I need to show you both something more."

Dr. Larson reached under her desk, and flipped a switch. A small panel opened on the wall, revealing three buttons. She walked over and pushed one as she motioned to Mary and Parks. The wall on the side of her office adjacent to the windows began to slide open, revealing a glass enclosure, and a hidden room. Mary approached the glass wall while Dr. Larson flipped on a light switch. The lights in the room brightened gradually, revealing sophisticated medical devices, and a hospital bed in the middle.

From Mary's angle, she could tell the bed had a patient.

"What, what, who is this?" she asked, confused.

Dr. Larson stepped close beside Mary, and took her arm.

"It's Bruce," Dr. Larson replied gently.

"Bruce," she said, pressing her face against the glass.

"Mary," Dr. Larson said, "I brought Bruce down here this morning. You and Parks are the only ones other than my nurses who know he's not still in ICU."

"But why? Why did you bring him down here?" Mary asked, her voice shaking. "I don't understand. Let me see him. Can I go in?"

Mary was becoming agitated as she looked at Bruce through the glass.

Dr. Larson gripped her arm tighter.

"Your husband is safe for now," she said comfortingly, "but I can't let you in yet. The room is sealed, and being purged to make sure there's no contamination."

Dr. Larson gently pulled her away from the glass.

Mary turned away, looking blankly into Dr. Larson's eyes.

"Come on over, Mary," Dr. Larson continued. "Just give me another moment to explain, and it should all make sense."

Dr. Larson led Mary back to her seat, and helped her sit down. She was deeply troubled, struggling to hold back her tears as she kept glancing towards the glass wall.

"I brought Bruce into my special facility this morning shortly after he came here. Years ago, I had this office built "off the plans" as they say. You are now part of a very select group who know about it. When they were building this facility after the struggle ended, I had some good friends who owed me favors, and they helped me design this part of the building. They were very creative in seeing no one suspected anything. There's a small elevator disguised as a storage closet from the third floor to the back of this special room. It sits at the end of the hall next to the back wall. You have to know it's there to operate it."

Dr. Larson glanced over to Parks again.

"I set this room up for people who needed special care. Management is always talking about efficiency instead of effective treatment. So over the years, I've brought people needing special medical attention down here, but this time I did it for security reasons. I don't want him disappearing like Kevin."

"Do you really think someone would want to kidnap Bruce?" Mary asked. "Why would anyone want to do that?"

"I don't have those answers, but I'm hoping Parks here can help find out."

"I'll look into it," Parks replied firmly.

Dr. Larson reached over her desk, and took Mary by the hand. It was a lot to absorb, and she knew Mary would need a moment.

"You can wait upstairs if you want, but I think it would be good for Parks to take you home for now. Your husband must rest, and there's nothing more you can do for him. Why don't you plan on coming back in about four hours, and I'll make sure you're called if there's a change before then."

Mary looked longingly at the figure stretched out behind the glass, and reluctantly nodded her head in agreement.

"Ok," Parks replied, glancing at Della as he led Mary to the door. "I'll make sure she gets home safely, and check around a little. I'm sure I can find out what's going on around here. In the meantime, it looks like you've got things well in hand."

CHAPTER 11

George left the hospital, hoping Bruce would be alright. He had to get back to his post fast, and let his superiors know what happened, and he also knew there would be plenty of buzz. His first stop would be to drop Bruce's cart off at the maintenance shop. It was in bad shape, and barely able to drive straight, let alone turn safely.

George rolled up to one of the open bays, and was greeted by the smells of diesel and oil and the sight of two greasy shoes protruding from under a large forklift. The cart's front wheel fell off just as he came to a stop.

"Hey, George," The main maintenance man said, rolling out on his creeper with a work light in one hand, and a wrench in the other. "What'd you do, run that thing into a wall or something?"

"Worse than that," George said as he climbed off. "Bruce Clawson was in an accident. I just came from dropping him at the medical facility, and he's in worse shape than this thing."

"Whoa...," The man said putting the wrench away in the tool chest, and wiping his hands on his coveralls. "That's bad. Is he going to be alright?"

"Don't know," George replied. "He was burned something awful."

"This thing looks like it's been through a war or something." The mechanic observed as he grabbed the handle bars, and pulled it into the shop. "The tires are even melted. How do you do something like that?"

"No idea," George replied, distracted. He had spotted Bruce's note pad on the cart floor. "Looks kind of like dross splatter on the fenders. Anyway, I'll need to sign out a loaner until you get this one fixed."

"If it can be fixed," he said, as they headed into the lockup to get a key. "This one may have to go straight to the scrap heap."

George rolled out towards his work station on the new cart. As the first responder, he was required to fill out the accident report, but it wasn't going to be easy, since he had no idea what happened. Yet he would be the one responsible for reporting the accident to the safety supervisor, and providing a narrative of the accident. Protocol demanded he make the report, but George didn't care much for paperwork. His strengths lay in his ability to keep a crew in line and focused, not in writing reports. That was his specialty, but today he would have to do more, like it or not.

He made the required calls, and started the accident report, but quickly became frustrated trying to answer all the questions. He put down his pen, and decided to go to the storage area. That might give him some answers, and help him figure out what happened. All he knew was the direction Bruce had come from. If he could retrace his steps, maybe it would make some sense. Besides, George wanted to get out in front of the investigation before senior management came down, and started snooping around. He didn't like being questioned, and not having answers.

George drove slowly through the outer storage area, looking for signs of the accident. He hadn't gone far when he noticed a faint black trail left by the cart tires as they melted. He followed it around several turns, and finally arrived at the edge of a wide pool of cooled dross.

He walked around the edge, trying to figure things out. There was the spot where the cart's tracks, immortalized in hardened metal, showed it was parked, and the clear tracks leading away, and out of the dross. But how did the dross get there? There was no container around, let alone one close to the spill site. But obviously, it had to have come from somewhere. This was shaping up to be more of a mystery than an accident. Logically, there should be a direct relationship between Bruce's injury and the accident site. But the only containers near the spill site were empty.

The scene just didn't make sense. He stood on the cart, and scanned the area. How could someone get hurt from hot dross spilled from a non-existent container? He would have a hard time filling out the accident report if he didn't get a break.

George took a few photos before pulling away and heading back to the office. He rolled the morning events over and over in his mind as he made his way along past numerous dross containers. Nothing added up. Then one set in the back at an angle caught his eye.

"Number seven," George said to himself as he wheeled around. "Bruce said something about number seven."

He pulled up, and checked the container. It was nearly full, and showed signs that dross had sloshed over one side. George examined the container closely. It was cool now, and had been put it in line for recycling. He pulled his radio, and made a quick call to one of the transporters.

In a few moments a large truck came rolling up.

"Put this container in the stockyard," George commanded the driver, "next to the ones needing repair."

Finally, things were looking up. At least he had found the source of the accident, but there were still no answers, just more questions. He followed the driver through the building and into the stockyard, where he put up a yellow tape barrier around the container to make sure no one would move it. When he returned to the office, the safety administrator was waiting for him.

"What happened here?" the man demanded the moment George came into the office. "We have a burn victim from some kind of freak accident or something. Do you have a report ready for me?"

"Not yet," George snapped as he put his radio on the desk, and sat down. "I've been a little busy trying to save Bruce's life. I'm going to need time to do some investigative work."

"Investigative work?" the man asked impatiently. "What investigative work are you talking about? From what I hear, a man got burned. End of story. I just need your signature on the bottom of the accident report, and I'll fill in the blanks."

George hated the focus on protocol and procedures that seemed more important than people. Management expected perfection, and hated anything less. But George was not about to be pushed around by some suit on this one. Bruce was not just his boss; he was his friend.

"I don't know what happened yet," George answered.

He pushed the paper away.

"There are things I don't understand, and it's going to take some time for me to figure this out before I can sign the report."

The safety administrator was annoyed as he paced across the floor. He was young and focused, mostly on his next promotion, and didn't want anything slowing him down, especially an accident. But he could see George was not going to give in easily.

"I'll give you till noon," he said, looking at his watch. "You have two hours to get this report on my desk. That's it. That's all you get."

George flashed him a hard look. The safety administrator looked slightly uneasy as he quickly exited the office, slamming the door behind him. George looked like a fighter. His crooked nose, narrow set eyes, and wide ears were imposing--add his broad shoulders and thick midsection, and he was a human fortress. He preferred to avoid violence, but if frightening the administrator bought him some more time, he would take it. He would have to come up with answers fast.

Then he remembered Bruce's notepad.

He pulled it from the inner pocket of his jacket, which hung by the door. Bruce had noted the typical things. Floors swept, tools put away, paper-work in order. Everything was ordinary until he came to the entry on container seven. Here, Bruce noted smoke rising from the middle of the container. Then he scribbled something George couldn't quite make out. He suspected it was after the accident, and Bruce was struggling to write.

"Boddy, Boady, Buddy," George said, trying to make out the word. "Wait a minute. What was that he said before passing out? 'Dead in number seven.' What could he have meant by that?"

Then it hit him.

"Body, body!" he exclaimed, jumping out of his chair. "Bruce was saying there's a dead body in container seven. That's what he was trying to write in his notepad--body. It's time to take another look at that container."

George grabbed his radio, and headed for the stockyard. He made it just as the transporter arrived.

"Pick that up, and follow me," George shouted over the roar of the motor.

The operator did as instructed, and followed George into an empty concrete bunker.

"Dump it right there," he yelled through the side window.

George hopped off, and walked to the side as the operator rotated the container, spilling its contents onto the floor. Hot dust and ash rose to the steel rafters above, sending a cloud through the building. The operator pulled away, and George got a good look at the pile of smoldering materials. He sent the operator back to production while he climbed into a small excavator parked nearby. He sifted through tons of smoldering dross, not sure of what he might find. The windows of the cab were getting hot, and he was sweating as he lifted the bucket into the air, sending a cascade of fine dust and debris flowing onto the floor.

A large, strangely-shaped object fell on the top of the pile, and slid to one side. George quickly jumped out of the cab.

His mind was racing as he grabbed a rake.

Using the tool, he pulled some tightly-wrapped material from the sticky dross, and spread it out on the concrete floor. The smell was sickening. He took another dig into the pile, and a blackened oblong object came out and rolled between his feet. He stepped back, and kicked it.

Looking up at him were the burned-out eye sockets of a human skull.

He jumped back as if it were a grenade. It couldn't be.

But lying there on the concrete, staring up at him blankly, was somebody's skull.

George was frozen.

Bruce was seriously injured, and now George had found a dead body, or at least part of one. He had no idea what was going on, but he needed a plan.

According to protocol, he should report this right away. But somebody had put a human body in a dross container, and Bruce nearly died when he discovered it. What would happen to him that same person found out that George knew about it?

He pulled a rag from the cab, and wrapped the smoldering skull. It was hot, but he did his best to treat it with respect. He knew this was once a person, maybe even someone he knew.

George stared at the smoking mess as he pulled away. There was no doubt he would have to report it, but to whom? Someone had obviously gone to a lot of trouble to cover it up, and George really didn't want to join Bruce in the hospital, or worse, the morgue. He would have to tread very carefully.

He loaded his cart, and was halfway to the medical facility when a security vehicle appeared around the corner.

"Not him!" George said to himself. "Now what?'

"What's going on?" Barron said, rolling down his window. "I heard there was an accident out here."

"Bruce Clawson was injured today. I was just checking it out for the report."

"And what have you found?" Barron replied, his eyes narrowing.

"Nothing. I didn't see anything that explains what happened. I guess we'll have to wait until Bruce can tell us himself."

"What's that all about?" Barron said pointing down the warehouse to where smoke was still rising from the pile George had been sifting through.

"One of the operators spilled some product." He answered, trying to play things down. "They'll be cleaning it up soon. I've got to get to the office and make my report. The safety guy seemed a little impatient."

George took off, not waiting for a reply, but he watched through the rear-view mirror on his handlebars as Barron drove in the direction of the smoke.

Security could only mean trouble. They never involved themselves in operations, so this wasn't good. George was getting more worried by the minute, but he had to make a stop at the one place he knew could help. He jumped in his truck, and went straight for Dr. Larson's office. Her receptionist said she was busy with a patient, but he insisted it was critical, and he had to talk with her right away. He had important information regarding the recent burn victim. Reluctantly, the receptionist paged the doctor.

"How can I help you?" Dr. Larson asked as she came down the hall.

"I only have a few minutes," George replied anxiously. "Is there someplace we can talk privately? I have something you need to see."

She waved him into a small office just outside the reception area.

"So what's this all about?" Dr. Larson asked, closing the door behind them.

"This," George said, handing her the wrapped skull. "I can't explain, but it may have something to do with what happened to Bruce."

Dr. Larson gasped as she unwrapped the package.

"Where did you find this?" she demanded.

"It was in the same container Bruce was checking when the accident happened," George replied. "I think Bruce found a body somebody didn't want found, and it cost him. You're the only other person who knows about this, and I don't even know if I should report it. I was hoping you could find out who it is."

"Where's the rest of the body?" Dr. Larson asked.

"In a pile of hot ash, or burned up," he replied tensely. "This is all I found."

"I'll run some tests, and see what I come up with. In the meantime, you go back to work, and I'll let you know if I find anything. Your secret is safe with me, so maybe you'll want to hold off on that report for now."

George was relieved, and thanked Dr. Larson, who put the skull in a sealed container. He nearly ran for the exit.

He signed the safety report, and told the safety administrator he couldn't figure out what actually happened. George was not easily frightened, but the whole incident had him spooked.

Later that morning, Dr. Larson took the skull to one of her friends who ran the forensic division. He said he would get to it as soon as he could, and send her the results directly. By the time she got back to her office, the phone was already ringing. He had sent the results directly to her computer. Several minutes passed before the report came onto her screen. Dr. Larson gasped as she read:

MATCH FOUND: KEVIN KNOBBS

Dr. Larson spent the first couple of nights in her office making sure things were going well. For his safety, Bruce had been staying in her special care unit, but she had other pressing duties, so she decided to move him to the third floor the following night after speaking with her nursing staff. Security was placed on high alert, and employees were required to show their identification badge to the security worker stationed by the nurse's desk before being allowed on the floor.

The new protocols required ten-minute bed checks instead of the standard twenty minutes, and Dr. Larson was feeling better about it. If there were any danger, she was sure they could handle it. Adding to her confidence, her best nurse, Darla, a tall red-head, was on night shift that week. Things were looking better.

Darla checked Bruce on schedule, and other than the fact his hand likely had to be amputated, he was showing definite signs of improvement. She made a double-check of the equipment before leaving for her next stop. She had just entered her next patient's room a few doors down the hall when she realized she forgot her clipboard in Bruce's room. Coming in, she grabbed it off the table, and was about to leave when something caught her eye. The color of the fluid in his IV bag should be clear, but instead it had a reddish tint.

Dropping her clip board, Darla pulled the IV from his arm, and quickly shut off the valve. Hitting the emergency alarm beside his bed, she checked his vitals. In a matter of seconds, nurses and hospital security filled the room.

"Who was just here?" Darla angrily demanded as she took the reddish bag off his stand.

They all looked confused as they said in unison they hadn't seen anyone pass by them.

"I want someone stationed by this door until I say otherwise," she said to one of the security personnel. "No one comes in or out of here without my permission."

She put a new bag and IV in, and stationed one of her nurses by his bedside. She didn't want him left alone for a second. Then she tucked the suspect bag under her arm, and headed to her office, where she quickly called Dr. Larson.

"I am heading in right now," Della said anxiously. "Is he ok?"

"Yes, I got there just in time," Darla replied. "I'm heading back right now to check on him again."

"What was in the bag you took off?"

"I sent it to the lab to be analyzed, and you should have the results when you get here."

Dr. Larson's good feelings evaporated as she made her way in. This was not expected. After all the precautions she took, someone had still managed to get to Bruce.

Something needs to change, she thought as she pulled into the hospital parking lot. I can't leave him alone for a minute without something happening. We need to find another means of protecting him.

She nearly ran to the room where Darla was double-checking everything.

"Ok, fill me in. How could this have happened?"

"I don't know," Darla replied. "There isn't a person on this floor that saw anything, and I wasn't gone more than a few minutes."

"We need to station one nurse inside, and another to take her place if she steps out. He cannot be left alone."

They agreed it was the best plan, and the only way to protect Bruce's life.

Meanwhile, Mary returned home to a dark, lonely house after spending hours at Bruce's side. The stress of possibly losing him was showing as she collapsed on the couch. Picking up the phone, she called their son, David, who was in finals at college, to tell him of his father's accident.

"Stay focused on what you have to do, and then come home," Mary said as David expressed the desire to leave immediately. "You know your father would insist you finish your finals."

David reluctantly agreed, saying his last one was later that day, and he would be there the following morning. Mary felt better just knowing he was coming, but there was little else she could do, so she started preparing food just to keep her mind clear. It wouldn't be wasted—like any young male college student, David was always hungry.

She laughed, remembering his high-school years and how hard it was to keep food in the house. The memories served to keep her from breaking down as the hours slowly passed. Exhausted, she went to bed early that evening.

"Hi, Mom," David said warmly as she walked into the kitchen the following morning.

David was a tall, muscular, dark-haired young man with steel blue eyes. Bruce and Mary couldn't have children, and adopted him when he was almost fourteen. That was when Mary and Bruce first met Dr. Larson and Kirsten, Parks' sister. Kirsten was working with Della for a special organization set up by the city fathers to assist citizens as they transitioned to the new order. It was their responsibility to match orphaned children with loving couples like Bruce and Mary. David had lost both his parents, but he was a strong, brave boy as he had proven when he escaped the Testers, and they loved him from the moment they met.

"David!" she exclaimed as she hugged him. "I'm glad you're home. I'm so worried about Dad."

"He's going to be ok, Mom," David said reassuringly.

"I know, but it's hard seeing him like that. I got a call this morning from his doctor. She wants to meet at noon, and I want you to come along. It may be good news. She sounded very positive on the phone."

Mary packed the food she prepared in a large lunch bag, and grabbed her coat. David had a lot of questions as they drove over, and his mom explained how things were not right, but Dr. Larson was keeping him safe in her special room. Parks was waiting in Dr. Larson's office when they arrived.

"David," Parks said jumping up from his chair, and grabbing his hand. "You're looking good, young man."

David pulled into Parks, and gave him a solid hug.

"And how are you, Dr. Larson?" David asked as he stepped back.

"I'm good but I didn't expect to see you. I'm glad you're here."

"Please have a seat," Dr. Larson said as she moved behind her desk. "I need to give you an update on Bruce, and more information regarding your friend, Kevin Knobbs. Did your mother tell you anything about that, David?"

"We talked a little. She said something about Mr. Knobbs's being attacked, and then going missing. She also mentioned some special precautions you've taken with my father as a result."

"That's correct," she continued. "Kevin disappeared under strange circumstances. He was taken by some mysterious orderlies we have no record of. That's why I brought your father to my special unit. It seemed too much of a coincidence that two supervisors from the Central Power Processor received grievous injuries a little more than a week apart. They were different circumstances, but something just didn't feel right."

"And you think it could have something to do with Dad?"

"I don't know anything for sure. We're just trying to do our best to protect your father."

"How is he doing?" Mary interjected, hoping for good news.

"I'm sorry to tell you that I had to remove his left hand. It was too badly burned."

Mary swallowed hard as David held her by her shoulders. "However, there is the possibility he may not need much skin grafting. The early application of the burn solution is working. But there's more. We had another issue last night."

"What kind of issue?" Parks asked, moving to the edge of his seat.

"It's hard to explain, but somehow Bruce's IV bag got changed."

"Changed?" Mary said, a dark feeling of dread filling her mind. "Like someone accidentally put the wrong one on?"

"It was no accident. His IV bag of saline was checked at 11:10 last night, and it was fine. Fortunately, my senior nurse Darla had to return to his room at around 11:13. That's when she noticed the bag had an off color, and she immediately removed it before any of the solution got into him. It was full of cyanide, and he would have died in a matter of minutes."

Mary gasped, and started to collapse as David grabbed her by the arm.

"My father's in danger," David said, holding tight to his mom. "We need to get him out of here right now!"

"You can't do that," Dr. Larson answered, "at least not yet. Exposing him to the outside environment would be too great a possibility of infection. He has to stay here a little longer."

"What do you propose then, if people are able to sneak in here and poison him?" Mary asked, her voice cracking.

"I called Parks, and we've come up with a plan I think you're going to appreciate. We've reported your husband's death to the authorities."

"You did what?" Mary replied, puzzled.

"We faked Bruce's death," Parks interjected. "We believe it's the best way to keep him safe and alive. Dr. Larson gave him a shot of something that mimics death before the medical examiner arrived. He certified his death as a result of the accident."

"Now what are you going to do?" Mary asked, looking somewhat relieved.

"We have a plan we would like to go over with you," Dr. Larson replied.

"Just a minute," David said. "I'd like to talk with Parks alone for a minute first if that's ok?"

Parks followed David into the hall.

"I know I can trust you," David said quietly. "Do you remember the day you found us?"

"I've never forgotten it," Parks replied. "You were quite the brave group."

"Well, you told us then there would come a time when we would be a force for change. I think that time has come, especially with what's happened to Dad. I'm part of a group of people who have been meeting to discuss that change. Several months ago, Dad and Mom came with Mr. and Mrs. Knobbs to one of our meetings. I was surprised to see them, and meant to talk to them afterwards, but didn't get the chance. I wanted them to know I was the one speaking from behind the mask."

"You always were the spokesman, as I remember."

"Well, we've been very careful to keep our meetings quiet and our activities secret, but now it seems we may have a mole, someone reporting on us to Management, and they may have recognized them, and reported back. Is there anything you can tell me, or have you heard anything?"

"No, and we're under charge to arrest anyone suspected of being a resister. What about this group you're talking about? You're doing a good job of keeping it secret, as I haven't heard anything about it until now."

"We've been meeting to discuss what we're all feeling. Management is surely up to no good. You must know that," David said looking solidly into Parks' eyes. "Look, we're the ones you rescued. We grew up together and went to the same school, yet never let on to anybody about our destiny. But we're not kids anymore. We're warriors preparing for battle."

David unbuttoned his shirt just enough to show Parks the crystal he gave him hanging from a silver chain around his neck.

"We're staying behind the scenes for now, but we need to know what's going on. I told Kevin he needed to talk to Dad and warn him to be careful, but I guess he never got the chance."

"I'm sorry to tell you, but Kevin's dead," Parks said. "Your dad found his remains at work."

"They killed Kevin?!" David said sadly, leaning back against the wall. "What about Mrs. Knobbs? She's ok, right?"

"We don't know. There's a missing-persons report out on her, but nothing yet. The main thing is, your dad is safe as long as people think he's dead. I say you go home and take care of your mom while we figure this out."

"I'll make sure Mom's ok, but I'm going to want to be involved. I'll do a little checking around and see if I can find something out."

Parks looked at David for a moment, remembering the day he pulled him and his friends to safety. He was bold, and committed to the freedom so many had given up in exchange for
"peace." He hadn't changed much, and if it was even possible, he was even more committed. It was a quality Parks admired.

"You do what you must, but remember there's a lot at stake. If things go sideways, there is no telling what might happen. It could be bigger than we know."

"Just a second," David said taking him by the arm. "We are more than a few. If needed, we'll come down on Management. But we're not just waiting. We're preparing for the future now."

They returned to Dr. Larson's office, and David sat next to his mother, hugging her shoulders.

"David is going to take Mary home," Parks said to Dr. Larson. "He'll help out with the funeral we'll create. Everything else is up to you."

"No problem," Dr. Larson replied. "I have nurses available who can keep an eye on him while he's down here if I'm busy. We'll make sure he gets better, and stays safe."

"Will I still be able to see him?" Mary asked.

"Maybe," Dr. Larson replied. "But it's probably best if you don't for a while. Wait until things have settled down. I'll show you how you can come here without being seen. Why don't you both get going--somebody will be in touch about the arrangements."

"Thank you so much," Mary said as they prepared to leave. "I can't imagine what would have happened to Bruce without you."

"What about Mary?" Della asked after they left. "She could be in danger too."

"David's with her now. She'll be ok."

"Did you know Kenzie has been volunteering here at the hospital? Darla is keeping her under her wing, showing her the ropes, but she's a natural caregiver. You did the right thing saving them that day."

"They're gifted children alright, but I still need to keep an eye on them. Things are happening that I don't quite understand yet. We'll talk more when I drop by later. You're going to be home, right?"

"I'll be home early tonight," Della said with a smile as she shut the door behind him.

The next several days would be critical but at least they had succeeded in removing Bruce from danger. Now it would be up to Parks and his investigative ability to find out what was really going on.

CHAPTER 13

The calm in the city was unnerving--like being in the eye of a hurricane. Management's system of control was getting more oppressive, even though it seemed things were sort of returning to normalcy for some people. But it was a new normal. One where disagreement wasn't allowed, and Management must be right all the time. There seemed to be little logic behind the constantly changing rules and protocols, unless the aim was to create chaos instead of peace. Jim Banner worked for the only independent media outlet in the area--HOT News. He was their weatherman, and a good one. His comedic nature and accurate forecasts made watching weather reports a highlight of most people's day. Calls and letters poured in constantly, making him the most popular celebrity in the city. Of course there were other stations, but they were kept under strict control, and people found them predictable. HOT News was different. They always strove for the truth, and worked to present it in the best way possible.

Jim liked working the obscure, out-of-the-way places. He would grab his crew, and show up in some random neighborhood for his early-morning broadcast. To make things even more exciting, someone at the studio would leak the location through a well-designed rumor mill. Once word got out, people showed up from all over the city, wanting to be part of the broadcast. Children and adults would crowd around, clamoring for a moment in the spotlight with Jim the Weatherman. Cadets were sent out to work crowd control, even though they weren't really needed. They just liked being a part of the show. Jim made it fun for everyone.

For the most part, Management could see no harm in allowing one competitor, and it even created an illusion of fairness. If anyone complained, they could point to HOT News as the "independent" station.

The day started off like any other. It was a cool, late-fall morning with a bite of winter in the air. He chose a spot in the upper section of the city at one of the facilities for non-productive people, and was busy unloading their gear for the morning show with the help of his crew. The city was divided into economic districts, allowing people and families who were deemed unproductive a place to go for retraining and evaluation. Here, citizens were processed, received new life goals, and learned new tasks designed to help them achieve personal satisfaction, and realize their full potential in life.

At least that was the selling point.

There were three separate Economic Diversity Divisions (EDDS) in the city: North, West, and East, all built essentially the same, with large buildings containing living quarters, retraining areas, exercise yards, and buildings that housed a variety of machinery, bunkers, and storage. These were home to thousands of city residents who had been committed for a variety of reasons. Most of the residents were older, sick, or disabled, but some were placed there for other reasons. But regardless of how or why people were there, EDDs were heralded as a progressive solution.

To sell the image, advertisements carried on controlled media outlets showed happy aged people tending beautiful raised gardens. They were heartwarming, especially when the advertisement zoomed in to catch "grandma" pulling carrots, and putting them in her basket. She wiped the sweat off her face with a dirty glove, leaving a smear across her forehead as she smiled into the camera. The ad then quickly cut to the network news anchors praising EDD for helping the "less productive" members of society find meaningful work in a stress-free environment.

It was a great sales tactic, and surveys showed it was working. People liked the idea that those less fortunate or in the later stages of life were being treated with respect, and given opportunities to live their lives with new purpose.

Jim's crew was ready to go inside the ten-foot high fence surrounding the complex as the crowd grew steadily. His excitement showed as the possibility of a serious weekend snow-storm loomed large. It was a bit early in the season, yet the Doppler radar indicated a real possibility of heavy snow with blowing winds.

The broadcast went as expected, with a large crowd of neighbors, and those who lived in the complex adding to the excitement. As soon as they signed off, Jim waded into the crowd to sign autographs, and talk with fans. His enthusiasm was contagious, and there were always some fans who decided to pursue a career in climatology because of his influence. Today was no different, and he seriously enjoyed the moment. He distributed signed autographed pictures of himself standing next to his specially designed black four-wheel drive.

People loved it.

The line was thinning, and the crowd had mostly dispersed when he noticed a young man pacing near the fence. He stayed in the back waiting until Jim was through.

"Do you want an autograph?" Jim asked kindly.

He shook his head.

Jim could tell the young man was nervous.

"How are you doing?" Jim asked in a friendly voice as he approached. "What can I do for you? Can I help you?"

"Yyyyess," the young man replied, stuttering.

"What's your name?" Jim asked gently, squatting down to look him in the eye.

Jim was 6'6", and his stature could be intimidating.

"My nnnamme is GGGrrreg," the young man replied.

"How can I help you, Greg," Jim said.

It was obvious Greg was upset. But Jim knew that meeting someone in his position was a bit overwhelming for adults, let alone this young man. Yet despite his impressive size and his fame, he had a way of making people feel at ease.

"I lllikked your bbbroadcaasstt," Greg said. Yyyou always tell us tttto follow our instincts and ppppayy attention to our environment. I need to tttalk to yyyou about something immmportant. Could I tttalk to you ssomewhere else?

Jim leaned forward, looking into his eyes as Greg looked intently back with a sincerity that impressed him. He also recognized deep concern in the young man's face.

"Why can't we talk here? I still have a few minutes before I have to leave."

Greg stepped back, wringing his hands nervously as he looked around.

"I ssshouldn't have sssaid anything!" he said as he started to walk away.

Jim stood, and took Greg gently by the arm.

"Just a minute," he said, "I can tell you're upset about something. I'm going to be in this neighborhood next week doing a follow-up on the weekend weather event. How about you come by and see me? I'll have a little more time, and maybe we can get a cup of coffee or something. You can tell me what's on your mind then. Sound good?"

Greg nodded once, then dashed off towards the main entrance.

Jim joined the crew in packing up the show. After a hectic broadcast, they were pretty much exhausted as they made their way through the gate onto the city street. As the van turned the corner, Jim looked over his shoulder just as the gate swung shut behind them. Something seemed odd to him all of a sudden. He had been by here many times, and had done several broadcasts, but he had never really noticed the walls and heavy gates. The armed guard secured it with a chain and padlock as they pulled away.

Suddenly it looked more like a prison than a place to send grandma.

The locked gate left a strange feeling in his gut; a feeling he would struggle to get rid of.

The main weather event Jim predicted skirted their area. It wasn't unusual for weather patterns to change suddenly this time of year, and he tended to the conservative side. It was better to be prepared than caught off-guard, he always said. But the change meant canceling plans for a follow-up broadcast.

Jim forgot all about his conversation with Greg until several weeks later when a letter arrived.

The mail at HOT News came to a central office, which in turn distributed it throughout the building. Jim was heading down the hall for a meeting with his producer and advertiser when the mail person spotted him.

"Jim, Jim, JIM!" she shouted, as he went speeding by.

He was a fast walker, and always running late, but slowed momentarily.

"Hi," Jim said as his attention turned. "You have some mail for me?"

She darted across the wide hall with a letter in her outstretched hand.

"I thought you might want this," she replied, smiling as she handed Jim a small envelope. "A nervous young man came by my office this morning. He seemed somewhat upset, and said this was very important, and you would want it. I had a little trouble understanding him. He stuttered something awful."

Jim took the letter, suddenly remembering Greg.

"Thanks. I'm sure it's nothing important. He's a fan I met," Jim said lightly, starting down the hall again. "You're the best. See you next week."

It was a long walk to the meeting as Jim stuffed the envelope into his coat pocket. He felt a little guilty for not following through with his promise to Greg, but rationalized it. After all, he was busy and the storm hadn't materialized.

He stopped and opened the letter anyway before returning to his fast pace. He had traveled those halls so many times, he could do it in his sleep, so reading and walking were no problem. Not to mention, people generally avoided collisions with him because of his size.

The letter was addressed to Jim Banner, Weatherman.

Obviously, Greg didn't know the address to the studio, or he could have mailed it. Jim figured he either got someone to bring him, or relied on a city bus driver.

"It took some effort to get this here," Jim thought to himself. "He must feel it is important to go to all this trouble."

The letter was written by hand. He immediately noticed Greg's good penmanship, spelling, and above-average grammar skills. He was surprised, as he understood that people who were placed in an EDD facility usually had some kind of debilitating handicap. But the writing style did not belong to a sub-productive, mentally handicapped person. This was the writing of an above-average, intelligent citizen. Jim's curiosity took over, and he stopped, and leaned against the wall.

Dear Mr. Jim Banner,

Thank you for speaking with me when you came by the complex. It was a great thrill to actually meet you, let alone talk with you. I've been your fan for years. I know you're busy, and I understand why you couldn't keep our appointment, but I was hoping you might have time to hear my concern, and why it's so important for me to speak with you. Here's my story. I hope you understand my urgency once you read it.

My parents died in a car accident when I was fourteen. I was left alone, as I have no other family. My dad worked in the Citadel as the chief accountant, and took good care of Mom and me. He must have made a lot of money, because after the accident, I was cleaning out the house, and found a suitcase full of cash. There was also a life insurance policy made out to me. I was able to cash the policy, and I put the money into a checking account my parents had set up for me. I used some of the money from the suitcase for living expenses, and the rest I was planning to use for college. The house was paid off, so all I needed do was pay the utilities and taxes.

It was pretty easy, and no one even thought to ask if I was alone, or if there were family members helping. I just kept to myself, and went to school. Dad taught me to be self-sufficient, and Mom made sure I could cook and keep house, so living alone was no problem.

A year after the accident, one of my teachers wanted us to bring our parents or guardians for a conference. I thought I could make an excuse and get out of it. I had done that before, and it worked. But this time, the teacher decided to drop by the house unannounced. It was a new "personal" approach the teacher's association enacted to meet parents who had not been able to make the regular conferences. When she came by, it was somewhat obvious I was alone. I made more excuses, but she became suspicious. She did her homework, asked around, and discovered my parents were dead. Needless to say, it was decided I should be moved to "safer," more controlled conditions. The house and everything in it was quickly sold, and, as far as I know, given to the EDD to pay for my room and board. They also took my check book, saying I was not old enough, or capable of handling it. I did my best to protest, and show them I was taking care of things with no problems, but as you know, my speaking abilities are rather limited.

I've been here at the East EDD for nearly four years. Actually, next Monday will be the fourth anniversary, which is why it's so important I speak with you right away. This facility was opened twelve years ago, and came to full capacity nearly five years ago. I know, because one of my jobs has been to take documents down to storage. I can speed-read and retain everything. My dad used to say I was a genius since I have a photographic memory and never forget anything. Anyway, I read as I went down the elevator to the basement storage unit out of boredom. It was then I began to realize the facility was taking in more "patients" per year than were being released, or dying naturally. I became curious, and started keeping track of people who didn't have visitors or family coming by to see them. People like me.

It was then I got scared. With every new wave coming in, room had to be made. I had five friends who were here before I came.

Three of them did not have visitors, and one day they were nowhere to be found. I did my best to find out where they went, but all I got was grief, and a dead-end paper trail.

I started counting the new residents arriving on buses. In the last six months, six hundred residents came in, but only two hundred left. You might be thinking I missed some, or counted wrong, but I'm telling you, I've been in charge of documents the entire time, and have seen the paper-work. No mention is ever made of the difference. How do you add continuously to a full facility without its overfilling? Something is wrong. Something I can't explain, but it's scaring me. I've seen the director glancing my way with her steely eyes.

I think they've noticed me.

Please come as soon as you can, and if you need money, I'll pay. I still have the suitcase.

Sincerely,

Greg Barrows

Jim folded up the letter, and put it in his pocket. He started off for his meeting again, a little puzzled.

It was incredible. But why come to him? It was obvious Greg had some issues, but even if he wanted attention, it was hard to believe he would go to that much trouble to make up a story. But he would need to have some facts to support that level of assertion. The EDD facilities were not designed to do anything harmful. They were meant to help people. But he would give him some time just the same, and make sure Greg was ok.

Jim returned to his normal pace, hurrying down the hall before leaving for the weekend.

CHAPTER 14

Several weeks later while monitoring an incoming weather system, Jim recognized a familiar pattern. It was a storm identical to the one he had predicted the day he went to the East EDD. Winter had officially arrived, so the likelihood of a snow event seemed even more certain than before. He quickly contacted his crew to set up a Friday morning broadcast. If he was right, this could be a nasty weekend, and a great opportunity to beat the competition once again.

The wind blew briskly, whipping against the side of his face as Jim prepared to go live. A large crowd had already gathered, and he scanned their faces, looking for Greg. He really wanted to speak with him after the broadcast, and hear his concerns. Maybe he could help him, and better understand what was going on. He had even driven his truck so as not to hold up the crew if he got into a lengthy conversation.

After the broadcast, he signed autographs and allowed fans to take pictures as usual, then helped the crew pack up their gear. To his disappointment, Greg hadn't made it. The letter had stirred his heart, and he had already spoken with the studio to see if he could find him a job. It would give him a shot at leaving the EEDD where he was so unhappy. Jim was impressed with Greg's writing skills, and felt they were good enough to work in editing at the network if he was interested.

As he headed towards his rig, Jim suddenly changed directions, deciding to see if he could find Greg. Battling the rising gusts of wind, he made his way through the large wooden doors that opened to a massive foyer. He was immediately greeted by an attractive young woman seated behind a solid oak counter.

"Hello," she said pleasantly, "May I help you?"

"Hi," Jim replied. "I'm Jim Banner, the weatherman. I just finished broadcasting from across your parking lot, and I'm looking for a friend. Could you help me find him?"

"Sure!" she replied enthusiastically. "Wow, I can't believe you're actually here. We were all watching out the window, and had it on the TV. Do you really think there's a bad storm coming our way?"

"Absolutely," Jim answered confidently. "You just need to be prepared, and you'll be fine."

Part of Jim's broadcast included providing common-sense advice. Fuel up, take extra warm clothes, water and food if you're traveling, but most of all, don't go out unless absolutely necessary. It was advice his followers appreciated.

"Who did you say you're looking for?" The young receptionist asked Jim never tired of the attention his job provided, especially from attractive young women. He scored many dates by being the "weatherman."

"I am looking for Greg Barrows," Jim replied, leaning just far enough over the counter to get a better view of her low-cut blouse. "You may even know him. I understand he has a job helping out with paperwork here. He's not easy to forget as he stutters a lot."

Looking down, she typed his name into her computer.

"I'm sorry," she replied, leaning forward, "There's nobody here by that name."

"Maybe you typed the name wrong," He said, pulling the letter out of his pocket. "His last name is spelled B-A-R-R-O-W-S. Mind if I come around?"

Jim was already making his way behind her desk before she could say no. He leaned over her shoulder, enjoying her perfume. She returned to the keyboard, and carefully typed it in again.

"Is that correct?" she asked, turning her face close to his.

"Yep, that's the right spelling," he answered, leaning in a little tighter.

She hit enter, and waited a moment.

"NO RESIDENT BY THAT NAME."

Jim straightened up, puzzled.

"That's not possible," Jim said, shaking his head slightly, "There has to be some mistake. Is there someone else I can talk to?"

The young woman became a little flustered, and her cheeks reddened slightly.

"I've only been here two weeks," she said defensively. "I just got this job, so I don't know how everything works, but I can call my supervisor if you like."

"Ok," Jim said brightly, patting her on the shoulder affectionately before walking back to the front of the counter, "I don't mean to suggest it's your fault. I'm sure it's just one of those stupid "computer" things."

She picked up the phone, and dialed.

In a few moments, a tall, stately woman in a dark suit came down the tiled foyer. Her heels clicked authoritatively as she approached.

"Jim the Weatherman," she exclaimed, stretching out her bony hand, "how great to meet you! My name is Lucy Lane, but you can call me Lucy. I'm the chief administrator here. I've been a long-time fan of yours and never miss a broadcast. How may I be of assistance?"

Jim took her hand, and shook it briskly.

"I'm looking for someone, but your wonderful receptionist can't seem to locate him through the computer," Jim said, glancing towards the young woman with a wink and a smile. "He's a nice young man I met nearly a month ago, and I just wanted to say hi. I'd like to give him a signed weather calendar, and maybe take him out for a quick cup of coffee. His name is Greg Barrows, and I understand he works in this office, running documents to storage or something."

Lucy backed away slightly with a puzzled look on her face.

"We have lots of workers and residents in this place, but I have to tell you I've never heard of anyone by that name," Lucy replied. "I've been here since the facility opened, and I'm sure I would recognize the name. Maybe somebody's pulling your leg, because there's no one "running documents" as you described. Everything we have is on electronic media. We send and receive by e-mail. Are you sure it was here he was talking about? Maybe he meant somewhere else."

Jim's face flushed a bit.

"I don't know what to say," he answered awkwardly. "I've met a lot of people, and had a lot of things tried on me, but I usually don't get tricked."

"I'm sorry you wasted your time. Maybe you'll have better luck with the weather this time, and come back next week for a follow-up broadcast."

He stood there for a moment, trying to piece things together. It didn't seem likely the young man was anything less than what he said, but who could tell? Maybe he had pulled some kind of weird trick.

"Anyway," Jim said turning to leave, "sorry for the interruption, and thanks for your time."

Jim was just about to the door when he turned as if he had just remembered something.

"Hey!" he said brightly, addressing the young receptionist as he returned to the counter. "If you're ever interested in seeing a broadcast live and in person, give me a call. I take people through all the time."

Jim handed her a card as she smiled, and blushed again.

"My personal cell number is on there," he said, as he spun about and headed out the door. "Call me."

Lucy and the young receptionist waved, wishing him a great day as the door closed. She quickly slid Jim's card into her purse under the desk as Lucy shot her a dark glance.

His mind raced as he walked across the parking lot towards his truck. What had begun as a normal broadcast and a fun morning had become a confusing, bewildering event. Jim studied people as much as he studied weather. He made his living understanding both, but this was not adding up. Why would Greg make this up, or play a trick. What would be the motive? And, Lucy, though convincing, was way too confident for Jim's comfort, especially when you have nearly ten thousand people under your care. There was no way she could know off the top of her head without even checking whether someone was or was not at her facility.

"And why deny Greg's existence?" Jim thought as he braced against a bitter gust of wind. "What purpose would there be? There's nothing to gain from messing with me. I couldn't care less. I just wanted to help a fan."

Reaching his truck, he climbed in and sat there for a moment, absentmindedly staring at the building. The thoughts running through his mind produced nothing, but he had a strange feeling something wasn't right. Heaving a sigh, he started the motor, preparing to leave. Then, he spotted Lucy standing in the foyer, staring at him through the window. As soon as she realized he saw her, she ducked off to the side and disappeared.

"Weird!" Jim said out-loud, "now that was weird!"

He took off for the studio, mulling over the events of the day as he drove, and a plan slowly began to form as his old investigative journalist skills began to rise.

"Maybe I should do a little more checking," he thought as he roared past a slow-moving truck. "I know some people who owe me some favors. I think I'll make a few calls, and do a little digging. That Lucy is a little too smug for my liking. And didn't Greg say it was four or five years ago his parents died? There should be something about them in the obituaries or accident files. I'll start checking the city library, and see what turns up. Maybe there's a simple explanation, and maybe there's not. Either way, I want to know."

There was a time when Jim was more than a weatherman. When he was younger, he trained as an investigative journalist, but when Management took over, he moved to weather, feeling it was a safer, less controversial, occupation. Besides, the hours and money were better. He had always hoped though to someday get back into the reporting game, and this might be just the opportunity he needed.

As soon as he got back to the main part of the city, he went straight to the library to look through the records. Chances were he would find everything he needed to prove or disprove Greg. Sure enough, there was a couple named Peter and Penny Barrows who were killed in an automobile accident about four and a half years ago out on the Eastside Mountain Road. Jim read the accident file, and looked up the obituary. There was no mention of a surviving son, or any other family for that matter. He searched deeper, looking for a birth announcement, something that mentioned Greg, but still came up empty.

He thought pushed back from the table, disappointed. Why would Greg be erased from the records, and who would want to do that? It would take somebody with a lot of power and influence. There would have to be way more to this than just Greg. He certainly didn't seem like he could be a threat, or dangerous to anybody.

He thought about calling his Uncle James and Aunt Lori. Uncle James had saved every copy of the Daily Gazette for the last fifty years, and kept them neatly folded, wrapped in plastic, and stored in the old barn. He had never adjusted to technology, and believed computers were unreliable. They could crash, and lose information, or be altered without people's knowledge. Newsprint was the only safe way to store information, he always said. It had always seemed like a strange idea, but now it could be very useful. Anyway, he hadn't seen them since the year before at the family reunion, so it would be fun to drop by and say hi.

He left the library with a sense of excitement that he hadn't felt in years. But the skies were darkening, and a cold wind whipped up, bringing with it the first snowflakes of the predicted storm.

CHAPTER 15

The drive to the county was beautiful; filled with long, winding roads shuttered by old farms, fields, and groves of trees. The snow came faster, bringing back memories of simpler days; days when people cared for their neighbors; days when a person felt safe. Good days. Those days were over, and life had become a daily grind life. Management's promises had sounded good at first. It wasn't until later that people understood the trade-offs. Giving up the city meant exchanging personal freedoms for guaranteed outcomes, but the only thing guaranteed was working more, getting less for it, and living in fear.

Jim turned onto the winding driveway that led through the groves of apple trees to his uncle's farmhouse. Even under the blanket of snow, he could tell the orchards were in good shape. Memories of warm summer days working with his uncle tending the trees flooded his mind as he pulled in front of their long porch, and stopped his truck. Just then, his aunt opened the door. She had obviously heard him coming, and waved excitedly as he got out.

His uncle and aunt were no strangers to winter conditions, and owned equipment designed to make their lives easier. Uncle James plowed the driveway with his tractor, and used a snow blower on the sidewalk. He still had to shovel the porch steps by hand though. They didn't make a machine for that, or he would have one.

"Hi, Jimmy," Aunt Lori exclaimed as he came crunching up the sidewalk. "It's so great to see you! Come on in out of the cold."

Jim came up the stairs to get a big hug from his Aunt. She was so positive, and she had an enormous heart. Walking into the house was like stepping back in time. He recalled countless fun afternoons playing games in the kitchen, and eating Aunt Lori's famous blueberry muffins. Everything was just as he remembered it.

His aunt wasn't exactly short, but she looked tiny next to his uncle, who was six-foot-nine. But even though he was a giant of a man, everybody knew who ran the house. His aunt may have been small and easy going, but she was fiery when she had to be, and kept her husband in line.

"Hey, big guy," His uncle said, ducking as he passed through the door opening as he came from the living room with the morning Gazette tucked under his arm. "It's great to see you again."

Jim smiled, and gave his uncle a solid hug before they sat down together at the small kitchen table overlooking the backyard.

"Man, it's been awhile." Jim said, looking around. "I haven't been in this house for years, but it hasn't changed a bit, and neither have you guys. You both look great!"

Aunt Lori laughed while his uncle reached for a freshly baked muffin.

"Hey, I saw your broadcast Friday, and you were right on," he said between bites. "It's been snowing pretty hard here since last night, but we had plenty of time to get the wood stacked in the wood box, thanks to you. We also love that neighborhood segment you do. Maybe you should consider coming out here for your next broadcast. You could set up on our porch. I bet it would bring out a lot of neighbors."

His uncle broke into a hearty laugh, winking at Lori.

"Oh, quit," his aunt said, filling their coffee cups. "You're impossible. Don't listen to him, Jimmy; he's always pulling something. You just relax, and have another muffin."

Jim smiled broadly, loving the banter between two of his favorite people.

"Not a bad idea, really," Jim replied, doing his best to look serious. "I think my audience may be interested in some country broadcasts. They're probably tired of all my city locations anyway. And you two, man, you could be my co-stars."

His uncle looked puzzled for a moment, then laughed.

"That's not why I came down to see you though," Jim continued.

"Why did you come down here anyway?" Uncle James asked. "There's not much exciting going on around these parts nowadays for a city boy."

"You mean other than missing you two guys!" Jim replied. "But what I really came down for is to see your newspaper collection."

"My newspaper collection," his uncle said, scrunching his face. "You came all the way down here to see newspapers? For what?"

"Well, I remember your collection vividly," Jim explained. "I helped Aunt Lori clean out the house, and put them in the barn that one summer. It was a lot of work, but I remember you had nearly every issue going back decades.”

"Every issue.” His uncle said proudly. "Got 'em all.”

"Remember when we did that?” Jim said, looking over towards his aunt.

"I remember,” Aunt Lori chimed, in glancing at her husband. "He had those papers in every closet in this house, and stacked on the porch to boot.”

She took a sip of coffee, giving her husband another hard look.

"It took Jimmy and me nearly two days just to carry them out to the barn,” she continued. "From then on I told you there would be no more papers left in the house. If you wanted to keep your precious collection, you were going to have to put them in the barn, or I was going to burn them. They make great fire starters on a cold morning.”

"Yeah, yeah,” Uncle James retorted, smiling. "They were so much trouble I know. I also remember paying him for helping you. Twenty dollars, I think. Anyway, what do you need with my collection?”

"It’s for a story I’m working on.” Jim replied, leaning forward to grab another muffin. "I need to go back about five years. I’m looking for some information on a family I recently heard about, and thought you could help.”

"Only five years, huh?” his uncle said, going for another muffin himself. "That shouldn’t be too hard. They’re categorized by decades. Why don’t we go on out and see what we can find. Hey, what’s wrong with that computer thing of yours anyway? I thought you didn’t need newspapers anymore?”

"Yeah,” Jim answered, "I usually don’t, but this is one time I think the hard copy is the best source.”

"And everybody thought I was crazy to keep all those papers,” his uncle said with a big smile as he looked with satisfaction at his wife.

"Make sure you boys bundle up,” Aunt Lori warned in her usual motherly way while ignoring her husband’s remark. "The nor’easter’s kicking up again, and that old barn’s pretty drafty.”

Finishing off the last two muffins, they put on their coats, and headed into the bitter cold. The wind was picking up under a bright blue winter sky. The sun, glistening off the thick snow, flashed brightly as the two men headed across the yard to the barn. A hard coat of ice covered the snow, and Jim's every step broke through it. He had the wrong shoes for this trek, but did his best to follow in his uncle's tracks. Even so, he got cold snow down his socks. His feet were freezing by the time they made it to the barn.

His uncle slid the large barn door open, knocking snow and ice off the track above. The ice hit with a thud at Jim's feet while the snow drifted down lightly. Some of it down his neck while they ducked inside. The older man reached around the large rough posts for the light switch. The lights came on, revealing a variety of old tools, lawn mowers, and the tractor he used to manage the orchard and grounds. The barn looked lonely, like it missed the old days of milking cows, and tending calves. A few old stanchions leaning against the far wall bore witness to those busier days.

Uncle James led the way towards a set of steps heading to the old haymow.

The barn was well built, but there were cracks where the wind whistled through, pushing in snow as they climbed. Jim didn't care. Tromping around in the barn felt great, like he was coming home to an old friend. Memories of good times long past filled his heart as he stepped lightly up the stairs behind his uncle.

It quickly became apparent that he had put some serious thought and energy into his collection. The cabinets were built from thick cedar, with labels identifying the papers by dates. It was impressive work; one which captured history in its rawest form.

A library of current events long past.

"Wow!" Jim exclaimed, stepping past his uncle to face the monster collection. "You really set this up nice."

He quickly scanned the cabinets to get his bearings.

"I remember stacking these in a big pile over in that corner." Jim continued, pointing to the far side of the haymow. "This is way better than I expected. I thought I was going to be digging all day, but you've made this easy!"

"Yeah, your Auntie gave me a hard time." His uncle replied, laughing. "She hates disorder, and told me to make this look good, or else. You heard her this morning. She threatened to burn them. So I built this, and now she's off my case. Go ahead, dig in," he said encouragingly, tossing a couple of empty boxes out of the way. "I'll help all I can. Its self-explanatory, but if you don't understand something, just let me know."

Jim sized up the layout. Each section was categorized by months, weeks, and then days. Following left to right, Jim pulled the section out for the date he had in mind. His uncle wrapped each month in plastic with a brown twine string, keeping them dry and insect-free. His uncle obviously knew what he was doing when he stored them, as they looked and felt almost like new. He flipped through until he found July, and came upon the twenty third.

The day of the Barrows' accident.

Thumbing through, he found the local section. Sure enough, under the Citadel report was a listing of accidents, just as he had seen in the version at the library.

"Maybe this was a waste of time," Jim thought as he sat down on a bench strategically placed for just such moments. "Hard to imagine anyone going to this much trouble; doesn't seem worth it somehow."

He found the report submitted by law enforcement. All the details were there. The wet mountain road contributed to a slippery surface that evening, and the Citadel provided support, helping investigate the crash site. It was a well-documented event.

"What are you looking for?" his uncle asked curiously, trying to read over his shoulder.

"Nothing new here," Jim said under his breath disappointedly. "The official conclusion: The driver spun out of control into the other lane, and hit an oncoming truck. Both occupants died at the scene." This confirms there is nothing to this, and I just wasted your time and mine."

Glancing up at his uncle, he folded the paper, and slid it back into the plastic.

"I might as well clean this up, and head out." He said dejectedly, looking out a cracked window at the blowing snow. "The wind is picking up, and the drive back is going to be difficult enough without battling snowdrifts too."

"Well, if you're sure there's nothing here," his uncle said. "You've got a great set of wheels there, and a little snow isn't about to slow you up, is it?"

"Obituaries, of course!" Jim nearly shouted as the idea hit him. "They should be entered a couple of days after the accident, when the funeral was announced."

Scanning through the papers, he found the obituary section. The Barrows were the third entry down, just under an old lady who passed away at age eighty-five. Jim read through the details explaining the location of services, who was going to be doing the service, what time, and so forth.

Then he gasped involuntarily.

"What? What is it?" His uncle asked excitedly. "What did you find?"

"Survived by their only son, Greg," Jim said blankly, lowering the paper.

"What does that mean?" His uncle replied, unable to hide his curiosity. "What's so important about an obituary?"

"Everything," Jim said, jumping off the bench. "Can I take this paper with me? I promise to bring it back so as not to mess up your collection. I just need to make some copies."

"Sure, sure, um…of course you can," his uncle replied, getting even more excited. "Your aunt would have a fit if I didn't let you take it. Besides, I've never been one for reading the obits anyway. Take what you need. This is for your story, right?"

"A big story, Uncle James," Jim said, running down the steps. "A giant story, no a colossal story. But I can't talk about it yet. I have more work to do, and need to get back to the city right away. I hope Aunt Lori will understand."

They headed for the house, and after some hasty explanations, Jim said his goodbyes, with plenty of hugs from his aunt. She packed a bag with some fresh blueberry muffins she had just baked, and made sure his thermos was full of coffee.

Waving as he headed down the driveway to the open road, Jim pushed his powerful rig along. The wind whipped snow off the ground, and new flakes joined in. His Aunt and Uncle stood in the living room window, waving as he drove off, but Jim's mind was already working overtime. In his briefcase was a story, a real story, a story only he knew. His excitement was growing by the second.

"Why remove the name of some obscure teenager, and deny his existence?" Jim asked himself as he plowed along. "Who cares enough to go to all that trouble? And who would have the authority? Lucy Lane? No, she's just a drone. But what could this really be about? Why hide the fact that a couple killed in a freak accident had a son? And where is Greg?"

Jim was full of questions, but getting the answers was going to be more trouble than he could even imagine.

CHAPTER 16

Jim got in late that evening, and headed straight for his apartment to begin researching. He needed help if he had any chance of getting back into the journalism game. He was acutely aware of the fact that reporters seemed to purposely steer clear of controversy, and often spoke a little too highly of Management. He felt there was a need for more.

"If you call serious reporting sending news teams out to talk to neighbors about wild dogs," Jim said to himself as he laid out his strategy, "or running stories on new cures for back aches, then we have it, we have a lot of it. But maybe it's time for all that to change."

He didn't sleep much that night as his mind continued working, trying to piece together a logical explanation, but nothing came. He knew he had to do something more than just find some old papers. Hard evidence and solid information were the only things that would break this open. But his newshound instincts were returning. What he needed was an insider with access, someone he could trust. He knew just the guy.

"Hello," said the groggy voice on the other end.

"Parks," Jim said. "It's Jim, your cousin. How are you doing this beautiful morning?"

"I was doing great until you woke me," Parks growled. "Do you realize it's Sunday, and not even seven yet?

"Hey, I thought you big bad BOJ guys never slept," Jim said, smiling.

"Yeah, and we eat nails for breakfast too," Parks retorted. "What's so important anyway? I haven't heard from you since the family reunion last summer."

"I'm sorry," Jim replied. "I've been meaning to call. Just been very busy at work you know."

"Alright," Parks said more evenly now that he was fully awake, "what's going on?"

"Hey, you know I wouldn't call if it wasn't important."

"Of course you wouldn't. What do you need?"

"I need a favor. I need to get into the East EDD."

"That shouldn't be too hard for you. Why don't you call and set up an appointment? I'm sure they'd welcome you with open arms."

"It's not that simple. I don't want to come in the front door. I want to come in the back side, and I don't want to be announced. I want to come after hours, so to speak."

"Let me get this straight," Parks replied, not sure if he heard Jim correctly. "The city's favorite weatherman wants to BREAK into an Economic Diversity Division after hours. I've heard some crazy things before, but this takes it. Are you playing with me?"

"I'm not playing, and I know how strange this must sound. I need to get inside unannounced. Something is going on in there that doesn't smell right, and I have information that needs to be confirmed. You're the only one I know who can move around this city unrestricted. You could get me in this Friday night. I understand they don't man the back gate. It's an automatic door where you need a pass code to get through or something. What do you say, Parks? Will you help me?"

"What's so important you need me to help you get into trouble? You're a weatherman, not a burglar. Have you been drinking?"

"Parks, you're just going to have to trust me on this one," Jim said firmly. "You're right of course. I've been a weatherman for a long time. But do you remember my days as a news reporter? I was good at what I did back then, and I have a story that's growing larger by the minute. I can't say anything more yet, but if I am right, you are going to hear the story of a lifetime, one that's really going to shake things up. I just need more evidence, and I'm sure I'll find it there."

The line was quiet for a moment as Parks thought over his request.

"Ok, OK!" Parks finally replied, with a sigh as he rolled his eyes. "I get the picture. But you know you're asking me to help you do something illegal. That's no small order. Even if I can get you in, there's no guarantee you won't get caught. Have you even thought about that? Then what will happen to your career? You'll go from reporting the weather to reporting on the inside of a Citadel cell. Not a good tradeoff."

"I know, cousin," Jim said quietly. "But it's the only plan that makes sense to me."

"Tell you what," Parks replied, sensing how important this was to him, "I'll help you, but only if you promise not to mention my name when you get caught. I don't have any desire to join you in jail."

"You got it. That's all I'm asking," Jim said with a sigh of relief. "In fact, I don't even remember having this conversation. Who are you again?"

"Here's the deal. I'll get you a code that opens the gate. A service code, not a security code. It should get you in, but after that you'll be on your own."

"Thanks, cousin," Jim said before hanging up. "I owe you one."

Parks was true to his word. Jim received the code later that week in an envelope with no return address.

The road leading to the back side of the East Economic Diversity Division was dark, and covered with a heavy layer of snow. Snow had been steadily falling all week, just as Jim predicted, grinding the city to a halt. The plows were doing all they could just to keep the main roads open, but nobody was even thinking about the back roads; they would just have to wait.

But Jim's black two-seat four-wheel-drive truck was quite capable of handling tough weather conditions. It had tremendous power, with a twelve-inch lift kit and all-terrain, knobby tires, which added to his weatherman mystique. He could go nearly anywhere, and he used it many times in blizzard conditions to report from locations nobody else could get to.

Tonight, he plowed his way along the winding road, staying in the middle, and giving as much room as possible from the deep ditches lining the side.

The back side was dark as he arrived. It was shielded by a ten-foot high rock wall surrounding the large facility. The glow from building lights illumined three strands of barbed wire strung along steel pipes embedded in the top of the wall. It was nearing 1 AM when he pulled off to the side, parking next to the service entrance. He could just make out the outline of two large gates through the blinding snow.

He trudged his way through, and flipped on a small flashlight fastened to the end of his key chain. Keeping it pointed down so he would not draw attention, Jim worked his way to the back gates. He was careful, even though it was unlikely anyone would be watching in these brutal conditions.

"I hope this thing opens," Jim thought as he surveyed the several feet of snow drifted against the mammoth gate.

Scanning with his flashlight, he spotted his target. Wiping the snow from the coded panel, he entered the six numbers provided by Parks. The electric motors sprang to life, and the gate moved slowly along a track, struggling against the heavy snow. Jim was thrilled. It looked like the door hadn't been in operation since the snow started flying, and seeing it open meant his plan was working. He let the gate open just enough for him to slip past before hitting the stop button on the inner panel. There was no point in opening it farther than needed, just in case someone was watching.

Quickly making his way along the snow covered area between the gate and the back of the warehouse, Jim headed for the building Greg had told him was off-limits. It seemed a little unusual for a facility that supposedly had a benign retraining focus to have such security concerns. These were the little things driving Jim's curiosity.

A large rollup door greeted him as he moved tight to the building. It was in line with the entrance gate to facilitate deliveries. Next to the rollup door was a regular walk door with a combination lock.

"Are you kidding me" Jim nearly said out loud! His frustration was mounting as he had expected some challenges to entry, but he didn't have a real break-in plan. He wasn't a professional thief, so he didn't bring tools or pry bars to force entry. His journalistic effort would come to an abrupt end if he couldn't get inside.

Jim's heart was racing as he looked for some alternate entrance, an open window, anything.

He had never thought past the gate.

The bitter cold was penetrating the layers of his clothing, so if he didn't come up with a solution soon, he would have to retreat to the warmth of his truck.

"What a revolting development. This isn't working."

Then a sudden gust of wind pushed him hard against the door, and it popped open as the wind shoved him into the building. Jim quickly grabbed the handle, catching himself before he fell onto the floor.

"What luck," Jim thought as he pushed the door shut against the blowing snow. "Someone must have forgotten to lock it. Yeah, and who would think leaving the door unlocked was a big deal anyway in this place? It's not like people are clamoring to get in here."

Switching his flashlight off so as not to draw attention, he scanned down the darkened hall as his eyes adjusted to the darkness. On one end, the hall dead-ended with another door. On the other, it opened towards the main facility Jim was eager to explore. Light coming from the next room barely illumined his way as he began to quietly move towards it.

He had taken only a few steps when suddenly someone grabbed him from behind, pinning his arms tight to his chest, and lifting him off his feet. Jim wrestled to break free, but it felt like steel bands wrapped around his body. Panic began to set in.

CHAPTER 17

Bruce's funeral was attended by hundreds of friends, family, and co-workers. Harry made sure everybody was aware of the small plaque they placed in his honor inside the office complex. Mary and David played their parts well, grieving in public. It all went off without a hitch while Bruce continued to recover under Dr. Larson's care.

David moved in with his mother while they considered their long-term goals. They planned to wait until his father fully recovered, and then David and other members of his band of resisters would smuggle his parents out of the city. In the meantime, they would keep up pretense so no one would suspect. But David still wanted to know who tried to kill his father, and he decided it was time to do some checking on his own. He started by meeting George one evening at the local pub.

The Bent Fork Bar was a popular gathering place for blue collar workers. Located along the West side of the city next to the industrial center, its lime-green florescent sign welcomed patrons with the image of a large beer stein being filled by a stately bar maid. It was typically full every night, and tonight was no different.

"I'm sorry about your Dad," George said as he pulled up a chair. "He was a good man."

"Thanks," David replied shaking his hand. "It's hard on Mom, but she'll be ok."

The waitress, a tall woman with a warm smile, brought some menus and silverware.

"Can I get a drink started for either of you?"

David ordered a porter, and George had his usual rum and coke. They made a little small talk while waiting for their drinks.

"I wanted to hear what happened to Dad first-hand," David said after their drinks arrived. "You were the one who found him, right?"

"He was in rough shape," George replied, taking a drink. "I didn't think he would even make it to the hospital in his condition."

"Did you notice anything unusual? I mean how did Dad get burned in the first place?"

"I've asked myself that very question a hundred times. I really don't know for sure. All I can say is he was burned by a splash of dross from container number seven. How it happened is a mystery to me."

"Container seven, I never heard that mentioned before. You know which one it was. Why is that?"

George suddenly felt uncomfortable. He hadn't intended to reveal any specifics about the accident, and was keeping quiet regarding Kevin.

"Well, I found evidence of a spill on container number seven, and put it together, that's all."

David could tell George was holding something back, and pressed a little harder.

"I believe someone wanted to hurt him, and it was no accident," David said bluntly. "He didn't die from his burns. Someone killed him in the hospital."

George's jaw hit the table.

"Your father was murdered?" he asked tersely. "Are you sure?"

"Keep your voice down," David said, looking around at nearby tables. "Yes, I'm sure--someone poisoned him."

George sat back, an astonished look on his face.

"I can't believe it. Who would want to hurt someone like Bruce? He was just an ordinary guy."

"I need you to tell me all you know."

"We can't talk here," George replied, leaning forward, and speaking in a hushed tone. "It's seven thirty now. I have some errands to run, so how about you meet me at ten at my apartment. I live up on Holly Street across from the bowling alley."

David agreed, and picked up the check. He wanted to get back and make sure his mother was ok anyway, so he didn't mind waiting.

After checking on his mom, he drove to George's place, and parked on the dimly-lit street. David climbed two flights of stairs to apartment twenty-two. The building was older, and showing signs of disrepair, but the neighborhood seemed nice enough. It was a little past ten when he knocked on the door.

"Hello?" David said, noticing the door was partially opened.

No one replied as he pushed it open. A strange haze hung in the room. There was a strange smell, and the place was a mess. Furniture was overturned, and stuff scattered everywhere. It looked like someone had been searching for something.

Then he heard a groan coming from behind an overturned couch.

"Are you ok?" David asked as he rolled the large couch off George, and knelt beside him.

He had a large gash across his forehead which was bleeding profusely. His eyes rolled back in his head as he attempted to stand up. He didn't make it, and collapsed onto one knee.

"I feel horrible." George said in obvious pain as David helped him to the couch.

David went into the kitchen to get some towels. When he returned, George's eyes were open, and he had managed to sit up on his elbows.

"What happened here?" David asked as he started wiping the blood off George's face.

George grabbed the towel, and it was then David noticed two of his fingers were twisted out of their sockets, and turned completely around.

"We need to get you to the hospital right away," David said grabbing him by the arm.

"Don't bother," George replied, pulling back. "I won't make it."

"Of course you will. It's just a few minutes from here."

George looked up grimly.

"I surprised a guy searching my apartment when I came home tonight. He was a small guy, with a medium build, and I thought at first I could take him. But he knocked me around like I was nothing, and then held me down with one hand. I couldn't move. It was like the guy was superhuman."

"You're going to be ok," David said encouragingly as he tried to get him up.

"No," George replied, pulling back. "You need to hear this. The guy kept going on about a magnifier, or looking glass, or something that belongs to them. The next thing I knew, he was twisting my fingers off, trying to get me to tell him what I did with it. I told him I didn't know what he was talking about, but he didn't believe me. Then he took out this small red glowing rock, and shoved it into my chest. I begged him to remove it, but he said I had to tell him where the thing was first. I can feel it inside right now, burning like fire. I guess he finally believed me, because he tossed me over the couch, and left. All I remember is seeing a dark mist filling the room before I blacked out."

David ripped George's shirt open to reveal a dark red glow in the center of his chest. He felt a pulsation coming from the crystal hanging from the silver chain around his own neck. It pulled away from him like it was magnetically attracted to the red glowing object in George's chest. David quickly lifted the chain from off his neck, and placed the blue crystal against the glowing red spot.

The crystal began to glow brightly, sending light pulsations through George's body. Suddenly, George sat straight up, and screamed a scream from somewhere deep inside. He convulsed backward, straightening out, and becoming stiff. David wasn't sure if he was dead or what, but there was nothing he could do but watch.

Then George's body went limp. David stood up, fearing the worst. He rolled George over onto his side, and the dark red stone fell out of his mouth, and onto the hard-wood floor.

"What the," George gasped as he opened his eyes and jerked upright on the couch.

"I guess it wasn't your time to go," David said softly. "Let's see about getting you to the hospital now."

David reached down to pick up the dark red stone, but it vanished in a puff of smoke before he could grab it.

"This just keeps getting better and better," David said in astonishment.

"He didn't find what he looking for," George said as David helped him to the car.

"What's the magnifier?" David asked as he drove George to the hospital.

"I don't know, but I think Kevin or your dad might have had it. Now they think I have it."

George was mumbling and rambling on as David raced to the Emergency room. He stayed in the waiting room until Dr. Larson was finished examining him. He had several broken ribs, a concussion, some internal injuries and three severely broken fingers.

"Thanks for calling," Parks said meeting David in the waiting room. "What can you tell me?"

"George Marshal has been investigating Dad's accident at the plant. I met him earlier tonight to discuss it with him. We were going to meet at his apartment later, and that's when I found him. Apparently, a small guy pounded him pretty good, and then shoved a red crystal into his chest without even breaking the skin."

"He had a crystal with that kind of power?"

"Yes but he was looking for something called a magnifier or magnifying glass. George thinks Kevin might have had it, and that's why they killed him. He doesn't know anything more about it--do you Parks?"

"I've never seen anything like that. What about the guy that attacked him, and the crystal you found?"

"I've got nothing. George is a big man, and whoever did this to him is powerful. Oh, there was this mist in the room George saw before he passed out. It was about the same as when the crystal vaporized before I could pick it up."

"This is strange business," Parks agreed. "Why don't you get some rest?"

David headed home as Parks went in to see for himself how George was doing and to touch base with Della.

Mary was baking when David came downstairs the next morning.

"Hi, honey," she said as she pulled a tray of chocolate cookies from the oven.

He quickly grabbed a glass and headed for the fridge for milk.

"Thanks, Mom!" he said as she set a plate of warm cookies in front of him. "Have you been able to see Dad?"

"Not yet. I can't go to the hospital without drawing attention, but Dr. Larson dropped by yesterday, and told me he's getting better every day."

David took another bite, chasing it with milk. He was happy, knowing his dad was recovering, but even happier to see the relief in her face. Eating another cookie, he noticed a small cardboard box on top of the morning mail. He reached over, and began to examine it. It felt heavy, and the label said to Mr. Bruce Clawson , but with no return address.

"Oh, that," Mary said, joining him at the table. "With all that's been going on, I forgot all about it. It came the day of your dad's injury, but I don't know who it's from."

David spun it around in his hand a couple of times before he noticed a small diamond symbol in one corner of the box. Recognizing the secret mark of their resistance organization, he excitedly grabbed the letter opener his mother kept on a nearby shelf.

"This is important!" he said as he slit the thick tape.

Underneath the wrapping paper was a silver object. He dumped it on the table for a better look. It was round, with a long, ornate chain. Picking it up by the chain to get a better view in the light, he saw a small blue stone set in the center. Covering its surface were dozens of unusual markings.

"That is really pretty, isn't it?" Mary said, reaching out and touching it. "It looks old. I wonder what it is."

David noticed a small slip of paper inside the box.

His eyes widened as he leaned forward and exclaimed, "This is from Kevin!"

"What do you mean?" Mary asked. "Kevin sent us this? Why? What does it say?"

"I don't get it," David answered. "He wanted Dad to get this to me. He apparently felt it was critical I got it. I have to go out for a while. Lock the door after me. Don't open it for anyone."

"Where are you going, David?" his mom asked anxiously.

"I need to see Parks," David replied. "He'll know what to do with this. But just to be safe, pull out Dad's pistol, and turn out the lights. Make it look like nobody's home. Call me if you hear anything, and I'll be right back."

David pulled into the alley behind Parks's apartment, hopped up onto his rear porch, and knocked. Parks let him in, and they quickly settled into the living room.

"You're never going to believe what came in the mail," David said, setting the object on the coffee table. "Kevin Knobbs found this, and mailed it to my dad before he was killed. The note he sent with it said it's vital to the resistance. What do you think it is?"

"I'm not sure," Parks replied, picking it up and examining it. "The small blue stone is similar to the crystals I have, but it's a little darker."

The engraving of three linked circles with the center one set with a beautiful crystal adorned the surface. Parks felt the crystal with his finger, and it pushed in slightly. Then the top of the object flipped open, revealing a larger blue stone, and small magnifying glass inside.

"That's cool," Parks said as he gently lifted the magnifier out of the object, and looked it over closely. It was about two inches in diameter, made from heavy glass wrapped in engraved silver.

Setting the magnifier onto the table, Parks pulled the crystal from the object, and held it up to the light.

"It seems a little blurry," Parks said.

"Why don't you use that magnifying glass?" David suggested.

Parks began to carefully examine the crystal with the magnifier. It was a beautiful stone, cut perfectly on every side. It had only one flaw. In the center was a dark spot, like an insect caught in amber. He drew it up close to get a better look.

Suddenly, he was pulled into the crystal. A man staggered past with a knife struck in his chest as another lay on the ground with blood oozing from his mouth. Everywhere there was death, and destruction. Everywhere there was chaos.

"Can this be our city?" Parks thought as a dark mist began to swirl.

The people fighting mindlessly were suddenly engulfed by the mist and a shadow began to emerge.

"Zender," Parks gasped, "the beast is back." "Run, RUN! Get out of here, he yelled as he ran through the streets, "You'll all be killed." But no one could hear him.

The beast rounded up the people like cattle to slaughter as the mist enveloped them. Parks watched helplessly as six bronze thrones came through the mist, and solidified. The people didn't even notice– they just continued arguing and fighting with each other, oblivious to their situation.

As he wondered what to do, six well-dressed men in sharp, pin-striped suits walked through the crowd, and took their places on the thrones. Each man had a brass scepter in his hand with a dark red globe on top. Suddenly, a bright light shot out from the scepters, and the people froze momentarily. They looked around at each other before disappearing into the mist. They were vaporized and the lights were gone.

"Parks, Parks, PARKS!" David shouted, shaking him by the shoulders. "Are you alright? Your face turned white as a sheet, and you started yelling."

"I'm alright," Parks replied, closing his hands tightly around the magnifier and crystal.

"What happened to you?"

"It was incredible," Parks answered. "I was in the city, and horrible things were happening. It's hard to even think about but people where killing each other mercilessly. Then they were taken by a power I can't even begin to describe. It destroyed those still alive. It seemed so real. Maybe it is a warning of something that's going to happen or might happen. I don't know, but I do know now why Mr. Knobbs was killed, and why George and your dad were attacked. This thing is powerful. Who knows what all it can do. We need to keep it out of sight, and not mention it to anybody. And you had better be doubly careful yourself. If they suspect you have it, you could end up like the others."

Parks was worried, and David knew it.

"We'll need to discuss your exit plans," Parks said. "Dr. Larson said your dad is getting better, and you'll be able to move him soon."

"What about the guy who attacked George?" David asked. "He may be the one who killed Kevin, and tried to kill Dad."

"I don't think we're going to find him, but chances are when he's ready, he'll find us," Parks replied. "In the meantime, we need to be smart, and keep quiet about this. If you're going to meet with your friends again, make sure you do it quietly. Whoever's behind this is watching, listening, and three steps ahead."

CHAPTER 18

"Hi, cousin," Parks whispered in Jim's ear as he squeezed him a little tighter. "Breaking and entering tonight, are we?"

Parks released his grip, and Jim spun around angrily.

"What are you trying to do, give me a heart attack?" he whispered, waving his fist in Parks's face. "What are you doing here anyway?"

"Oh, I just thought if anyone were going to arrest my cousin, it might as well be me," Parks replied quietly, no emotion showing on his hard face. "Keep it in the family so to speak."

"You're here to arrest me?" Jim asked, somewhat stupefied. "What are you talking about? You're the one who gave me the code to get in here."

"Well, maybe I'll arrest you later," Parks replied, his smile gleaming in the dim light from the hallway. "Why don't we see what you're getting yourself into first? No use wasting a good breaking and entering."

"So, you're why the door was unlocked," Jim whispered, glancing down the hall. "I thought it seemed a little too easy."

"Yeah, yeah," he said under his breath. "Let's get this show on the road so I can have you in jail before breakfast. I hate being hungry."

"And try to be a little quieter, would you," Parks continued light-heartedly. "I heard you coming before you even got that truck of yours parked, and you sounded like a troop of Testers plowing through the snow."

Jim couldn't deny he felt better having Parks around. He was used to going it alone, but this was new territory. He would need all the help he could get.

They turned the corner, and headed down the hall towards the light. Jim stopped short, hearing voices coming from around the next corner. Parks moved in front, and flattened himself on the floor. Parks could hide out in the open if he wanted to. He had a way of becoming invisible, or nearly so. From where he was, he could see the front and one side of a large black bus. There were several big men in uniform standing next to the opened door.

Someone was barking orders just out of sight, and the voice sounded familiar.

Jim got down on his belly, joining Parks, and peered around the corner to get a better look. As they watched, a line of people came into view, and began boarding. They were a combination of elderly, semi-disabled, and young people, all looking very sleepy and confused.

Jim shot a look towards Parks, who shrugged his shoulders.

After a few minutes, the line ended with a woman dressed in a dark suit. Jim instantly recognized her. Lucy Lane, the woman from the main office. She walked over to the driver, still barking instructions. The echo in the large building obscured her words so they couldn't make out what she was saying. Two of the security guards stepped onto the bus, and shut the door.

The motor roared to life, and bright headlights momentarily blinding Jim.

Parks and Jim quickly slid back out of sight as the large overhead door next to them began to grind open. Bitter gusts of the cold north wind whistled into the building, driving snow with it as the door rose. They stood up with their backs to the wall, and looked at each other. They had no idea of what was going on. The only sound was the bus revving as the driver shifted into gear. Lurching forward, it slowly passed, breaking into the cold night. The darkened windows revealed only outlines as it moved along.

Once the bus had exited the building, the door immediately began to close. Parks and Jim jumped through the opening, and Parks ran in the bus's tracks as it moved through the deep snow towards the outer gate, Jim tight on his heels. The bus slowed briefly as the outer gate opened, and began plowing through the deepening snow onto the darkened street.

Jim and Parks stopped as they watched it disappear into the night.

"Where's your truck?" Parks demanded as the bus's rumble faded away. "If you want your story, we're going to have to get after that thing."

Jim was already sprinting through the deepening snow towards where his rig was parked.

"Come on!" he shouted over the howling wind. "Get your butt in here!"

He had already remotely started the truck, and it was warming up as they jumped in. The wipers brushed at least two inches of fresh snow off the windshield as they pulled out. The weather was turning from bad to worse.

"Where do you think they're headed?" Jim asked as he pulled into the bus's tracks.

"This road leads to the city wall on the back side. After that, you're talking the outer region, and then nothing but wilderness."

It was easy to track the bus through the virgin snow, and before long, they were hot on its tail. Jim kept his lights off to avoid alerting the driver. He could see just enough to stay on the road and out of the ditches. Drifting was becoming an issue, but fortunately, his truck was equipped for such conditions. The bus did most of the work, plowing through everything in its path.

A cloud of snow blew over them as Jim pulled up tight. It lessened any chance the driver might have of detecting their presence, but it didn't make driving any easier. He couldn't see anything but the back of the bus, and swirling snow. He nearly rear ended it several times.

It lumbered steadily along, heading towards the outer wall, several miles away. It quickly became obvious they weren't stopping anywhere inside the city. Soon, the outline of the giant wall surrounding the city emerged. It was impressive--built from steel, rock, barbed wire, and concrete. Its stated purpose was to keep wild animals out, but it worked equally well to keep citizens in.

The main entrance to the city was manned by guards with automatic weapons, but this one was one of two gates of lesser importance, which used electronic controls and alerts. If either of the lesser gates were opened, a signal was sent to the central computer which activated cameras, and alerted security. Under normal conditions, a security team could respond within minutes.

There was nothing normal about that night, though. No one would respond anywhere quickly, and any unauthorized movements would be tough to deal with. But both men suspected there was nothing unauthorized about the bus they were following, and their suspicions were quickly confirmed as the giant gate opened before the fast-approaching bus.

"Who has automatic gate openers for this?" Jim asked in amazement.

"I couldn't guess, but they would have to be well-connected," Parks replied, watching the bus speed through. "I didn't know equipment like this had even been installed. This entrance is seldom used, but somebody apparently needs it, or this never would have been set up."

The bus throttled down slightly as the driver checked his clearances before roaring through. Jim cuddled close to the rear of the bus, hoping the billowing snowy back-draft would hide them from the cameras. Detection would spell disaster now, as he was sure someone would let the driver know they were being followed. Not to mention they needed to make it through before the gate shut to have any hope of solving the mystery.

As soon as the bus cleared the gate, the diesel revved again, blasting through the heavy snow towards an area known only as "the wilderness." Behind them, the gates closed, sealing in the city once more. There were no visible roads, but the driver seemed to know exactly where he was going.

Jim backed off a bit to follow at a more comfortable distance now that they were outside the city. There was little danger they would be spotted with his lights off, and the bus driver would have no reason to think he had a tail anyway. The wilderness was unfamiliar territory to most, but Parks had spent his youth out there, and he knew it well. He also knew it wasn't much to look at; just rocks and brush.

"Where do you think they're going?" Jim asked as they motored along, maintaining a safe distance.

"I have no idea. There's nothing out here, especially in these conditions. Hard to imagine they're going on a field trip."

They followed the black bus for nearly two full hours, plowing its way through drifts and around rocky outcrops. It was difficult to imagine they were even on a road. Finally, the bus crested the top of a knoll, and began a short descent into a flat area about the size of a half-acre. The brake lights came on as the bus began to slow, and Jim waited at the crest to see what was going to happen next.

Air brakes sounded as the bus slid to a stop.

Jim backed out of the bus tracks, and into a bank of snow. The snow, still falling steadily, quickly covered the front windshield with a fresh blanket of white, effectively obscuring their presence. Parks's side window offered an open view of the activity below. He lowered it as Jim shut down the motor, and they watched the unfolding drama. The cold wind chilled them, but they kept it open. On the bus, someone was shouting orders.

The bus doors opened, and the two guards with their semi-automatic weapons stepped. Jim and Parks watched in horror as the men ordered the ragged group out. Once off the bus, they stood there silently, shivering in the cold.

As if on cue, a wolf began to howl. Others joined in, and they sounded uncomfortably close. The passengers huddled together uselessly, defenseless.

Jim started to open the door, but Parks grabbed his arm.

"Wait a second. They're getting back on the bus. It doesn't look like they're going to shoot them."

The guards, keeping their weapons pointed at the group, got back on the bus. One of the men grabbed for the guards gun and got a boot in the chest for his effort as the doors closed behind them, effectively sealing the fate of the ones left behind. The diesel motor wound up as the bus lurched up the hill towards where they were sitting. Jim considered ramming it, but he quickly realized it would do no good. His truck would barely make a dent in that monster.

They could only watch as it roared past. Slowly, the sound of the bus churning through the snow faded into the distance, while the darkness of the night enveloped the lonely group huddling below. The wolves howled again, and they sounded closer than before.

"Why didn't you stop them?" Jim shouted angrily, "you could have shot the driver with that Nullifier thing of yours. It's going to take at least two hours to get back to the city, and even longer to get transportation back, and they'll never last twenty minutes in these conditions."

"I didn't bring it," Parks snapped, "or I would have used it but there was no way I could have guessed we would end up out here."

CHAPTER 19

They sat quietly for a few seconds, stunned by the sheer magnitude of the unfolding events below.

Parks broke the silence first.

"We need to do something right now."

Jim felt helpless as he pulled out of the snow bank, and headed down the hill, his lights illuminating the shivering band of humanity. It seemed like a hopeless situation. He could only haul two passengers at a time, including himself. Parks jumped out of the truck into the deep snow as an older gentleman stepped forward to meet them.

"Who are you guys?" he said through chattering teeth. "What do you want with us?"

"Don't be afraid," Parks answered calmly. "We're here to help. We need to find shelter right away."

"What shelter?" The old man replied, covering his eyes as the wind gusted again. "We're in a blizzard in the middle of nowhere."

"We'll find some shelter in the rocks above," Parks answered. "I know this terrain. There's bound to be a rocky crevice where we can get a fire started, and there's plenty of gas in the truck. It won't take long to get something going."

"We can try," the old man said as he looked over at Jim's truck.

The wind whipped up again, stinging their faces as they began their feeble rescue effort. Parks pulled the man from the snow who had been kicked by the guard. He was breathing and alert but could have several broken ribs. Jim shouted over the howling wind for them to follow him as he pointed towards the nearby mountain. But just as they were getting started, the ground under their feet began to shake and vibrate intensely. Then a loud and grinding sound like some huge machine rose above the wind.

The people looked at each other, confused. Some of the older people fell into the snow from the vibrations. A hundred feet or so away, a snow bank lifted into the air, and a long sliver of light appeared just above the thick layer of snow. Swirling snow devils danced along the edges of the ever increasing opening. The silhouettes of a dozen or so figures slowly rose from the bowels of the earth.

Parks worked his way around to the front of the freezing group, positioning himself between them and the approaching strangers. Jim joined his side, prepared to do whatever was needed to protect these folks.

But, as they got closer, Jim could see the figures more clearly. They weren't carrying weapons. They were dressed in Arctic gear, and some of them were pulling sleds. They looked more like a rescue team than like enemies."

"Who are you?" Parks shouted as they came within hearing range.

One of the men in the front removed his face shield, and pulled back his parka. He was an older man with a friendly face.

"Sorry to frighten you," he shouted over the howling wind. "We're not here to hurt you. We're here to help."

He looked the man over carefully, and shot a quick glance at the group.

"Ok! We need to get them out of this weather right now," Parks agreed.

The man waved his group forward. Jim and Parks helped an older woman into one of the rescue sleds, while two others pulled a handicapped man from the snow, and onto a second. Everybody grabbed an arm as they headed towards the light.

Jim hit his remote, shutting down his truck, and turning off the lights. The darkness surrounding them stood in stark contrast to the bright opening ahead. In a few moments, they were there.

The lid was huge, with two giant hydraulic cylinders on each side supporting a heavy metal roof covered by tons of snow. A ramp, extending deep into a cavernous underground facility, welcomed their arrival. Parks made note of the distinct markings painted on the ramp, which suggested it had been used for something special in its distant past.

They blinked several times from the bright lights as warm air rose to greet them. It was a welcome relief from the frigid world outside. As soon as the last person passed below ground level, the metal roof slowly lowered behind them, just as a strong gust of wind blew a large section of snow from the side. It slammed onto the ramp, seeming to protest their narrow escape. The noise echoed through the chamber as the roof sealed tight again.

When they reached the bottom of the ramp, Parks saw a massive underground facility It spread in every direction as far as the eye could see.

"What is this place?" Parks asked the older man.

Just then the speaker on a walkie-talkie their rescuer was carrying sprang to life.

"Be there in one minute, sir!" the voice on the other end declared.

"Great!" the man replied. "Looks like we've got a full house tonight,"

"What is this place?" Parks asked again.

He only smiled, looking up at Parks before turning to address the crowd.

"It's going to take some time to explain," he announced. "But you need to know we're here to help. This is not a place you need to fear.. We have nothing to do with those who brought you, and if they knew, you wouldn't be here at all. But they don't know. They sent you into a blizzard to die, and as far as they're concerned, you're wolfsicles about now."

The hum of approaching electric motors interrupted him as headlights emerged from a side corridor.

"Colonel," the driver of a small train announced as he pulled to a stop, "let's get these people on board. I hear they're serving some hot soup down below, and these folks sure look like they could use some."

"All aboard," the Colonel said with a friendly voice as he hopped on the front, waving his hand encouragingly.

Younger assisted older until everyone found a seat. Then the Colonel turned around on the front seat, and grabbed a microphone. Taking on the persona of a theme park announcer, he pointed to interesting features as they rolled along.

"On your left are the steam lines heating this place." He said, steadying himself as they lurched forward. "There are over two million feet of piping, and only one plumber. You can only imagine the overtime we have to pay."

The riders looked back and forth at each other for a moment before realizing he was making a joke. They tried a laugh, but it wasn't much.

"I'm sure you're all wondering what's going on, and I am going to help you with that," he continued, sensing their anxiety. "This place was used by others years ago for military purposes, but we like to think of it now as an Island; our own little oasis in the middle of a brutal world. For some reason, it was abandoned and mostly forgotten, fortunately, I was stationed here briefly when I was younger. I saw this place a couple of times from above, but never knew the extent of this underground paradise. It was quite a surprise to find all this."

The train picked up speed as it flowed through seemingly endless tunnels to another part of the facility. Parks was certain he had seen the driver somewhere before, but he couldn't place him. He was a large man with dark curly hair, but where had he seen him?

"After I left and was assigned to another area," the colonel continued, "they must have decided to move all operations underground. The buildings were dozed to look as if everything were gone. They effectively erased this place from the map. I've been down here almost six years now, and still haven't discovered every secret. There are tunnels going in all directions to who knows where. Anyway, we're getting close to our destination, and all your questions will be answered soon enough. Just, please wait until we come to a complete stop before getting up. I haven't lost anyone yet, and I don't intend to start now."

Some people laughed nervously as the colonel sat down, while others just looked blankly forward. The train slowed as they wound around a narrow bend, and into a brightly lit docking station. Several nurses waited at the station, ready with wheel chairs and gurneys if they were needed.

A bank of doors opened off to one side, and one of the nurses stepped forward, greeting the passengers as it came to a complete stop.

"Hi, my name is June, and we're here to help," she said with a smile. "Come on in. I'm sure you're chilled from being outside. We'll need some information to help us better understand your situation and needs."

Passengers and nurses worked together to help the ones with special needs, and they all followed June down a short tunnel into a large dining hall. They were in awe, and somewhat frightened, but the smell of hot soup was an encouraging welcome.

Parks and Jim hung back, waiting for an opportunity to speak with the Colonel, who was overseeing the procession from the front of the train. Once the last passenger had disembarked, they headed for the Colonel. He spotted them coming, and waved them over.

"I know you have questions," he said as they hopped up next to him. "It's obvious you're not here under the same constraints as the rest of these folks. I imagine one of you is driving that nice vehicle all covered with snow and ice parked outside. How about we go over to my office and sit a spell. I can fill in a few gaps for you."

"Just a minute," Parks interrupted, leaning forward to address the driver. "Why do I think I know you? You look familiar somehow."

"We met at the river," the driver responded.

Parks sat back for a moment, puzzling.

"At the river, when did I meet you at the river?"

"The day I left the book for you to find," the man said smiling. "I put it in the birch tree at the last minute, hoping you would see it."

"The book," Parks exclaimed, "of course. I remember now. It was you who left it there? But why, and how did you escape, and what happened to the one who died?"

"There are many ways in and out of here," the man continued. "Our job was to separate you from your partner, and hand it off. We were hoping to get a chance to explain, but after two weeks of being shot at, we decided to get out, and make our escape along the river. We were going to try again some other time, but that's when my brother took the fatal shot. I put the book in the tree, and ducked underground with his body."

"He was your brother," Parks said quietly. "I'm very sorry for your loss. My partner doesn't respect life. He just knows how to kill. But why the book--why was it so important you risked your lives?"

"I don't have all the answers," the man replied. "We were told you were the one who would understand what it means."

"This must all seem quite unreal to you, I know," The Colonel interjected, stepping off the train, and starting across a wide aisle towards a set of elevators tucked around the corner of a large auditorium. "But this place is for real, and there are mysteries which will have to wait--for now. What is important is for you to learn the opportunities this place presents."

Jim and Parks followed him as the train pulled away.

He noticed the colonel was limping slightly on his right leg, and that he wore a leather glove on his left hand. When they came to the elevators, the Colonel removed a special card that hung on a chain around his neck. He inserted it into the slot next to a bank of buttons, the door opened, and they stepped in.

The elevator descended slowly at first, and picked up speed as they went.

"It just takes a few moments to descend over four hundred feet," the colonel said, continuing his tour guide persona. "This elevator was installed to move dignitaries and important people out of harm's way in a hurry. I only started using it recently as we have begun to fill up. There are nearly six thousand people living here now, and more coming nearly every week. It's a good thing this place was built for an army. With a little more help, I think we could take a lot, but running this place gets more and more complicated as people keep getting dropped off."

"Here we are," the colonel announced as the elevator glided to a smooth stop.

The door opened to a large foyer with shining marble flooring and walls. The room was equipped with a rounded central desk obviously meant for security purposes, but there was no sign of security.

"Follow me," the Colonel said, passing the long, ornate desk to a nearby office.

They entered through tall wooden doors into an office with dark cherry paneling. The Colonel seated himself behind a matching dark cherry desk the housed a bank of closed circuit monitors sitting off to his left. The screens switched between rooms in the facility and outside cameras.

"So that's how you knew the bus was here." Jim said, pointing to one of the monitors.

"That, and some sensors buried in the ground," he replied, glancing over towards the outside snow scene.

Parks and Jim took seats in leather bound chairs as they watched the monitors sweep the areas.

"Believe it or not, I know you both," he continued pointing his gloved hand at Jim. "Jim the Weatherman, I've seen your broadcast many times and I love your forecasts. Then there's the famous Mr. Parks! You have the book Sterling gave you. I was once responsible for deciphering it, but couldn't. Words would appear and then disappear. It was impossible. Ah, but the parchment was different. It had the face of a man. A man nobody knew until I saw you in the city one day. That's when we decided to deliver it to you in hope you could unlock its secrets."

"Book? What book? Jim interrupted excitedly. "Is this something I should know about?"

"It's still a mystery to me," Parks answered. "Whatever secrets it holds may never be revealed. But why not just come to me in the open with it?"

"We couldn't take the chance," the Colonel replied, leaning forward, and putting his elbows on the desk. "We'd be dead men if we exposed ourselves to one of the main security men from the Citadel. So we tried to help you "find" it." It just didn't work out the way we planned."

"What's so important about a book?" Jim insisted.

"It was discovered in a cave by a family hiking in the wilderness many years ago," the colonel replied, "sealed in a clay jar. They sold it to a collector from the city who had it for about two years, so the story goes, but began to have mental issues, nightmares that wouldn't stop. Eventually, he blamed it on the book and sold it. It continued a similar path through many other owners until, one day, it was donated to the city museum. But, then the museum curator began to experience the same horrible nightmares. That's when it was turned over to the military for examination and I first got a look at it. They required me to examine it."

"Required to examine it?" Parks asked. "Does that mean you were forced to?"

"Yes, and I didn't enjoy it," he answered. "Fortunately, I didn't have it long. It was taken from me, and sealed in a lead box. It wasn't until I came here that I met the men who could decipher it, at least somewhat. Sterling and his brother were the only ones who were not affected. Somehow they figured out you were the one it was intended for, and risked everything to get it to you. Sorry to hear you haven't discovered why yet."

"Interesting," Parks said thoughtfully. "My nightmares pretty much ended when I got the book."

"What inspired both of you to come out here?" The Colonel asked, changing the subject.

150

"I'm in the middle of an investigation," Jim replied quickly. "It came to my attention citizens were disappearing from the East EDD, so we broke in to discover a black bus being loaded with people, and taken away in the middle of the night. We followed the bus, and you know the rest. What's your story, Colonel?"

"Well, I'll give you the short version. I spent my youth in the military. Not the current version, a much older one. When the struggle was underway, I was part of the resistance. We got trapped against the cliffs on the East side of the valley, under heavy assault from the Testers. That's when I got hit. I lost my left hand, and my left leg just below the knee."

He removed his glove, revealing a mechanical hand attached to a metal sleeve connected at the elbow. Reaching out, he picked up a pencil from his desk with the metallic fingers.

"Quite a sight, isn't it? I keep the glove on most off the time as it's not my most attractive feature. I would show you my leg and foot, but I would have to take my pants off, and I think we can do without that."

The colonel smiled slightly.

"My men had some Management uniforms they stripped from some of their fallen," he continued, slipping his glove back on. "We were planning a counter attack intending to infiltrate their ranks in disguise, but we never got that far. The Testers hit us hard and fast, and before I knew it, I was done. I don't remember much after that, but I do remember my men dressing me in the uniform of a colonel. I guess that's where my nickname started. Anyway, they put me out where I would be found, and made a break for it. The next thing I knew, I was in the city hospital in a bed, with all kinds of tubes coming out of me. It wasn't like I was well known or anything, and the stolen ID belonged to a man that was part of one of the units we hit. Since I was severely wounded, nobody thought to check me out. They assumed I was him."

He drifted off for a moment, staring at the back wall as he remembered the events.

"I tried to find out as much as possible on the conflict, and then heard the City Fathers signed an agreement with the outsiders. As you all know, that's when Management took power. I thought about escaping and getting out of the city, but a one-legged one-armed man didn't have much chance. So I decided to find another way. I convinced the doctor to give me rehabilitation outside of the hospital. They had an opening in the library for someone to organize books at night. I started there and had only been there two weeks when the file building mysteriously burned."

The Colonel smiled broadly at the thought.

"They managed to put it out," he continued, "but not before a large section of personnel records were destroyed."

"Hey, I covered that fire," Jim interjected, "the fire marshal's investigation indicated it was accidental. A short in an outlet behind a large file cabinet I believe."

The colonel smiled even wider.

"Yeah, accidental," he said emphatically. "Shortly after the fire, the medical staff assigned me to their new so-called "Economic Diversity District" on the East side, where I was to recover from my injuries, and learn a new trade. That's where you were just investigating. Anyway, the retraining amounted to little more than teaching me how to type one-handed. Not much of a future with those "dynamic skills.""

The bitterness in his voice was unmistakable as he tapped his metal fingers on the desk.

"Most of the time, I wandered around the facility, talking with other "inmates," as we started calling ourselves. I was probably the most vocal, and complained about everything. It made a lot of people uncomfortable, especially that bitch Lucy. Anyway, one night, several large goons showed up at my door. They said we were going on a little outing. I hobbled along to where a large van was waiting. This was before they got that new black stealth bus you followed. I hopped on board to find about a dozen or so of my fellow inmates. It was a hot summer night as they drove us out here and dumped us off."

"We were the first group taken out," he continued taking a long breath. "They were just looking for a convenient spot, and found this area perfect since it had a large turnaround area. It was a scene very much like you saw a bit ago, only it was summer, not winter. They shoved us out, and took off for the city. I thought they might shoot us at first, but they decided there was no way we could get back through the brutal wasteland. Leaving us out here to die of thirst or starvation kept their hands clean. Did you know it gets up to a hundred and twenty degrees during the day in the summer? If the heat didn't get us, there were plenty of hungry animals."

The colonel sat forward in his seat.

"That night, it was a full moon, and none of us had any idea where we were. We sat together on some rocks, trying to come up with ideas, but it was hard to find any in the dark. We just huddled around, waiting for day break, and taking inventory of our situation. It certainly looked bleak. No water, no food, with crippled and old people everywhere. There was a certain sense of panic and dread. But it was then I recognized the outline of one of the entrance blocks. The military disguised electronic controls for approved entry personnel as stone blocks. You couldn't miss them once you knew what you were looking for. I could hardly believe my eyes, and started laughing. Of course, the folks thought I had gone nuts, but I had one of my friends help me to the block. My only concern was my old code, and whether it would still work. It had been nearly 20 years since I worked at this site. When I entered my code, it didn't work, but I remembered that if you enter your old code in backwards with a few special commands, the system would reset. I gave it a try, and the screen went blank for a moment before the cursor appeared. I was trained in cipher technology, so it didn't take long to reset my password and gain entrance."

The colonel leaned forward, taking another deep breath.

"You guys must be exhausted," he said, rising from his seat. "There's a couple of couches in the next office that have served well in the past if you're interested. I can explain more in the morning."

Parks and Jim stood to their feet.

"That's an amazing story," Jim said. "I want to hear about everything. But we need to get some rest, as you say. There's nothing we can do tonight anyway, with that howling storm outside, and I'm curious to see what's coming next. After the day we had, I expect to find a little girl chasing a large white bunny down a rabbit hole."

The colonel chuckled, and smiled.

"Fair enough," Parks confirmed. "Tomorrow will be a new day."

CHAPTER 20

David sent a thought through his crystal to the other key members of the resisters requesting a meeting. He needed to discuss recent developments, and see if anyone had a clue about what was going on. The blowing snow was piling up as he rounded the bend, following tracks made by other members. Everybody had four wheel drives, or rode with someone who did. Empty windows with torn curtains stared back at him as he drove past an old abandoned farmhouse. He remembered playing inside once with a friend as a child. That seemed like a million years ago now as he pulled around behind the dilapidated old barn and parked next to Kenzie's bright red sport runner. Light shone through a large hole in the wall as he made his way through the deepening snow. A gust of wind dusted the entrance as he stepped in.

"Hi, David," Burke exclaimed. "That's quite the storm. I hope we won't have to spend the night here."

"Not a chance," Kenzie laughed. "You guys can ride in the back of my rig if you can't make it out."

"I can take that princess fairy truck you drive anytime," Joshua crowed. "I've had mine up the mountain through Devil's canyon. You don't even like to get mud on your tires."

"Hey, guys," David interrupted. "Enough. I didn't call you out here to discuss off-road trucking."

"Why did you call us out on such a rotten night?" Troy asked as he put another piece of wood in the fire box of the small potbellied stove they set up for meetings like this.

It was glowing bright orange as they huddled around and warmed themselves. A piece of iron pipe served as a makeshift chimney, taking the smoke just high enough to dissipate above their heads and through the siding. The barn was a fitting place to hold their meetings, as this was where Parks had found them that fateful day so many years ago.

"I'd like to wait for everybody before I begin," David said as he sat on a large block of wood. "Where's everybody else?"

Just then another set of lights appeared through the cracked barn window.

"It's Kirsten!" Isaac said. "She's by herself though."

Burke took one of the oil lanterns off a hook, and met her as she entered.

"That's not a fun drive," Kirsten said, brushing the snow off her sleeves. "It's a blizzard out there."

"Just the kind of night we need," David replied. "There's no chance we'll be discovered or interrupted. Where are Aaron and Normand?"

"Normand said they called him into work." Kirsten answered. "One of the other drivers couldn't get out of his driveway or something. I don't know about Aaron. He hasn't been at a meeting with us in a very long time anyway."

"Do you think we should wait?" Joshua asked.

"On a night like this," Kenzie replied, "I don't think so. Let's get started. You called this meeting, David--what's on your mind?"

"Here's the deal," David began as they all found something to sit on. "We've been holding our secret meetings for five years with no issues. But now all of a sudden, things are happening, and they're not good. Some people I know have been seriously injured, possibly kidnapped, or even killed, and we have no explanation why. I called Parks for help, and he said we should put our heads together. I'm thinking there may be a mole in our midst."

"A mole," Burke said. "You mean somebody is spying on us?"

"That's exactly what I mean. Kevin Knobbs was killed, and his wife is still missing. My dad was in a suspicious accident, and I spent last night rescuing another man who was attacked while investigating my father's accident. Dad told me Kevin was upset after our last meeting, and that he may have recognized someone from work. It all adds up to one thing, we've been found out, and need to take things to the next level."

"What are you proposing?" Kenzie asked as she scooted closer to the stove.

"First, we need to get my parents out of the city."

"You mean your mom, right?" Troy said.

"You guys don't know this, but my dad isn't really dead. We faked his death because someone was trying to kill him too, and they nearly did."

"Man, I'm so happy to hear your dad is alive. But if they believe your dad is dead," Joshua interjected, "your parents should be ok."

"I don't think so," David answered firmly. "Whoever these people are, they're not about to give up. They're looking for something they want, and that's why they killed Kevin, attacked Dad, and another man. If they think there's any chance of finding whatever they're looking for, my mom may still be in danger. I want to get them out of the city and somewhere they can't be found. Besides, Dad can't hide indefinitely."

"David's right," Kirsten replied. "Do any of you have any ideas how we can help them?"

They looked blankly around at each other, their faces glowing in the light of the lamps.

"I know!" Burk said excitedly. "Why don't they go out and stay with my cousins in the country. They have a big house, and I'm sure they wouldn't mind."

"That's a generous thought and great idea," David answered. "But I know my dad. He would never feel comfortable staying with somebody very long. We have to think of something else."

"Wait a minute," Troy said, standing up and moving next to the stove. "Why not get Parks involved? He knows of hiding places outside the city wall. You know, caves and such. Maybe we could move them to one of those for now."

"That's pretty risky in this weather," Kirsten interjected.

"I don't mean right now!" Troy answered defensively. We'll wait until the storm dies down and then see what he has.

"I'm not sure how much time we have," David said. "But it's a good suggestion. Maybe something we should all consider the way things are going."

"I'll follow up with Parks and see what ideas he has." Kirsten said looking over towards Troy. "In the meantime, I suggest we stay where we are until further notice. Certainly no one is chasing us in these conditions."

"I agree." David replied. "I'm sure I can keep my folks out of harm's way for a while."

"Good. And I'll see what kind of solution Parks has. However, if they are looking for this thing David was talking about, they may hurt more people, and we can't let that happen. In the meantime, David, why don't we send your folks to my Uncle Jim and Aunt Lori's place? They live out in the country too, and have a small apartment they built for my grandparents when they were still alive. I've stayed out there a few times, and it's very quaint. Nobody would think to look for them there, and I know they wouldn't mind. They could stay there until we get an answer from Parks."

"That's a great idea!" David exclaimed. "I just need directions if you're sure they'll be ok with it."

"I'm sure! Now what about this mole thing; does anyone know anything about that?

They all looked at each other, and said "no" in unison.

"I think we'd best keep low until we know more of what's going on," Kirsten said quietly. "If Management is on to us, they'll be watching, and looking for opportunity. In the meantime, you guys quietly look around, and see if you notice anyone suspicious. Don't take chances though. We'll be in danger like never before. I say we meet back here in a week and discuss our findings."

They said their goodbyes, put out the lamps, and slogged into the heavy snow. The wind was whipping up as Joshua floored his rig, sending a wave of snow over the hood of Kenzie's truck.

"We'll see about that!" Kenzie exclaimed to Troy, who was riding with her. She quickly downshifted, roaring up tight behind Joshua. The road was narrow, with a ditch on one side, but she saw her opening as they rounded a bend. Joshua did his best to stay in the middle of the road and keep her behind, even though the road had widened enough for two vehicles. Kenzie punched it, lurching to his left. Joshua saw her move, and swerved to block her advance. That was all she needed. Joshua's truck plowed into a small drift. He couldn't pull out of it quickly enough, and watched helplessly as Kenzie zoomed by. She made sure he got a full windshield of snow as she roared past.

But David was more interested in getting home than playing in the snow. He was worried about his mom, and wanted to be sure she was ok. It was nearly one AM when he came in and checked on her, and went to bed.

"Mom," David said, poking his head into her bedroom early the next morning. "I have to go out for a little, while but I should be back about nine."

"Ok, honey!" She replied, sitting up in bed. "I'll have breakfast waiting for you when you get back."

"Just remember our signal." David said as he closed the bedroom door. "Three knocks, and then I push the doorbell before opening the door with my key. That way you know it's me."

Mary got dressed, and headed into the kitchen to get things ready. She had just started the coffee when the doorbell rang.

"I didn't hear any knocks," she thought as she peered around the corner at the door.

The doorbell rang a second time as she moved into the living room, and peeked out from behind the curtain. When she saw who it was, she ran to let them in.

"Jackie!" she said as she opened the door. "What are you doing out on such a nasty morning? Come on in before you freeze."

Mrs. Cantrell was a little old lady who lived across the street. They had been neighbors for years, and Mary used to help her with her flowers. She was old, and needed a cane, so Mary thought it strange she would venture out in this weather.

"Oh, I'm alright," Mrs. Cantrell said as she took off her scarf. "I was hoping to find you at home. I wasn't able to make it to your husband's funeral, but I wanted to give you my deepest sympathy."

Mary helped her take off her coat, and hung it in on the rack by the door. She led the way into the kitchen, glad for some company, even though it was strange to see the old lady during such severe weather.

"The coffee should be ready in a minute!" she said cheerfully as Mrs. Cantrell took a seat at the kitchen table. "I was just about to start breakfast. David should be home anytime now."

"Oh, David's back? I thought he was still at college?"

"He's done now, and is staying with me for a while. He worries a lot about me, the dear boy."

Mary poured a cup of coffee for both of them, and sat down next to her at the kitchen table.

"How are you doing?" Mrs. Cantrell asked as she took a sip of coffee. "I know how hard it is to lose a loved one. My husband passed away ten years ago today. There's not a moment that goes by I don't think about him."

"I remember him," Mary replied. "He was such a nice man. But I'm doing ok. It was so sudden, I guess it just happened, and then it was over."

Mary got up from the table to start mixing pancake batter for breakfast. She didn't want to appear insincere, since Bruce was not really dead. As she worked, she tried to think of other topics of conversation, but nothing came to mind.

"I think you may have something that doesn't belong to you," Mrs. Cantrell said quietly. She stared intently over her bifocals at Mary.

"What?" Mary replied absentmindedly as she poured in the milk, and returned the container to the fridge.

"You have something that doesn't belong to you!" Mrs. Cantrell said loudly.

"I have something that what?" Mary said, pulling her blender out of the drawer.

"You have something they want," Mrs. Cantrell nearly shouted as she slammed her coffee cup onto the table. "They told me you took it, and they want it back."

Mary dropped her blender onto the counter, and stepped back against the sink. The kindly old lady she had known ever since they moved to the neighborhood looked different somehow. Her face was scrunched up, and her eyes were narrowed, with a look she had never seen in them before.

"I, I, I don't know what you mean," Mary stammered.

"You have it! I can tell!" "The frail woman said as she stood up, and moved menacingly towards Mary, who slid behind her island counter. "Kevin sent it here. Didn't he?"

Mary was horrified as the old lady rounded the counter. She had nowhere to escape to, and she was strangely afraid of what an eighty-year-old ninety-pound woman might do. Suddenly, three knocks came at the door followed by the doorbell.

"Hi, Mrs. Cantrell," David exclaimed as he entered the kitchen. "I haven't seen you in years. How are you doing?"

The old lady turned, and pushed past David, knocking him into the wall. She scurried to the living room, grabbed her scarf, and slammed the door behind her as she headed into the cold.

"Wow!" David said when she had gone. "She's plenty strong for an old lady. What's gotten into her?"

Mary quickly explained the events as David's face turned from confusion to deep concern.

"We're leaving right now, Mom. You can't stay here any longer. I went by the hospital, and Dr. Larson said Dad is ok to travel. Kirsten has made arrangements, and we're going to get you and dad out of the city. I wanted to wait until tonight, but that isn't going to happen now. I'll get your suitcases, and meet you at the truck."

David looked across the street as he pulled out onto the snow-covered roadway. Mrs. Cantrell was standing at her window, glaring at them as they left.

"Here's what's going to happen," David explained as they worked their way across town. "We have arranged for you and Dad to travel with Kirsten. No one will suspect you're in her truck. I'll go a different way and, if anybody is watching, they'll follow me."

"Are you sure, son? I feel like I'm not going to see you again."

"You'll be ok, Mom, and Dad will be with you. We'll come out to see you once I know everyone's safe. This is the only way I can be sure you guys will be ok and we can take advantage of this bad weather to get you to safety."

David pulled into the rear of the hospital where the ambulances were kept. Kirsten was waiting with Bruce in the backseat.

"I love you, son!" Bruce said getting out, and hugging David.

"I love you too, Dad, but you guys have to get going. We can't afford to have anybody see you now!"

Even though her truck had dark windows, Mary covered them both with some blankets as Kirsten drove off. David left a different way where he could be easily seen if someone wanted to follow him. He figured he could lose a tail if he needed to but, for now, would make himself an easy target. But what his mom said about Mrs. Cantrell seemed nearly unbelievable. It was hard to imagine an old lady acting like that but he totaled most of it up to his mother's stress and his overreacting. But he needed his parents out of the city and this was as good a catalyst as any. So, with them safely away, he forgot all about it.

CHAPTER 21

When Jim opened his eyes, Parks was gone.

"So it wasn't a dream after all," he thought, rolling off the long leather couch.

He left for the elevator, and worked his way through the dark hall lit only by trim lighting running along the edge of the ceiling. Next to the elevator panel was a red call button.

"Do you wish to come up?" A warm female voice asked.

"I do," Jim replied. "This is Jim Banner. We came in last night, and I need to see the Colonel."

The door to the elevator opened, and Jim stepped in. He was not sure which button to push, but the elevator started on its own.

"Somebody must know where I'm going," he said to the elevator door, "because I sure don't."

In a few moments, it came to a stop, and the door opened onto a new floor.

He stepped out, and was greeted by an attractive young lady sitting behind a large polished marble counter.

"The Colonel is just down the hall to the right," she said pointing.

"Ok," he replied, stepping forward, and leaning against the counter. "I'm Jim, and you are?"

"My name is Iris," the young lady replied, returning a friendly smile.

"Thank you, Iris," Jim said over his shoulder as he started walking down the hall. "It's really nice to meet you!" he continued, spinning around and walking backwards. "Hope you're still here when I come back."

"I'll be here!" she said brightly, her checks turning a slight shade of red.

He turned, and just about ran into Parks coming out of the colonel's office.

"So, there you are," Parks said with a smirk. "I thought you were going to sleep all day."

"Hey, Colonel," Jim said, ignoring Parks' remark, "I thought people here were like from the Island of Misfit Toys or something."

"Oh, you must be referring to Iris," the colonel answered, glancing over his shoulder. "No, we're not all old, disabled, or useless. Iris is an only child, dropped off by our Management friends some five years ago when she was barely fifteen. Her father was quite wealthy, and held an upper position at the Citadel. I understand both her parents were killed in a car accident off East Mountain Drive. Anyway, she was hustled into the retraining facility for about a week, and then shipped out here. She's the only one I've ever seen brought out solo. I think someone had their eyes set on their family money or something. She was a pretty scared young lady when we found her."

"That's totally wrong!" Jim said angrily. "It's not even human to drop a young girl off like that."

"And especially one who is still mourning the loss of her parents," the colonel agreed. "Anyway, it took some time to convince her we weren't going to hurt her. The older ladies helped a lot. You would be surprised at what a talented, caring group we have here. Hard to imagine anyone would dump valuable people like this as if they were worthless."

"Five years ago," Parks said quietly, a frown burrowing across his forehead. "That's about the time Barron got his second promotion. He took Robert Watter's position when he and his wife died in a car accident."

"Watters?" the colonel replied, his voice rising. "That's Iris's last name, Iris Watters."

"I always wondered what happened to Bob's daughter after the accident." Parks replied. "We were told she ran away. They were good people. It's great to know she's ok."

The corridor ended at two large double doors the colonel pushed out of the way as they entered what appeared to be a control room.

"CCColonel." A young man said, turning from a console full of gauges, dials, and buttons. "Gggood to see you sssir."

"Good morning, Greg," the colonel said with a smile."I've some folks here who would like to see you."

Greg jumped out of his seat at the sight of Jim.

"Jjjim," Greg cried, wrapping his arms tightly around, and hugging him. "Wwwoww! I never expected to see you again."

Jim grabbed Greg's shoulders, pushing him back gently.

"Young man," Jim said, looking intently into his eyes, "I'am glad to see you too. I thought you were dead. Man, if it wasn't for you, I would never have investigated or found this place. You're the reason we're here. I came looking to find out what happened to you."

Jim laughed with genuine affection, and pulled Greg in for a second hug.

"TTThannk you," Greg replied, "ttthank you for coming for mmme!"

"There will be plenty of time for reminiscing later," the colonel said, stepping forward and putting his hand on Jim's shoulder. "Greg has work to do, and we have things to discuss. Greg is our technical engineer. You see, this place has a self-replenishing cold fusion reactor buried deep below. It's designed to run for millennia, but some of the calculations built into the program were causing power-downs. However, in the short time since Greg arrived, he's reprogrammed the computer, eliminated brown outs, and increased efficiency. This place is humming right along, thanks to him."

"We'll have that conversation I promised yet," Jim said, giving Greg a friendly slap on the shoulder as he headed back to his station.

"Ttthanks," he gushed, easing behind the command console.

"I had some men bring your vehicle in out of the cold this morning," the colonel said as they walked down the hall towards the elevators. "If you take the tunnel, you can get to the city a lot faster, and avoid the snow entirely."

"Tunnel, what tunnel?" Jim asked.

"There are underground tunnels that stretch in many directions," he replied. "I've followed a few of them as far as I could before I had to turn back. The one I'm talking about runs under the city, and ends up behind the Citadel in an old, abandoned warehouse. I used to worry someone would use it to find us, but over the years, I have grown to believe no one knows it's there. I think it was designed to move volumes of men and equipment in a hurry, probably in the event of an attack of some kind."

Jim smiled warmly, waving at Iris as they stepped onto the elevator.

The door opened on the floor just below where they started the night before as the colonel led the way out.

"We appreciate what you did last night," the older man said as the men made their way towards the people-mover station. "And Parks, you're not alone on your journey. Whatever comes of the book and the parchment, you're linked to us somehow. Our paths are different, but we want the same thing--freedom. Management is dangerous, and if they find out about us, they will come. They're patient, waiting for the opportunity to destroy anyone who stands in their way. We'll need to be smarter, stronger, and ready if we're to be victorious."

"I don't know about all that," Parks replied. "I just have a lot of questions I can't answer. I want to understand why the old book is so important. I'll come back and speak with Sterling when I can."

"That's a good idea," the colonel said. "I believe Sterling may have more information. However, we need to be thinking about our next move. There's no telling what could happen if we're discovered, and I don't want people getting careless."

"You can trust us," Jim replied. "We'll keep your secret safe."

"Your secret's safe," Parks confirmed, "at least for now. But I suggest you remain vigilant, and be ready should anything change."

The colonel nodded as they all shook hands before getting into Jim's rig.

"Let's get these blasted doors open," the colonel shouted to several of his men. "From here, it's a direct drive to the city. Just remember when you get to the other end, look for a control panel. Enter the code I gave you this morning, and the ramp will drop down. Reset it before you leave, and check for "prying eyes," although in this weather, I doubt anybody will be hanging around an old, abandoned warehouse."

They pulled into the tunnel, and as soon as the nose of Jim's truck cleared the doors, a row of lights on the ceiling of the tunnel came on, giving clear view of the roadway ahead. Jim watched in his rearview mirror as the doors closed behind them, and he hit the accelerator, heading down the center of the tunnel. No matter how fast he drove, the lights came on ahead of them, lighting their way. Every so often, they passed access vents and ladders ascending to the top of the tunnel. Parks noted their locations, figuring they were there for ventilation, or escape if needed.

"All the years I spent in the wilderness," Parks thought, "and I never spotted one. They must be well disguised."

The tunnel was perfectly straight, meaning whoever designed it had chosen the shortest distance between two points. It could have handled several large transport vehicles side by side easily, with room to spare.

A half hour or so passed before Jim broke the silence.

"So, what were you and the colonel discussing this morning before I got up?"

"What do you mean?" Parks responded.

"Oh, come on, Parks," Jim said insistently. "I saw you two coming out of that office. I'm sure you weren't watching cartoons."

"Hey, don't worry about it," Parks replied, glancing at Jim. "You've got enough on your mind. We all have things we need to work on.

"You're right about that. I intend to expose the wrongdoing at that horrible place they call the East Economic Diversity District." Jim said leaning forward on the steering wheel. "I'm going to wake people up. I am going to make a special report, and expose them."

Parks tensed a little.

"Jim, there's way more to this than you know. I don't think you should do anything drastic yet. This will be no easy take-down. I'm pretty sure somebody is watching, and may already be suspicious of you."

"I have to do something, even if it's risky. There are a lot of people out there like Greg and Iris and their families. They're being thrown away like they're nothing, and I plan on finding out what the real agenda is, and who's running the show."

The lights in the tunnel began to change from white to yellow then to red as they approached the end. Distance signs appeared along the tunnel sides, instructing them to slow and prepare to stop. Jim eased up to the heavy steel barrier protecting the exit ramp while Parks jumped out, and located the panel. He entered the code the colonel had given him. In a few seconds, a section of the tunnel ceiling lifted above them, and a hydraulic ramp lowered, allowing Jim to drive up to the inside of a large, aging warehouse.

Parks, following on foot, located the hidden panel behind a steel column just as the colonel had instructed, and closed the tunnel exit. Together, they brushed dust over the ramp seams and their tracks, erasing any trace of their arrival.

The door at the end of the warehouse was open, revealing wind-whipped snow devils as they exited. Their tracks would soon be covered by blowing snow, eliminating any evidence of their presence. Jim maneuvered through the many abandoned warehouses before finding the exit to the main road. The streets were plowed and empty, except for the occasional abandoned car stuck in a snow drift. It was obvious people had chosen to stay home on this bleak Sunday, and wait for better weather. Even the diehard skiers weren't out. In his rig, Jim had no problem powering through the drifting snow as he headed towards Park's apartment.

"Just drop me in the alley, and I'll walk to my apartment from there. I don't think we should be seen together."

"Thanks for all you did, Parks," Jim said sincerely as he rounded the corner. "I really appreciate your help. Just keep watching my show, and you'll see what I can really do. Hey, one other thing, what do you know about Harry Allison?"

"Harry?" Parks asked, "The head of the Citadel? What about him?"

"Just curious what you think of him," Jim said slowing to a stop.

Parks took a long look at Jim before stepping out of the truck.

"He's his own man, but he may be involved somehow with this whole mess, and possibly other bad things too," Parks replied before closing the door. "Steer clear of him, and try to keep your reporting low-key for now. This is not something you want to rush."

CHAPTER 22

After two weeks of severe winter storms, the weather finally let up. City crews got busy making travel possible again, but Jim hadn't been sitting around, waiting for the roads to clear. He had been preparing for the return of "Jim the Investigative Reporter."

The colonel had given him a list of the people who had been dropped at the island, as they had come to call the hidden facility in the wilderness, to help in his investigation. He made several more trips to his uncle's farm to further mine his newspaper library, and confirm each story. Jim was meticulous as he cross-referenced, and double-checked his research. Reports that had been filed on-line and copied to microfilm were compared against the newspapers. Most of the names on the list were mentioned in the obituary section as "died of natural causes." Considering they had been dropped in the middle of a wilderness with no provisions, it was an accurate description. He also found stories similar to Greg's. Some people on the colonel's list were not on the official record and it was these Jim chose to focus on most. Exposing a systematic elimination of people would be a powerful revelation indeed.

"This is good stuff," Jim said to himself. "Now I just need to get it to the right people, and bring this sorry business to a crashing end, and expose whoever's behind it."

His first major challenge was finding a way to get the information to the public. He needed a stage to present his case, and that was where Frank came in.

Frank was Jim's producer; a short heavy-set fellow with a round face. If there were such a thing as a perfect producer, Frank would have fit the description. He loved the energy, and being in the middle between cast and crew. On one side, he was an effective motivator, keeping his crews on schedule. On the other, he knew how to soothe his temperamental stars. It was a tight wire, but he walked it successfully, and his skills had made "HOT News" the number one most-watched station in the city. Fortunately, HOT News's success also made it risky for Management to take it over. They allowed HOT News to operate outside their tightly-controlled system to keep from causing a stir.

Jim finished his early morning broadcast to the tune of ringing phones. People throughout the city requested him to come to their neighborhood next. But Jim's concerns weighed on him as he headed to Frank's office.

Pushing the door open, he walked in without knocking. Frank was just finishing up a phone conversation, and waved him over.

"Jimmy, my man," he said, hanging up the phone. "You hit another home-run this morning. People are really tuned in, baby! They're loving it; LOVING IT! I'm thinking you're coming up on a nice bonus."

Frank knew his stars so well, he could usually tell what they were thinking. He was sure Jim was looking for a raise, and at any other time, he might have been right. This time, however, he couldn't have been more wrong.

"Thanks, boss," Jim said with a smile as he eased into one of the plush chairs set around Frank's desk. "I can always use a bonus, and a million bucks would be just fine."

Frank leaned back, frowning a bit.

"But one of these will work for now," Jim said as he reached over, and pulled a cigar from a box on his desk.

"You had me there for a minute," Frank laughed, breathing a sigh of relief. "You've been doing great, but not that great."

"No worries. That's not what I'm here for anyway," Jim continued, running the cigar under his nose before depositing it in his coat pocket. "Remember the old days when we worked together, reporting events as they happened? We were a great team. You and I built HOT News into the powerhouse it is today."

Frank leaned back, nodding in agreement as he folded his hands over his round belly.

"But hey, you seem to be backing off a little of late," Jim continued wryly. "Covering events carefully, politically correct as people say now-a-days. It seems you've been reluctant to dig into real issues, and expose the darker side of things."

"Hey-Hey-HEY," Frank answered defensively. "We take a pretty aggressive line with the information we get. You know that. People still consider us their main news source, and respect our place as a watchdog for the public. I haven't suppressed any true stories. But we have to be sure before broadcasting, and bringing accusations. Good journalism requires accuracy, not half-truths. Not to mention, there are plenty of people who would like to see us shut down, and would use any excuse to make that happen. We have enemies, you know."

He knew he had Frank going now, and pressed his advantage.

"You can't get ahead in this business without making some enemies," Jim replied calmly, leaning back and crossing his legs, "but I'm not here to talk about past successes or present problems. I am here about principle; the principles that drove us to keep broadcasting, even while the city was being taken. The principles which helped our friends to safety by secretly reporting troop movements. And you, you were exceptional in convincing them we were in favor of the takeover, even as we did our best to undermine their arrival."

"Oh, I remember all right," Frank replied, leaning back and glancing over at one of the awards he'd won for best broadcasting. "But the fact is, we were needed to secure public opinion. They wanted a quick transition, so overlooking some transgressions made sense. We quickly shifted gears, and began encouraging citizens to cooperate once it became clear it was over. We made it easier for everybody, and you know as well as I do it would have been far worse if we hadn't. There are still times I wish we had continued to fight, but it was a judgment call."

Frank sank deeper into his black leather chair.

"But that was then," Frank continued as he reached forward, and took a cigar from the box. "We surrendered, right? We can't change that now."

"I get that we had little choice, but it wasn't our call. The City Fathers agreed to that deal. But maybe there's something we can do now. Management seems to have it made, taking and doing whatever pleases them, but I have information that could start us back on the road to sanity. Maybe it's time for 'Jim the Reporter' to make his return."

"Jim, the Reporter!" Frank exclaimed, nearly falling over backward. "It's been a long time since I heard that phrase. Are you telling me you want to stop being the most well-known weatherman this city has ever seen, and go back to reporting? Are you nuts? Why would you want to do a thing like that?"

Jim leaned forward, taking another cigar from the box. This one he lit with the gold-engraved lighter Frank kept on the desk.

"It's not as crazy as it sounds, and I'm definitely not nuts," Jim replied, taking a draw from the lit cigar. "Look, we all thought we were doing the right thing by avoiding casualties. The City Fathers made a good argument, and we bought it. But the change we were sold and the change we got are not the same thing. Since then, we've buried our heads in the sand, thinking Management has our best interests in mind. Believe me, that's where I was until just a short time ago. I thought that my safe life was a good one. It seemed worth the minor inconveniences from Management. I was wrong. It's nothing but a fantasy. I've seen what they're capable of doing first hand, and what they're saying is just a bunch of lies."

Frank moved the round, heavy silver ash tray into the center of his desk. Reaching forward, he grabbed the desk lighter, and lit the cigar he was fondling.

"Hey," Jim said, "I thought you gave those things up."

"I have," he replied, inhaling deeply as he spun his chair towards the window.

There was silence for a few moments as Jim watched smoke curling over the top of Frank's chair.

"We've known each other for a long time," Frank said, looking outside. "In fact, I know pretty much your whole family, and there's not a more honorable, honest family in this city. I know you believe you're on to something, and hope to make a difference, and I know you will try. The problem is, I know other things too. Things I've never told anyone, not even my wife." Frank continued to stare out the window as he talked. "But I have to warn you, my friend, whatever you're planning could be big trouble, bigger than you can even imagine. Are you sure you're willing to jeopardize your career? If you're wrong, you may lose way more than just your career."

He slowly spun his chair around, and flicked the cigar ashes into the ash tray.

"I'm not afraid, and I'm not wrong!" Jim said boldly. "What I have is big, but I have no way to know how deep or high this goes. I'm just on the scent. I need to act now, because if I don't, more innocent people may die. It's that important."

"You're saying there are people who have died?" Frank asked.

"I've said enough for now," Jim replied as he extinguished his cigar in the ash tray, and got up. "Look, I don't want to hurt you or

HOT News. I love this place; I always have, and if you don't want to be involved, I'll find another way. You have a lot at stake here."

He turned, and started for the door.

"Hold on there," Frank exclaimed, pulling his cigar from his mouth as he jumped from his chair.

He grabbed Jim's arm, and pulled him around.

"Don't get me wrong here. Just because I'm cautious doesn't mean I'm not interested. And we've been through too much together to separate now. Look, Jim, I don't know what you've got going, but if it's that important, I'll need time and more information in order to make a decision. Why don't you tell me about it?"

"I can't just yet," Jim replied, feeling relieved by Frank's statement. "I have to do more checking first."

"Fine, but if you're so dead set on becoming a reporter again," Frank continued, squeezing his arm, "you'll be more effective if people continue to think you're "Jim the weatherman." That way, you can do your thing, and not be noticed. Also, I believe I can free you up a bit by giving some of your work to that attractive young meteorologist we hired last year, you know, the one you've been mentoring. I think she's ready to take a more active part in your program, and it'll give you some time to work on whatever "newsworthy" project you have going. What do you think, Jim, sound like a plan?"

He stepped back, sticking out his right hand in a handshake gesture.

Jim grabbed Frank's hand, and pulled him tight to his chest.

"Thank you, Frank. I'll keep you informed as things move ahead. I'll let you know what's happening within the next couple of weeks."

Frank watched from his office window as Jim drove out of the parking lot. He was good at reading his stars, but this one had taken him completely by surprise. Sitting back at his desk, Frank reluctantly picked up the phone…

CHAPTER 23

Jim headed home to get some much-needed rest, and to plan his next move. Somehow, he had to find a way to get what he needed quietly, and without drawing the wrong attention. That wouldn't be easy, but he did understand Management's system.

Directives came down from the Board of Directors, which was made up of six mysterious men. These were the ones the City Fathers handed power to when they surrendered. Their directives filtered through a complex managerial system to ultimately become law. It was an inefficient, yet effective means of dictating people's daily life. The one thing not tolerated was a break in the chain. No one went over the head of their respective area manager who was responsible for carrying out the will of the Board. The repercussions for anyone crazy enough to try were serious and well-known.

Jim had an advantage others didn't have. Since he worked for the only independent news organization in existence, he didn't have to follow the prescribed system. It was the only "loophole" in this well devised scheme, and it gave him the freedom to skip all the ladder rungs, and go straight to the top.

Lucy Lane, the head of the East Economic Development District, was obviously deeply involved, Jim thought as he sat down at his kitchen table with a hot cup of coffee. She was the one he saw that night, commanding the men who loaded people onto the bus. That meant she was at least partially behind the euthanasia policy, but Jim didn't know if she was acting alone, or receiving orders from higher up.

He took a sip of coffee as he considered his options. At some point, he was going to have to risk exposure if he was going to get to the bottom of this.

Harry, the head of the Citadel and city security, looked like a logical starting point. Parks had seemed a little suspicious of him, but he did say he was his own man. He would just have to be careful with his approach.

Jim called ahead, and got Harry's secretary, Birgit. She was excited, talking to the famous weatherman, and quickly cleared a spot on Harry's schedule. Jim arrived right on time, and even though the guard recognized him, he still checked his name on the gate list. But before Jim could enter, the guard slid an extra sheet of paper in his window with the clipboard. Jim obliged, and the guard smiled broadly, opening the gate while sliding the paper with Jim's autograph into his top pocket.

Following directions to the underground parking garage and the visitor parking spaces, he found the elevator to the upper floor where senior management offices were located. The door opened to a modest reception room manned by an attractive middle-aged woman. She was around from behind the desk in a flash, almost before he had stepped off the elevator.

"Hello, Mr. Weatherman," she said enthusiastically, "I'm Birgit. We spoke on the phone earlier when you called. Can I get you a cup of coffee or some tea?"

"You can call me Jim, and thanks for the offer, but I'm good. Is Harry available?"

Birgit hit the office intercom.

"Sir, Jim Banner's here to see you," she said brightly.

"I'll be right out," came the reply.

Approaching footsteps sounded from behind a pair of heavy wooden doors separating the foyer from the main offices.

"Jim," Harry exclaimed, greeting him warmly as he stepped into the room. "I've been a long-time fan of your show, and have to admit you're much taller in person."

"I get that all the time," Jim laughed. "It's all those talking head shots that make me look short."

"Come on down to the office," Harry said with a broad smile. "Did Birgit take good care of you?"

"She was more than gracious," Jim said, shooting a quick smile over his shoulder.

The two men headed through the doors down the hall to his office. Harry's office was a half-circle, with large glass windows overlooking the cadet training yard. Jim stepped in from the tiled hallway onto a plush carpet, and followed him to the window. Several new cadet squads were going through their routines.

"Impressive, aren't they?" Harry said proudly.

"Yes, quite impressive," Jim responded, as he scanned the group below. "Quite a nice view you have here."

"Thank you!" Harry replied as he turned, and stepped behind his desk. "I like to see the men in action."

Jim followed, sitting down in one of the office chairs as Harry leaned forward with his elbows on the desk.

"To what do I owe the privilege of having the city's most renowned weather celebrity sitting in my office? I told my wife you were coming in to see me this morning, and it was all I could do to keep her from coming to work with me today."

"It's really my privilege. I've heard great things about this place, and you, but I don't think I've ever actually been inside. I hope you don't mind, but I need to get right to the point. I came here to talk with you about a situation, and see if it's something you could help with."

"I don't know much about weather other than what it's doing right now. I don't see how I could be of much help…"

"Oh, it's not a weather problem. It's much more than that. It's a long story, but let me give you the short version."

Harry sat back in his chair with an interested, somewhat puzzled look on his face. Jim was a little nervous exposing his intent, but he had no choice. He needed someone on the inside who could do something, and Harry would be perfect if he were interested. Even Parks didn't have that kind of authority.

"Certain information has come into my possession regarding one of the Economic Development Districts where people are sent to retrain and learn new life skills. It seems some patients or patrons, whatever you want to call them, have been disappearing."

"Disappearing? How? Like walking out and leaving the facility?" Harry interjected.

"I wish that's all it was, but I am afraid there may be more to it than that. Let me explain. I met a young man at one of the facilities when I was doing an onsite broadcast. He was a resident there, and wanted to talk with me. I assumed he was just a fan, but I later learned he was quite concerned about things he saw happening with folks at his facility. Anyway, we had a meeting set for the following week, but I got delayed. When I went to meet him several weeks later, he was nowhere to be found. I checked with the staff there, and they said they had never even heard of him."

"Not surprising." Harry stated flatly." They're big places with populations of nearly ten thousand people each. You couldn't expect them to know everybody. Maybe he was transferred. They do move people around sometimes."

"That's what I thought at first too, but as I asked more questions, they said they had no record of him at all."

"Well, that is strange, but what does that have to do with me? Wouldn't that be more of a problem for missing persons, or the facility itself? Could be they're having problems keeping their systems working right."

"Exactly! So I checked the records at the city library, and there's no evidence the young man I met that day ever existed. I looked at birth records, news reports, anything I could find, and there was no mention of him. However, there was mention of his parents. The obituaries confirmed his parents were killed in a car accident, but there was no mention of a surviving son. No birth record. No mention in the paper or computer records."

"Maybe you've just made a mistake," Harry answered somewhat defensively. "Maybe you got the name wrong, or somebody was playing a trick on you. I'm sure there's a logical explanation."

Jim became a little nervous with Harry's continuing litany of excuses and his defensive attitude but he needed to stay calm.

"Oh, I'm pretty sure this is no trick, at least not on me," Jim said keeping his cool. "I found some old newspapers confirming both his birth date, and the date of his parents' demise. He was clearly mentioned in both. Somebody removed this information from the public records, and expunged it from private files. They wanted it to appear as if he never existed."

Harry got up from his desk, and stepped back to the window. He stood there for a moment with his hands clasped tightly behind his back, watching the Cadets work out.

"Quite a story for a weatherman," he said without turning, "but I still don't know why that would be of interest to me. We don't do missing person investigations, and there's no evidence of a crime. Why bring it to me?"

Jim leaned forward in his chair, folding his hands between his knees.

"I thought you might be interested in what could be a serious problem and could possibly even affect your position," Jim continued in a soft voice, being careful to maintain respect. "My research indicates this may be bigger than just one person."

Jim's stomach was turning over when Harry suddenly spun around, and returned to his chair.

"Tell you what," he said with a smile as he leaned back, taking a fresh look at Jim, "how about coming up to my house tomorrow night, say, around seven? My wife would love to meet you and, in the meantime, I could put more thought into what you've said. I can ask around a bit and see if anyone has heard of something like this going on. I'm sure it would be tough to keep secret. If I come up with anything, we could discuss it then, and you could bring what evidence you have of this "problem" with you. You can present the facts so we aren't relying on speculation. Unfortunately, I have another meeting in a few minutes so I can't talk now anyway. What do you think, Jim? My wife makes a killer lasagna."

"Sounds great!" Jim said, relieved by Harry's change of attitude as he got up from his seat. "I'll be there at seven. Thank you for seeing me, and for listening."

"Great, great," Harry said, escorting him back to the reception area. "Birgit, would you please give Jim a map to my house. He's coming by for dinner tomorrow night."

"Oh, lucky you," she said flashing a huge smile towards Harry. "Just a minute, I'll print you out a copy."

He took the directions, and said a cheerful goodbye before leaving. On the way down, he couldn't help thinking this went better than hoped. Not only did he have the manager of the Citadel working on the case, but he was going to his house to discuss the issue personally.

It was a great start, and he was finding the new "Jim the Reporter" to be a powerful force indeed!

CHAPTER 24

The next day passed quickly as Jim compiled his papers, preparing for his evening meeting with Harry. The bulk of evidence sprang from his research on people the colonel had mentioned, and copies of newspapers from his uncle. It was damning proof that something dark was going on at the EEDD. Jim intended to pull back the curtain, and see what was really going on there.

The trip to Harry's house was long, dark, and winding. He hadn't realized Harry lived above the Cliffside estates in the large mansion at the top. The severe weather was over, but gusty winds still blew wisps of snow off rocky ledges as he drove past. The nearly hour-long drive took him by sharp turns, graveled roads, and a road maintenance site where snow plows, dump trucks, and other heavy equipment were housed.

It had been years since he had been up that way. He used to ski cross-country through the valleys and hills scattered throughout the area. Perhaps he should come up, and ski again before all the snow was gone.

He continued the climb, his rig powering through the slushy snow and melting ice.

He realized it was the same road where Greg's parents had died.

Harry's house came into view at last. It was quite impressive, with heavy, wrought-iron gates guarding the main entrance. He pulled past a huge yard filled with barren trees still hibernating from the winter's grip as he made his way to the front of the house, lined with huge columns along the walkway to the main door.

He parked along the curb, and made his way up to the front entrance. Low lights illuminated the path, with an exterior chandelier hung high above wide double doors, stopping his approach. A beautiful melody played when he hit the doorbell, and the sound of clattering heels could be heard approaching inside. The door opened to reveal an attractive young woman dressed in a tight-fitting maid outfit.

"Good evening, sir," she said politely. "May I take your coat?"

"My coat and my heart," Jim said with a smile as she helped him with his overcoat.

"Thank you, sir," she responded. "Please follow me; the Mr. and Mrs. are waiting for you in the drawing room."

He passed several ornate marble statues and numerous oil paintings as she led him towards two tall glass doors that opened into an exquisitely furnished room. Stepping in, he was greeted by a large, open room with dark paneling and high ceilings. A stone fireplace stood at the far end of the room, flickering invitingly.

"Your guest has arrived," the maid announced before closing the door, and returning to her duties.

Harry and his wife stood up from their chairs by the fire.

"Jim," Harry exclaimed, "glad you could make it! This is my wife, Autumn."

"I'm so excited to meet you," she said, shaking his hand vigorously. "I watch your show all the time."

Harry's wife was a thin woman about five foot four with an attractive smile. She wore a dark green, tightly-fitting dress that accentuated her bony shoulders and protruding rib cage.

"It's so great to meet you!" she gushed with a huge grin surrounded by a generous portion of red lipstick. "I was just telling Harry how much I love your program. It's like we're right there with you when you do those on-site programs. I never knew the weather could be so interesting."

"Thank you very much. My crew and I work hard to make sure people have fun, and are well-informed."

Autumn didn't waste a moment. She continued talking about her interest in television, and how she almost took a career in broadcasting. She peppered him with questions, and ultimately pressed him for an audition, claiming she could do as good a job as the new weatherwoman.

Unfortunately, dinner didn't provide much relief.

"This is a beautiful home you have here," Jim said, seizing the moment as Autumn sipped from her crystal wine glass. "Didn't this belong to a famous family once? How did you manage to get it?"

"Oh, that's a great story," Harry bragged. "I got this place for nearly nothing when the previous owners died tragically years ago. The home went up for auction, and I made the winning bid. I couldn't have asked for a better deal."

The maid brought in the first course, and Autumn resumed telling him about her "experience" in journalism, and how she once had a bit part in a play that received some notoriety. Jim did his best to be polite, and tried numerous times to shift the conversation to what he'd come to discuss, but she would have no part of it.

Eventually, the main course arrived. A beautiful, tasty lasagna, and Jim was quick to compliment his hostess on her excellent recipe.

"Oh, it's nothing," she replied. "Our maid brought that recipe with her when we hired her. I've never really been much of a cook. Harry married me for my good looks and high energy."

"Honey, you're just being modest," Harry scolded his wife gently. "You know I've always loved your cooking. It's just nice you don't have to slave over the stove anymore."

Jim felt awkward, realizing Harry had lied about his wife's cooking. It wasn't a big deal, but seemed strange nonetheless.

"I'm expecting an early spring this year," Jim asserted, changing the subject. "The hard winter we're having is off the charts, but it should be close to over now, and I'm predicting a mild spring and summer."

His ruse worked, and dinner ended nicely. Harry invited him to join them in the sitting room. It was smaller and more intimate, with comfortable, overstuffed chairs and couches surrounding a rock-faced fireplace. Logs glowed brightly on the hearth as they took their places.

Jim hoped this would be his opportunity to talk seriously, but it soon became obvious Autumn was not about to let up. She seemed to have an endless supply of personal success stories revolving around experiences in media. Harry didn't seem to mind, and even encouraged some of her drivel. Jim stayed patient, waiting for the conversation to die off.

"Stunning," he commented seizing the moment.

Hanging over the fireplace was a beautiful oil painting of the house in the summer, with all the gardens in full bloom. The artist focused on a child, maybe six years old with blonde hair, playing in a field of flowers. Beautiful purple, yellow, and white flowers surrounded her.

"What kind of flowers are those?" he asked.

"Those are irises," Autumn responded, joining him by the fireplace. "The painting came with the house."

"She thinks it's valuable," Harry interjected.

"It is valuable because it's so beautiful. It's my favorite. The painting is called "The Garden of Iris." I just love it."

Jim stood studying it for a moment before returning to his seat, as Harry stepped behind a dark cherry wood bar.

"What can I get you?" he asked. "I can make just about anything as long as there's alcohol in it."

"I'll take a glass of red wine," Autumn said.

"Make mine a rum and coke if you have it," Jim replied.

Harry mixed up a margarita for himself, and presented the drinks on an ornate solid silver tray.

Sitting down, Harry switched to a new subject. This time, he focused on the architecture, and explained in detail how the art in the home was at least as valuable as the house itself.

Jim had only taken a few sips from his drink when he noticed the room was starting to spin a bit. His vision blurred slightly, and he felt a little nauseous as he worked to maintain his composure. Standing to his feet, he staggered back a little.

"I am not feeling too good," he apologized. "Maybe I should be going."

Harry and Autumn stood up, each of them taking an arm.

"You do look a little pale," she said.

"You really do," Harry replied echoing her concern. "Do you need to lie down or something?"

"No, I think I'll be alright. I've been working hard lately, and maybe it's starting to catch up with me. It might be better if I headed for home. We could reschedule for another time if you don't mind."

"Sure," Harry said sympathetically. "I'll have Birgit give you a call next week, and set something up. We really do need to talk."

Autumn was obviously disappointed as Jim said his goodbyes. He wobbled slightly as the maid helped him with his coat. The brisk air on his face felt good, and helped clear his head while he walked to his truck. They watched from the entry window as he drove out the driveway.

He kept telling himself to drive slowly as freezing rain started pelting his windshield. Squeezing the wheel tightly, he bit his lip slightly to increase focus, but it didn't help much. As he wound down the mountain, each corner became more of a challenge, but he refused to yield to the waves of nausea and pressure building in his head. Then he caught himself drifting off the road around a sharp corner.

"I just need to keep it steady," he said out loud. "Focus, man! Focus!"

He approached one of the sharpest corners, and barely navigated it before drifting into the oncoming lane. His eyes drooped shut only for a second when suddenly, he was confronted by blinding lights. Slamming on the brakes, he cranked the wheel to the right, slamming into a guard rail. The force sent him spinning several times before he came to a stop on top of an ice-packed snow bank.

He sat there for a moment, confused, and unable to focus. Then the left side of his face and the interior of his truck lit up brightly. Looking out the side window, he shielded his eyes with his arm, trying to figure out what was happening. In a second, he was slammed so violently, the side air bag deployed. It pushed him hard against the seatbelt, which cut into his waist as it trapped him against the gearshift.

Suddenly, the sound of a revving diesel motor penetrated the cold dark night. He felt his truck lift off the ground, and even with his head swimming, he knew he was moving. The back-up alarm sounded from whatever equipment had him. Suddenly, the truck lurched forward. Even in his drugged state, he knew he was hanging over one of the highest mountain drop-offs, in the clutches of some mechanical monster. His only hope was to get out. He clawed frantically for the seat belt release button, but couldn't find it. Jim figured he would kick out the front windshield, and jump to safety before he and his truck were dropped, but quickly realized that was not going to happen as his truck shuddered.

Adrenaline pumped into his bloodstream, allowing him to overcome the nausea and confusion. His rig slowly tipped forward, sliding ever closer to destruction, when suddenly, it stopped. Jim ripped at his seat belt, but it still wouldn't give. He punched the air bag to no avail. Then he remembered the emergency tool he kept in the glove box. Retrieving it, he stabbed the airbag, cut his seat belt, and broke the window in a matter of seconds. The diesel motor was revving again as the hot air from the motor blew through the broken side window into his face. The backup alarm began to beep as he lurched backwards, away from the cliff. In a few moments, he was back on the road, and the machine was backing away.

A shadowy figure appeared in front of the lights as he kicked open the door, and climbed out.

"Jim, Jim, are you ok!" the voice from the darkness shouted.

He might have been foggy and confused, but there was no mistaking his cousin's voice.

"Parks? Is that you?" Jim said bleakly, as his knees buckled slightly. "What are you doing?"

"Just saving you again, as usual," he replied, grabbing Jim's arm before he fell down. "Seems like this is getting to be a regular job for me," Parks continued, as he helped him to the truck bumper. "Maybe you should consider hiring me full-time."

"What?" Jim said as he grabbed his head, and slumped forward.

"If I were to venture a guess," Parks replied, squatting next to him, "you were the subject of a hit, as it were. Not to mention, you have either been drinking heavily, or somebody gave you something. I think your new investigative career may need to be reconsidered in the light of recent events, unless you're working on a death wish."

Jim put his hand on Parks' shoulder and stood to his feet, shaking his head to clear his mind.

"Are you going to be able to drive?" Parks asked, surveying the damage to his vehicle, and assessing Jim's condition.

"I think so," he replied, taking a few steps forward. "That bastard Harry must have put something in my drink. Fortunately, I only took a couple of sips. I hate to think what I would be like if I had drunk the whole thing."

Jim literally fell into the front seat as Parks let go of his arm.

"My truck was built to take punishment, and most of the damage is to the side," Jim said as he turned the key.

It revved without hesitation.

"What a mess," he lamented as he looked over what was left of the once-beautiful interior. "Why did you hit me with that machine you were driving?"

"I didn't run into you!" Parks responded sharply, pushing the bent door shut. "The guy you want to talk to is taking a little nap in the cab right now. Look, let's get out of here. I parked down the road next to the equipment yard. I'll drop this thing there, and follow you. There's an all-night coffee shop along the River Road, and you look like you could use some good coffee."

Parks followed as they made their way down the mountain, and across the bridge to the coffee house. Jim's mind was finally clearing as the effects of the drug wore off. Thoughts raced through his mind, but nothing was adding up.

His meeting tonight had been pretty weird, but there had been no indication Harry was out to get him, or would try and drug him. He seemed eager to meet again, and tonight was obviously more about his wife. Maybe Parks was right, he thought as they approached the coffee shop. He needed to be more careful how he investigated. Harry's involvement changed everything.

They pulled into the parking lot, and got out. Jim's legs felt like rubber as they entered the brightly-lit shop. Parks went to the counter and placed their order while Jim took a booth overlooking the parking lot. Since they were the only inside customers, there was no concern about being interrupted or overheard. Truckers and night shift workers made up the bulk of the coffee business in this part of town. They liked their coffee fast, and mostly through the drive up window.

Parks delivered two coffees as he slid in across from Jim.

"I don't know how you like yours, but I like mine black," he said.

"Black is fine," Jim replied, sipping from the steaming cup. "Why are you up here, and what's going on?"

"You're treading in some deep water. These are some dangerous people you're dealing with."

"Yeah, I get it," he responded, his head still throbbing from the night's events. "Frankly, I never expected this."

"It's a nasty situation, I agree. But lucky for you, Birgit likes me as much as she likes you. I was at the club last night having dinner like I do on Fridays, when she came in. She sometimes hangs at the club. Anyway, she saw me and came over. We talked a bit, and she told me you had come up to the office to visit Harry, and were going to his house tonight for dinner. I immediately thought something was wrong, because I know Harry hates entertaining. All the top brass are very private and secretive, and Harry's no different. As Birgit was going on about meeting you, and how exciting it was, I became suspicious. Why did you think you could go to Harry with your information anyway?"

"You said he was his own man. I thought I could trust him."

"You totally missed it. I never said you could trust him. He came from outside. He's Management!" Parks took a sip of coffee, and a deep breath.

"Fortunately, I know where Harry lives, so I parked several miles up the mountain in one of the side roads overlooking the main road, and waited. I saw him go by around five, and then at about six thirty, you passed. I decided to wait a little longer, and sure enough, about an hour later, here comes General Olliver.

"It was just starting to get dark, and he didn't spot me, so I dropped in behind with my lights off. I followed him up the hill until I saw him pull into the equipment yard. He never looked around to see if anyone was watching. Probably wouldn't expect anyone that time of night. Then I heard him warming up one of the snow plows, and moving it around. He was making a lot of noise, so I walked up the road to get a better view of what was going on."

Parks looked around, and leaned over the table.

"I moved around the buildings," he continued, lowering his voice, "keeping low and out of sight. Suddenly, he roared around the building, driving one of the trucks with an attachment on the front I'd never seen before. It looked like a modified forklift or something. I ducked behind some bushes as he passed, and then ran after him on foot. After about a mile or so, he stopped and turned out the lights, just sitting there idling. I waited behind the truck and out of sight until you came around that sharp bend."

"I sort of remember that part," Jim said slowly.

"I didn't know how I was going to save you after he had you up in the air. But right as he was about to dump you into the canyon, he rolled down his window to make sure he wasn't too close to the edge himself. As soon as he opened the window, I jumped on the running board, reached in, and pulled the emergency brake. He caught me with an elbow to the jaw," Parks continued, rubbing his chin.

Jim slammed his fist on the table.

"Olliver was your boss! What's going on here, Parks?"

"Keep your voice down," Parks warned, looking hard into Jim's eyes. "This is not the time. Anyway, he knocked me back, and nearly off the side board. He's a big, powerful man, you know. But then I caught him square in the temple, and he crumpled over. I pushed him to the other side of the cab.

"I was surprised he didn't try to hit me with his other hand, but then I noticed his right hand was blue. The book calls it crystal sickness. He must have used one of the crystal blades at some point to hurt someone. The warnings are real, and you have to be careful not to use them wrongly."

"How could that be? You're the only one who has those."

"Not exactly. He confiscated one several years ago when I was showing the cadets how it worked. He hated how I did things with them. But he must have used it on somebody. That's the only way I know of to get crystal poisoning."

Parks looked out the window, remembering what Dr. Larson had said about Kevin Knobbs. How he was stabbed, but showed no evidence of external injuries. It seemed that General Olliver must have used the blade to kill Kevin.

"But that's not important now," Parks continued. "What's important is I kept you from the bottom of that canyon."

"That's a fact!" Jim replied.

"I hope you realize this is only the beginning," Parks warned as he took his final sip of coffee. "You have started something, and you're making important people nervous; so nervous, the head of the Citadel wants you dead. If Harry is involved, you know it's big. I hope you have the stomach for this, because it's only going to get worse."

"We're going to need more help," Jim replied. "And come up with a plan to get the word out."

"I'll see what I can find out," Parks replied, getting up from the booth. "But you're going to need to figure some things out on your own. Just don't plan any more dinner dates without asking me first."

Jim left a good tip on the table, and followed Parks to their rigs. The brisk, early-morning air felt good on his face.

"Keep in touch," Parks said as Jim caught up, "and keep your head on a swivel."

Suddenly, Jim grabbed Parks' arm just as they were about to separate, and gave him a solid hug.

"Thanks again, cousin," he said with genuine appreciation.

Parks felt a wave of satisfaction as he returned the hug. Jim may have grown up easy, with things handed to him while Parks had to work for everything he got, but when it really mattered, it was Parks, his country cousin, who saved the day, and his life. Jim's appreciation was a good feeling.

They were about to part ways when Jim froze.

"Iris!" he nearly shouted. "It was Iris in the garden."

"What are you talking about?" Parks replied, pausing for a moment.

"The painting at Harry's house," he exclaimed. "The child in the Garden of Irises, "it wasn't about a garden full of flowers. It was about Iris, the pretty gal we met at the Island. The one the colonel said lost her parents in a traffic accident. It had to be their house Harry bought. He may be behind more than we think, including murdering women and children."

"That makes a lot of sense, but you had best keep that information to yourself. We can't accuse Harry of murder, and it would probably be impossible to prove anyway. He's done a good job of covering his tracks."

Jim nodded reluctantly. Even though he was plenty mad, he knew Parks was right. Getting Harry would be important, but he needed to do more than that. He needed to bring down the whole system. His next move would involve HOT News, and getting the word out to the people. Then maybe they would have a chance to set things right.

The two men roared off into the night.

CHAPTER 25

Harry kissed Autumn, and headed for his morning meeting with his subordinates. He was looking forward to giving a butt-chewing session like they had never had before. Information had to stay in-house at all times. Letting people outside the Citadel know anything was not to be tolerated.

Harry loved the drive off the mountain. It gave him a sense of power - descending from above to those below. He knew the roads would be slick this morning, but the danger thrilled him. Also, he was still tingling with excitement as he remembered the move he had engineered the night before.

Turning the stereo up in his custom red convertible sports car, he slowed nearly to a stop on the final sharp curve to see if he could spot Jim's rig below. Unfortunately, the low-lying clouds and mist hid the valley floor. He had wanted the first look, but resigned himself to waiting for it on the morning news.

"Won't that be great," he laughed, "when HOT News is the first crew on-site."

He roared towards the gate. The guard hustled to open it and salute as he drove past, not even slowing down. Pulling into his marked spot, he headed for the elevators. A few lower employees shared the ride up. They all said their respectful greetings, and Harry nodded his approval, but mostly ignored their presence by staring at the doors, and tapping his briefcase impatiently. Normally, he would take his private elevator, but today he had to share the public one. His was undergoing maintenance and repairs. After several stops along the way, the elevator doors finally opened on the top floor, and Harry stepped out, relieved to get away.

Birgit was putting the coffee on as he breezed past, and headed for his office.

"Good morning," she said cheerfully.

"Good morning." he responded lightly.

"How was your dinner with Jim last night?" she asked before he could disappear through the office doors.

"Oh, it was really nice," Harry said, holding one of the doors half open. "Autumn had a great time."

"It must be so exciting to have a celebrity over for dinner," she said giddily as he closed the door, and hustled down the hall for his office.

Birgit liked her job, even if Harry was not the greatest boss. He was more demanding than personable, but she didn't care. She had learned a long time ago people cared most about themselves, and what they could get from you. Harry was no different. So she did her job with excellence, and never allowed her feelings to show.

Harry's office door was equipped with a combination lock entry system which he reset every week. Being head of the most important department in Management's system, he felt the need to set an example for the rest of his managers. Entering, he headed straight for his desk to prepare for the day's meeting.

Sunlight poured in through his windows, and he forgot to turn on the lights. Organizing his paperwork while the computer system booted up, he suddenly felt uncomfortable. The hair on his neck bristled as he glanced around the room. His office was the most secure in a complex surrounded by walls, gates, guards, and military personnel, so where was this feeling coming from? Scanning the room, his eyes fixated on the shadowy area at the far end. Straining for a few moments, he finally shook his head, returning to the work at hand.

"Just my imagination playing tricks on me," he thought as his computer screen lit up.

He typed the meeting itinerary, and focused his thoughts.

"Simple," Harry thought to himself, "I'll let my managers know the consequences of leaking information. I'm sure most of their seats will be wet by the time I am finished."

The uneasy feeling returned.

Glancing up, he thought he saw something move in the shadows.

"Harry," came a deep voice.

He jumped to his feet, shoving his chair into the wall as Parks' tall, broad figure stepped into the streaming sunlight.

"What the...Parks! Is that you? Are you crazy, startling me like that? How did you get in here, anyway?"

He stood glaring angrily as Parks approached, and stopped in front of his desk.

His anger shifted from hot to cold, and his stomach tightened as the Order's most powerful leader put both fists on his desk, leaned forward, and looked hard into his eyes.

"It's not how I got in here you should be worried about," Parks said evenly, "but how you're going to get out!"

Harry slid down into his seat, and leaned as far away from Parks as possible.

"Are you threatening your superior?"

"Threatening!?" Parks replied, drilling his stare into Harry. "I don't threaten."

"Speak, then, and this had better be good, because you're way out of line, and I don't have time to deal with you right now."

Harry's mind raced. He'd never seen Parks like this. He had watched him work before, subduing criminals in the city, and knew what he could do if he wanted to. But Parks was always cool and collected, even in the middle of a fight.

Here was an angry version of him, with only a desk between them, and Harry was becoming more concerned by the second. His best bet would be to reach the firearm in the bottom drawer of his desk, but he had to get to it, and it was locked. With Parks so close, that could be a problem.

"We have an issue to discuss, Mr. Allison," Parks said.

"We do?" Harry asked. Beads of sweat formed on his forehead as he slid his left hand into his coat pocket, feeling for the desk keys. "What kind of issue?"

"The issue is you," Parks responded, his voice becoming deeper, and sounding more like a growl than anything. "I have watched you for years as you have taken whatever you wanted, but this time you've gone too far. Last night, you tried to send my cousin off a cliff. He came to you about a conspiracy, and he'd be dead now if it wasn't for me."

"It's not me, Parks," Harry pled.

Parks' eyes changed from green to a dark red, and pierced into Harry's being. Harry tried to break free from his stare, but couldn't. He was frozen with fear.

"I don't even know your family," Harry meekly asserted as he slowly leaned forward, positioning his hand next to the drawer.

Suddenly, Parks grabbed Harry's wrist, lifting him off his seat. He slowly increased the pressure until the key dropped onto the desk, and bounced to the floor.

"This is your one and only warning," Parks growled, as he pulled Harry's face close, his feet dangling in midair. "Anything happens to my family, and I'll be back."

Parks threw him to the floor with a thud. As Harry rolled to his side, he spotted the key within reach, and grabbed it. Scrambling behind his desk, he grabbed his revolver, and brought it to bear on Parks.

But Parks was nowhere to be seen.

Harry opened his office door cautiously, checking both directions, and could hear Birgit talking to someone in the outer office. Creeping quietly down the hall, he hoped to surprise Parks. Shoving the door open, Harry burst into the office, waving the revolver wildly about.

Sharon, one of the other office managers, screamed, and Birgit dropped the coffee pot she was holding. It shattered on the tile floor, splashing hot coffee on them both. They screamed again.

"Where is he? Where is he?" Harry shouted as he rushed past, heading down the hall towards the outer offices.

The doors were all locked as Harry tried each handle. Satisfied the rooms were secure, he headed back to find Sharon wiping the coffee off her legs, and Birgit mopping up the floor.

"Where is he?" Harry demanded, still brandishing his revolver.

"Where is who?" Birgit answered, somewhat angry and confused as she wrung coffee into the sink.

"Parks! Who else?!" Harry snapped, his eyes darting around the room.

"Parks, we haven't seen Parks. What are you talking about?" she exclaimed as Sharon echoed her sentiments. "We were here making coffee for your meeting this morning. Why would Parks be here? I didn't see his name on the list."

Harry lowered his revolver, realizing Parks had escaped. But how? He cautiously moved down the hall, returning his revolver to waist level as he continued past the office to his private elevator. Warning tape covered the elevator doors. Harry ripped off the tape, and tried to pull the doors open. They resisted for a moment, and then opened several inches. Putting his foot into the opening, he forced them the rest of the way.

The elevator was at the bottom as he leaned over, looking down the shaft. Staring into the darkness, Harry strained to see or hear something, but there was nothing.

"You think you can threaten me?" he said to himself as he locked himself in his office. "We'll just see about that."

Harry sat down, and picked up the phone.

CHAPTER 26

Harry's bedside phone was ringing as he rolled over, squinting to see the time.

"5:45 AM? What idiot is calling this early?" he said, fumbling for the answer button.

"Yes?" he mumbled into the receiver.

"Morning, Harry," said the gruff voice on the other end.

"Bert? Is that you?" Harry said, sitting up. "What do you want this early in the morning?"

Bert was the Manager of the city's three EDDs, and came into power with Harry during the takeover. They both had led part of the advancing force, and were rewarded with prominent positions once the city had surrendered.

"I guess you haven't been watching the morning news," Bert squeaked.

"No, I haven't," Harry whispered, leaning forward, and covering the mouth piece so as not to wake Autumn. "I was sleeping, like most reasonable people. My first meeting isn't until 9:30."

"Who is it, Harry?" Autumn asked, rolling halfway over, and peeking out from under her sleep mask.

"Hold on, Bert," he said, dropping his feet into his slippers as he got out of bed. "Go back to sleep, dear, I'll be back in a minute."

Autumn flipped her mask down, and turned over.

Harry quietly shut the bedroom door behind him as he headed down the hall to the kitchen. Flipping the lights on, he pushed the door open.

"What's this all about anyway?" he said sternly, squinting as his eyes adjusted to the bright lights.

"It's about that "problem" you said you were going to handle for me," Bert said, his voice rising again. "The problem is on TV right now."

"What channel?" he asked sharply, grabbing the kitchen TV remote.

"HOT News," Bert shouted into the phone. "Which other channel do you think would carry this? Are you friggin' kidding me?"

"Hey, give me a minute to wake up before you start yelling, would you."

The TV flickered to life, and there was Jim, talking about some mysterious disappearances. He was showing old copies of newspapers, and comparing them to public and private records.

The differences were glaring.

"My phone started ringing five minutes after he started his broadcast," Bert said. "Dave Castle wants me to come to his office first thing this morning, but I'm not going alone. You're coming with me."

"Relax, Bert, relax," Harry said, pushing his chair back from the table. "Dave's a good guy. He'll just want to know what HOT News is up to. You know, what they have going with this."

"What HOT News has going?!" Bert said incredulously. "They're exposing our business; the business we've been working for years."

Harry watched Jim for a few more minutes while Bert ranted.

"We have some options here," Harry interrupted. "First of all, who says "Jim the Weatherman" is anything less than a kook. Second, all we need do is put some pressure on his boss. Next thing you know, Jim's out of a job. We just need to put a cork in it."

"You're not getting it, man!" Bert shouted." It's not about Jim, it's about us. Dave wants answers. I didn't find out till this morning when Dave's secretary called to instruct me to tune into Jim's report. Apparently, he kept the broadcast location a secret so no one could intervene, but it should have been obvious. He held it outside the main gate of the East EDD. The one we have been doing most of our work at. We're done, Harry, but I am not going down alone. If I go, we all go!"

"Ok, OK!" Harry replied smoothly. "But getting emotional isn't going to help matters. Give me a chance to get dressed, and meet me at my office. It shouldn't take me more than an hour to get there, and then we can go up together. He's going to want to hear from me eventually anyway; might just as well get it over with."

"Ok," Bert said, his voice relaxing a bit. "One hour. I'll be there."

Autumn was snoring slightly as he crept in, and dressed. His thoughts were dark, and he could only suppose how Dave might react. To add to his troubles, he had yet to report the death of his second in command, General Olliver.

Harry had gone up to the equipment yard after Parks left his office to check things out, and found General Olliver's body. It appeared Parks had left the truck running with the heater on, but that didn't help him. Harry blamed Parks, and was convinced he was responsible for the General's death. He had an enforcement team out looking for him.

While Harry pondered his next move, Jim finished the broadcast, and headed back to the station. He was solo on this one, using only the mobile broadcasting equipment. That way, no one else could be blamed or held responsible for any fall-out. He knew he was going out on a limb this time, but he was not a man to back down.

As he pulled into the parking lot behind the studio, he saw lights on inside. Sliding back the side door to the van, he began unloading video equipment. Just then, three of Jim's crew came rushing through the rear side doors, and started grabbing equipment.

"Thanks, guys," Jim said as he closed the van door. "Did you catch my special broadcast this morning?"

Chris, Jim's senior assistant, looked over with a big smile.

"Man, that was right on!" Chris said, throwing a bag full of cords and mikes over his shoulder. "My mom was in that place several years ago, and I tell you it was creepy. Not that you would actually see anything going on, but there was this feeling I couldn't shake. I was never so happy the day I got her out of there."

Danny and Ray, writers for his weatherman program, nodded in agreement as they carried the last of the equipment inside.

"The boss is looking for you," Danny said as they came up the steps and through the rear entrance. "He was here early this morning. I saw his car in the parking lot when I got here at five thirty. He wants you in his office ASAP."

"Thanks again," Jim said holding the door for them. "I appreciate the help. I'll head on in and see him. Hey, Danny, I'll need to see you later in the cut room when I'm done, so don't go anywhere. We have a lot to discuss."

Jim booked it down the hall towards Frank's office. He had whacked the hornet's nest pretty hard, and now it was time to see how many bees came out. Jim was bold, fearless, and sometimes reckless, but it was those traits that had once made him a great

194

reporter. Frank was well aware of his star's strong points, but they could also put him and everybody around him in danger. That was part of the reason he had agreed to let Jim become the "Weatherman."

"Jim!" Frank exclaimed, rising from his chair as he came in.

The smell of cigar hung in the air as Jim shut the door.

"That was one broadcast for the ages," Frank continued, waving him over. "Our phones have not stopped ringing. You touched off a real firestorm--set a match to things, you might say. Folks want to know what's going on in that EDD, and I have a growing log of people who want someone they knew, who also disappeared for no apparent reason, investigated."

Jim leaned over Frank's desk, pulling a cigar out of the case before sitting down. He ran it under his nose, inhaling deeply as he closed his eyes. Running it back and forth in his fingers for a moment, he then slid it into a cigar case he took from the vest pocket of his coat, and returned the case to his jacket.

"Tell you what, Boss," Jim said, leaning back and crossing his legs, "I'm going to hang onto this cigar for another day--the day we celebrate a new era for our city."

He leaned his head back, gathering his thoughts before continuing.

"The broadcast this morning could go just about anywhere. Whoever is behind this deal might be involved in a lot of other things too. Seems to me they've been doing most anything they want, and no one's been paying attention. We've exchanged common sense for money and false security. We were duped."

"It's begun already," Frank replied, lighting up a cigar, and taking a long draw.

The smoke curled out of his nose as he shot a couple of smoke rings up at the ceiling.

"We have to keep out in front of this thing. They'll be looking to quiet us down, but so far, it looks like you caught them off guard. None of their stations have issued a response yet, but I know it's coming, and probably fast. You're going to need to get out of sight for a while. I have a place you can stay until your next broadcast. In the meantime, I'll divert questions, and build interest around the follow-up broadcast at the same time. A few teasers will keep people tuned in, and spread the word in such a way they'll be reluctant to get too aggressive. Curiosity is our friend, but it can turn against us, so let's try to do this right."

"Thanks, Frank," Jim replied. "You know how to work a plan, and that's what I love about you. I'll take the unmarked van, load it with some mobile equipment, and wait for your signal. I have a few taped interviews which should prove interesting, but better that you don't know too much yet."

"That's fine, but you had best get your butt out of here fast. I'm sure I'll be having some visitors dropping by today."

The two men shook hands. Neither one could know what was coming, but they both assumed it would be bad. They had been through a lot together over the years, and built a bond of trust. Now that bond was to be tested again.

Jim quickly left the studio, double-checking to make sure he wasn't followed as he navigated the city streets. He felt a rush of excitement at the thought he might actually be doing something meaningful. It was a feeling he hadn't had since the takeover.

In the meantime, Harry impatiently waited at the elevator door, the light indicating it was still on the top floor. As he stood there formulating exactly what to say, Bert grabbed his arm.

"I'm not feeling too good." Bert said, looking flushed. He had just returned from the men's room, where he deposited his morning breakfast.

"Relax," Harry said, pulling his arm away, "Just keep your mouth shut, and let me do the talking. I have a plan. Trust me!"

Stepping into the elevator, Harry pushed the top floor button.

"The plan is simple," Harry said, glancing towards Bert's distraught face. "Dave's not going to do anything against us if we stay together. The board's likely looking for a scapegoat, but once we identify the real culprit, the pressure is off."

The elevator was nearing the top floor as Bert stared at Harry, a fearful look clouding his face.

"What culprit?" he asked bewilderedly.

"Parks, who else?" Harry said smugly as the elevator glided to a stop.

CHAPTER 27

Harry exited the elevator into a luxurious reception area of Management Central Control, with Bert tight on his heels. It was intended to impress and intimidate. A monument built to affirm power and status. Polished marble floors, crystal chandeliers, rare paintings, and ancient statues overwhelmed the senses. Both men had been there before, but the feeling of awe quickly returned. The enormity of excess easily separated the haves from the have-nots.

Harry strolled confidently towards a shiny, ornate desk manned by an attractive young woman while Bert distracted himself on an oil painting of a half-clad woman.

"We're here to see the President," he said assertively, leaning forward on his elbows, "and, we're expected."

The young woman looked up over the computer screen at the two men with a plastic smile outlined with dark lipstick.

"Your names are?" she asked politely, sitting back to get a better look.

"Sorry," Harry said, returning the smile, "Bert Parsons and Harry Allison."

Running her manicured black nail down the guest book, she checked appointments for the day.

"You don't seem to be on the list," she said, closing the book. "Maybe you have the wrong day?"

"We have the right day," Harry said insistently, still smiling. "We were called in this morning by Mr. Castle. He's waiting for us."

She reached over, hitting a button on her phone.

"Mr. President," she said quietly. "There are two men here who say they have a meeting with you, sir; a Mr. Parsons and a Mr. Allison. Yes, I will let them know."

"You're expected," she said, returning the phone to the receiver. "You may take a seat in the waiting area next to the conference hall."

She pulled out a floor map, and circled their destination with a red pen.

"Just follow the hall to the right," she continued, pointing across the cavernous room toward two large carved marble columns. "It is just past the statue; you can't miss it."

"We know the way," Harry replied, still smiling.

"Thank you for your help!" Bert gushed, pushing past Harry. "You've been a big help!"

"Come on," Harry said, heading across the hall. "We don't want to keep Dave waiting."

"Parks? Whatever in the world is going on in that mind of yours, Harry?" Bert asked quietly as he caught up. "Parks can't be connected to this. He's head of your BOJ Order, and one of the most popular, respected personalities in this city."

"Exactly," Harry said under his breath behind a fiendish grin, "Who else would have the influence to make something like this happen? Who's to say Parks and his trainees aren't behind every problem we have in this city? They don't behave like normal officers, do they? They claim to be above reproach, never taking a bribe, or taking advantage of a citizen. What if it is just an elaborate cover for their real agenda?"

"Who's going to buy that?" Bert replied, rolling his eyes as they passed through two marble columns. "I think you're losing it, man."

"I don't think so!" he snapped, shooting a glaring look at Bert. "I have it on good authority the intervention team sent to arrest him on suspicion of the murder of General Olliver found evidence of jewels, gold, and money linked to three of those mysterious disappearances HOT News featured this morning."

"General Olliver's dead? Parks killed him?"

"Yes. It's not about us; it's about Parks. Always remember that."

Bert looked dismayed and confused, but Harry returned to his normally placid expression forged from a lifetime of manipulation and control. He had learned early on if you put up enough smoke, people would have a hard time finding the flames. The rest of the long walk went by in silence. As they approached the two massive ornate doors, one opened from the inside, and a very large man, Dave's personal assistant, stepped out to greet them.

"Good morning, Mr. Parsons and Mr. Allison." The man said. "You may come in now. Mr. Castle is ready for you."

They walked briskly past the massive fellow, and Bert looked up with a weak smile.

Dave's office took up a quarter of the entire upper floor; its vastness emphasized the importance of his position. Bert was acutely aware of the large man shadowing them as they approached his gold-plated desk. The back of a large leather chair greeted them, and they could faintly hear a muted conversation coming from the other side. They strained to make something out as they stood waiting.

After a few moments, the chair spun around, and a sharply-dressed man came into view.

Bert tried to appear calm, while Harry shoved his hands deep into his pockets.

Dave gestured with his free hand for them to sit down, and spun his chair back towards the large window that looked out over the city. Both men tried to hear if anything being said might be about them, but Dave's voice was too soft to distinguish words.

Finally, Dave came back around, and returned the phone to its hook.

"Good morning, gentlemen," he said smoothly, "How nice of you to make this meeting. I hope your drive over was pleasant."

"Good morning, Sir," they replied, nearly in unison.

Dave rocked back, clasping his hands under his chin while he looked at the two men.

"So, that was quite a news program this morning, don't you think? I trust you both were able to catch it."

They nodded their heads.

"Well, what do you make of it?" Dave continued, seeming somewhat disinterested as he leaned his head back.

Harry scooted forward in his seat, folding his hands, and placing them on Dave's desk.

"I've been all over this since it broke this morning, and I believe I have the answer. Even though it took us by surprise, it also confirmed our suspicions. May I explain?"

"Please, by all means continue," Dave replied, closing his eyes, and snuggling into his chair as if he were about to be told a bedtime story.

"Ok," Harry said, taking a deep breath. "It seems the leader of the famed BOJ Order has become subversive and destructive. Our fair citizens have been taken advantage of, and now, even killed. I was just informed before coming here this morning that Parks is responsible for the death of my second in command, General Olliver."

Harry lowered his gaze, and clenched his fist, moving it up and down in a stabbing motion for effect.

Dave opened his eyes, and sat upright in his chair with a puzzled look.

"Ollie's dead? What happened?"

"It seems Parks ambushed him just outside of town." Harry continued, looking serious and angry. "I don't have all the details yet, but it appears he tricked the general into meeting him alone at one of the equipment sheds just outside of town. General Olliver was killed by a blow to the head. My crews said they found his frozen body when they went up to do some equipment maintenance yesterday."

"This is serious!" Dave responded, sinking into his chair. "But how do you know it was Parks who killed him? General Olliver had plenty of enemies."

An awkward silence ensued for a moment as Harry quickly formulated an answer.

"It had to be Parks. We found one of his special weapons near the General's body. He must have dropped it during the fight."

"But why would he do such a thing? What's his motive?"

"Well," Harry said, rising to his feet with his fists clenched tightly. "It appears Parks had all of us fooled. I have always had the highest respect for him, but I learned of late there was tension between him and the General. He didn't like some changes Olliver was making, but I never thought he would resort to violence. Maybe he suspected the General was onto his EDD scheme."

Dave raised his eyebrows somewhat, and pursed his lips.

"What about you?" He asked, shifting his gaze to Bert who was sitting there quietly, trying not to be noticed. "Do you have anything to add to this?"

"Well, not really sir, I just learned about it." Bert said calmly, clenching his hands tightly so they wouldn't noticeably tremble. "I had no idea people were disappearing. My nursing staff hasn't mentioned any irregularities in their reports. Someone on the inside must be working with Parks. I intend to examine my staff thoroughly, and get to the bottom of this."

Dave rocked back, glancing between the two men, while chewing on the end of his pen.

"Curious. The heads of both the Citadel and the Economic Retraining Department are expecting me to believe they have no knowledge of these events that have now become public. Not to mention one of our department heads is dead, and we have to tell people he was killed by one of his own staff, who just happens to be one of the most beloved people in the city to boot. Don't think you can fool me into believing you two were just innocently standing by while things were going down. Do either of you have a clue how that makes you look, let alone how it reflects on me? This is a mess, and I hold you both responsible."

"We'll get this fixed right now, sir," Harry responded, seizing the opportunity. "You don't need to worry. It will be taken care of."

Dave leaned forward, and put his hands flat on the desk.

"The Board is meeting tonight, and I can't say it will come out well for either of you. We have all profited since taking this city, and avoided unnecessary "punishment" for those who oppose us. We even let that puny station "HOT News" stay on the air. But with your little deal coming out into the open, we may have to shut it down for good."

Dave reached into his desk, and pulled out a piece of paper. Writing for a moment, he folded it, put it in an envelope, and handed it to Harry.

"The instructions on that sheet of paper will put an end to what has been allowed here." Dave said with a stern voice. "Harry will carry them out to the letter, and then wait for instructions. Bert, your involvement is less strategic, but no less important. I will contact you when the time comes. Now get out of my office!"

They both eagerly jumped out of their chairs to leave.

Without thinking, Bert extended his hand towards Dave in hopes of a handshake, but Dave just spun his chair towards the window without saying another word as the large man grabbed his arm, and pulled him towards the exit.

The door slammed with a thud behind them as they exited into the hall.

"That went well," Harry said, hustling for the exit.

"Do you really think so?" Bert asked, working to keep up. "I don't think Dave likes me."

"Oh, don't take him wrong. He treats everyone that way--doesn't mean a thing."

Harry picked up the pace a little more. There was much work to be done.

CHAPTER 28

Bert was distracted as Harry opened the envelope, and read the note Dave gave him. As they approached the elevators, he slid it back into his pocket.

"Things are going to work out just fine," Harry said to Bert as he pushed the call button. "Dave is king when it comes to working these types of situations. I think he already has a plan. Hey, I have to get back to my office to coordinate the pursuit of Parks, but before I go, I need to get something out of the Citadel. Can you come with me for a minute? There's something I want you to see."

The elevator arrived with a ding.

"I need to get back too," Bert said as they got on the elevator. "Dave's counting on me, and I'm sure some of my staff watched the broadcast this morning. I need to get a lid on this right away."

"It'll only take a moment. You really need to see this."

"You'll have to make it quick," Bert said reluctantly.

Harry nodded in affirmation as the elevator doors opened on the bottom floor, and he led the way across the yard towards the back entrance to the cadet training rooms. The area was deserted this time of the morning while the cadets and trainers worked their morning routine on the other side of the Citadel.

They chatted along the way, discussing possible scenarios and outcomes. Bert was noticeably nervous, but Harry continued to comfort him, insisting things were better than they looked. Arriving at the lower entrance to the training rooms, they entered through two double doors, and headed down the empty hall. Harry walked quickly, with Bert tight on his heels, and in a few moments, they arrived at a door sporting a restricted access sign. Harry unlocked and opened the door as Bert followed him in, and hit the lights. On the opposing wall was a long row of lockers with combination locks.

Harry opened locker 66.

Bert was beginning to get curious. He had never been in this section of the Citadel before.

"What is it? What are you after?"

Harry retrieved a long, slender, ornate box and set it on a nearby table. Turning his back slightly just enough to hide the contents, he opened the box. Then he turned back towards Bert with a long, curved crystal blade in his hand, which he drove deep into Bert's chest. Bert's eyes widened, and his mouth opened in shock as he stared into Harry's face. He stumbled back and looked down, the handle pinning his tie to his chest in the center of his button-down vest. Bert slumped against the wall and slid to the floor, his eyes still staring straight at Harry.

Harry pulled the blade out of Bert's chest, but there was no blood on his suit. He pushed Bert's tie aside, and unbuttoned his shirt to confirm there was no mark on the skin either. Harry was morbidly thorough as he re-buttoned Bert's shirt, and repositioned his tie. He quickly returned the blade to the box, and put it back in the locker. He checked the hall before dragging him out.

Harry locked the door, and called for emergency services on his mobile phone.

They arrived within minutes, doing everything they could to revive Bert, but to no avail. There was no question he died from some internal hemorrhaging, probably a heart attack.

"Take him directly to the morgue," Harry instructed the paramedics. "I'll write a report to the coroner explaining what happened since I was the first responder."

"Ok, sir, will do," the senior responder replied.

The walk back to his office was satisfying as he contemplated his next move.

"This is working out fine. I now control the spin on this event, and should be able to muscle it through without any interference. The blade belongs to Parks. Everybody's seen him use it in exhibitions where he sets up a blind target behind a thick metal plate, and throws this knife at the plate. Somehow, the blade breaks the target behind the steel without leaving a mark on the metal. It'll be no problem to pin this on him once the autopsy is complete, and I'll make sure Dr. Larson is keenly aware of my concerns."

Once off his private elevator, he arrived at the main office to inform his staff of Bert's tragic demise.

The shock was obvious. Bert had been around a long time, and was a likable character. He had tried to date Birgit once or twice, but she knew better when it came to that old fox. Still, he would be missed.

"Bert would want us to carry on," Harry said. "We will always remember him as our friend, but also as a great administrator. He would want it that way."

"If you could just give the family a call," he said to Birgit, who was sniffling. "That would be a big help. The rest of you may have the day off."

Harry turned, and headed for his office.

"That goes for you as well," he said, glancing back at Birgit just before the door shut.

Settling in behind his desk, he took the envelope Dave gave him from his coat pocket, and re-read the note before securing it.

"Bert is no longer useful. You know what to do."

He slid the letter into the drawer, and locked it. There was a lot to do if he was going to get a handle on this reporting business.

Suddenly, a sharp pain shot up his right arm. He pulled his arm tight to his chest, massaging it vigorously. His hand appeared white, like all the blood had drained out, and it was cool to the touch. He shook it a few times, and the pain in his chest lessened slowly.

He called Birgit on the intercom, hoping she hadn't left yet.

"Birgit, get me a doctor's appointment right away!" he said.

"Sure," she replied. "I'll call right now. Are you ok? I'll be right down."

"Don't bother; I'm fine," he answered, "just the shock of losing Bert."

Harry needed to stay on schedule. There was no way with the rapidly changing situation he could afford any disruption. Dave was counting on him. The pain emanating from his hand to his shoulder and radiating into his chest could be a problem, but first on his list was getting Parks. He knew he could stick General Olliver's death on Parks and, maybe Bert's death too. It was a believable story, blaming him for everything, including the disappearing residents at the EDD. If all went as planned, Jim would get discredited too, now that he knew they were related. All he needed to do is show how they operated as a team, with Parks helping Jim from the inside. What more evidence would he need? It was a family business. He just needed to produce some documents showing that Parks was under investigation for suspicion of embezzlement and other crimes that would link him to the disappearances.

Not a problem for the head of the Citadel.

"After all," he mused out loud, half laughing, "who else has his level of influence as the leader of the BOJ? Nobody really understands what he does anyway. If I paint it as a cover for his real motives--stealing money, property, and murder--people will turn on him in a second. This is going to be easier than I thought."

He sank deep into in his chair with a sense of satisfaction as he pondered the possibilities.

"Frank is taking some liberties though," he thought as he massaged his arm, "thinking he can actually operate that station independently. He's making some serious assumptions. Maybe I should throw him in the pot with Parks and that blasted "Jim the Weatherman." I'll get rid of the lot of them, and then we'll see this city change. No more dealings with those who resist. Just simple math. Subtract resistors, add more for me, equals a really good time."

His smile changed to maniacal laughter as he threw his head back. Things were shaping up better than he could have imagined.

Just then, Birgit rang in.

"I have the doctor's office on the line. Can you make eleven?"

"Eleven will work fine."

"Ok, I'll let them know."

"Ten," Harry confirmed checking his watch," just enough time to make a few quick stops and set this ball rolling."

He packed his briefcase, and headed for his private elevator. It was finally working again, and he wouldn't have to ride down with his staff anymore.

Lucy was a good candidate for Bert's job, he mused. She was eager, willing, and she knew the system. He would stop by before seeing the doctor.

Harry knew the word was traveling fast, but he still needed to get out and talk to his department heads. He would recommend her to Dave, even though she didn't come with them when they took the city. She was a native, but he admired her ruthless attitude. She was sharp and cruel, willing to dump people into the wilderness with no remorse. He fondly thought of her as a female version of General Olliver.

A perfect day, he thought as he pulled through the gates of the East EDD. Nothing but blue skies ahead. But the pain in his arm intensified.

CHAPTER 29

Dave leaned back with his hands behind his head, thinking of his conversation with Harry and Bert. He had a board meeting tonight, and needed to be ready with some answers. Harry had called to let him know he had taken care of things. It was a step forward, but more needed to be done, and he would need some solutions in hand. The board wouldn't be in a mood for excuses.

"Hello," Dave said picking up his phone.

"Hi, Honey," his wife Doris said cheerfully. "Are you coming home tonight before your meeting?"

"I hadn't planned on it." Dave replied. "I have a lot of preparation to do."

"There's something really important I need to talk with you about," she said insistently. "Can you please come home first?"

"Well, if it can't wait."

"I'll have dinner waiting when you get here," she said, sounding relieved as she hung up.

He left had the house early that morning before she was up, so they hadn't had a chance to talk as they normally did, but he wondered what could be so important. She wasn't usually so insistent. He went back to his preparation, putting a plan together to present to the Board.

This whole business was starting to bother him. He didn't like having to answer for the dealings of his team, but it went with the job. Tonight, he would have to be at his best. No telling how things might go. He finished up at the office, and left for home in his chauffeured limousine. His personal assistant served in various capacities, including driver and bodyguard. Dave wasn't afraid; just cautious.

Doris was waiting anxiously as he came into their palatial home. She had dinner ready, as promised, but gave no indication of what was on her mind. After dinner, they settled in with a cocktail, and she finally opened up.

"Do you have to go to your meeting tonight?" Doris asked as she fixed him another drink.

"Yes. There are some important issues we need to deal with."

She snuggled in close to Dave, and began crying.

"What's wrong, Doris?" he asked as he slid his arm around her shoulders.

"You're going to think I'm crazy," she answered, smudging her eye shadow as she wiped her tears with a napkin. "I had a horrible dream last night, and I can't get it out of my mind, it was so vivid. I never remember my dreams, but this one was so real."

"It was only a dream, dear. It can't hurt you. Why don't you tell me about it?"

"There was a group of men who were planning to destroy our lives, destroy our city. They surrounded you as a dark cloud appeared, and then the darkness covered you. I searched for you, but couldn't find you. When I woke up, you were gone, and I was alone, all alone. Are we in some kind of danger? I saw the broadcast on HOT News. Is there something going on you're not telling me?"

"There's no problem. The Board is aware of the broadcast, and we're going to discuss it tonight, but it has nothing to do with me, and it won't hurt us."

"It really scared me, though," Doris said. "It felt so evil."

"Just a dream," he reassured her, as he pulled her tight to his chest, "no need to worry."

She managed a weak smile as they finished their drinks before Dave got up to get ready for the meeting.

He arrived early as usual. It bothered him that they always met so late at night, always at midnight. He put his papers in order, and gathered his thoughts before heading for the board room. Dave entered the modest room, outfitted with a large wooden table surrounded by seven plush chairs. There was so much opulence in this place, and yet the board room was oddly mundane. It sat at the end of a long hall, guarded by a solid oak door. A little brass plaque sat to one side, identifying it. Not much for the most powerful group in the city.

Inside, a row of small chandeliers ran down the center, providing adequate lighting. The outside walls were windowless, with another door standing at the far end of the room. That was the board's entrance. It allowed them to enter and leave without having to speak with anyone.

Six average-looking older men in dark suits were gathered around the far end of the table, discussing among themselves as Dave set his briefcase on the table and sat down.

"Mr. President," one of the men said when they had finished their conversation. "Thank you for coming. We're glad you could make it tonight."

Dave was appointed to the presidency shortly after the city fell, but he still didn't know these men's names. They were known only by the numbers set in brass name plates positioned in front of each of them. Somehow, they reminded him of old friends or next door neighbors, and he never questioned why the most powerful men in the city were as average as they come.

"Good to see you all as well," he replied, moving right to the subject at hand. "I understand you were alerted regarding a certain broadcast yesterday. It's being dealt with as I speak. We are taking steps to ensure this is stopped. It's totally under control. I have my report right here."

He set a stack of papers on the table for the board members to review.

"This meeting is not about your report," Number six interrupted. "We know all about the broadcast, and have been tracking the situation. But there are other problems brewing you don't have a handle on, and that's what this meeting's for. Tonight, we need to talk about you. We need to know what you remember."

"What I remember?" Dave asked, looking up from his notes, and sitting back. "I'm sorry, sir, I don't understand. I thought you would want to hear my strategy, and take a look at my plan…"

This was not what Dave was expecting. He was ready to unveil a carefully designed plan to stop resistance in the city, but they didn't seem at all interested, and he was beginning to get more than a little nervous.

"Do you remember anything before we came here?" Number Five asked. "Before we took the city, I mean."

"Of course," he answered quickly, not sure where this was going. "I was leading the advancement as we came over the mountain. It was my charge that first bridged the wall. We were driven back, but then they surrendered."

"What about before that?" Number One asked.

Dave sat there for a moment, dumbfounded.

"Before that," he answered, his mind searching for information, "Before that?"

Before that, he had no memories.

"That's what we thought," Number One said, leaning forward. "You still don't remember anything. But that's good. We wanted it that way. You needed to fit in here, and we couldn't have you troubled by your past. But it's time for you to remember, time to bring you back, so you can get working again. We chose you because you're clever and cunning, but you need to know what is expected. Follow us for a moment, please."

The six men rose from the table, and opened the rear door. They filed through one by one as Dave dropped in behind, confused at best. He was surprised to find another long, windowless room. He knew this building, and had walked the grounds many times, but there was only a stairway out back. Where did this room come from? The room was dark as the door closed behind him. The only light came from a dimly-glowing object set on a table in the middle. There were no chairs, just seven octagon raised platforms surrounding the table. Each man stepped up and took a position on one, and Number Two took Dave by the arm, leading him onto the seventh platform.

Dave looked blankly around at the six.

The six stared at the globe sitting before them. It began to glow a dark red, and rose from the table as it began to spin.

Dave's eyes widened as he glanced about at their stoic faces. His instincts screamed for him to run, but his legs were concrete, and his feet bolted to the floor. The room became a brilliant dark red as a beam shot from the globe into the foreheads of all seven men.

They were now connected.

Sights and sounds came as memories forgotten or blocked out flooded in. Suddenly, he was in another city, one he had forgotten. The landscape was devastated, and filled with dead bodies. He saw himself stepping over people he once knew; friends and family. He was alive, walking through death and destruction because he had agreed to do anything, anything to survive. He had made an agreement with the Six.

They spoke to him in a unified voice.

"You agreed to our conditions, and we let you live because we felt you could be useful in finding the Gifts. They were not in your city, or any of the others we destroyed. But ten years have passed, and we're running out of time and patience. We need to know if they're here or not."

"I've been searching ever since the fall of the Zender," Dave said defensively. "You said that was the sign they were here. The man called Henry Parks could have them."

"We've thought of him," The Six continued. "But crystals are not enough. Does he have the book and the parchment too? What about the silver cord and the Magnifier? If he is gathering these, he is dangerous and must be destroyed, but not before we know for sure."

"He never talks about those things," Dave answered. "He doesn't show anything. I have thrown everything in his path, and he doesn't respond. If he had the parchment, he would know of the portal. He would do something to reveal it, but he hasn't. It could be someone else. I have heard of others with crystals too, but how can I know for sure?"

"We know the Magnifier is here. Someone has taken it, and you're going to have to find out who. Whoever has them all will try to stop us, and we must stop them before it's too late. Therefore, the city must suffer more. They must suffer until they are revealed."

Darkness flowed from the globe through the Six and swirled like coal dust around them, filling the room. Their appearance changed from sharply-dressed men to dark, vague figures. The blackness in the room weighed on Dave as horrible thoughts and evil imaginations filled his heart with darkness. He was becoming darkness itself.

The six turned in unison towards him, opening their mouths, and out flowed streams filled with vile creatures. The streams joined as one, and penetrated Dave's being. The globe continued to spin, spewing out darkness for a few more moments, and then it stopped.

"I remember now," he said, his eyes black from the inside. "We must find them. We must find them all, especially the book and the parchment. They hold the secrets of time."

"What about the city?" they asked coldly, "we need more energy."

"I have that in my thoughts too. These people are weak. They want justice and fairness, but I will give them only pain. I will make them hate, and then they will fight. Chaos has already started with the broadcast. It will bring forth the resisters, and then we'll crush them."

"The City Fathers were wise not to resist," they said in unison. "They feigned surrender so we couldn't draw their energy. Somehow they must have known about us and our coming. Somehow, they managed to avoid the Zender we sent. You must defeat their wisdom, and bring us the Gifts. Our future cannot exist beyond this universe if we lose the timeline."

"I'll find them, and I know your names. I remember now."

"You will not speak of it. Our names cannot be spoken until the Gifts are destroyed. You will see to it."

The men returned to their normal appearance as the red globe settled onto the table.

Dave smiled darkly as an idea came to him. He could turn the broadcast into an opportunity, an opportunity to destroy all resistance and find the Gifts.

"What about your wife? Will she be a distraction?"

"No need to worry; I'll take care of her," Dave answered coldly as they filed back into the board room. "She won't be a problem. I'll see to it."

He left the meeting, and headed for home. The Six had restored his memories, and he knew his former life again. He was on the city council when they came, and secretly met with them, agreeing to hand his city over on the condition he would be given power and not be killed. They agreed on condition he gave full allegiance to their plans. He managed to convince some others, like Harry, Olliver, and Bert, to join him, even though it meant destroying their own people.

A feeling of power coursed through his being as his chauffeur pulled off the main road. It was nearing three AM, so he knew his wife would be sleeping when he arrived. He had a simple plan.

"She won't feel a thing," he thought, smiling to himself as they motored up the long driveway, passing ornate statues and tall hedge rows. "But the Gifts, they're more complicated. The Six want them destroyed, but we'll see about that when the time comes. Could it be Parks? Maybe, but I must find out for sure. Maybe I can force him out, and make him reveal what he has. But even if it's not Parks, so what? Either way, I am rid of him."

His limousine rolled up his driveway, dropping him at the front entrance. Doris left the front house lights on as usual. Dave sent his driver home, and headed into the house…

CHAPTER 30

Jim pulled into the darkened driveway off Midway Street. Frank's hideaway was little more than a rustic cabin along the far end of West Lake. He had inherited it years before from his great aunt. She owned it outright, and since many of the property records were "accidently" destroyed by the colonel, there was no record of it.

He drove close to the cabin, and shut off the van. Heading along the rocky path towards the darkened front door, Jim flipped over a fake rock in the window box next to the door where Frank kept the key.

The door squeaked in protest as he pushed it open. It had been some time since anyone had been there. He felt around, locating the light switch behind the door. A strong, musty odor, mostly from a lack of heat and ventilation hung over the room, but it was otherwise clean and neat. Frank kept a stack of kindling ready in the fireplace with several pieces of dry wood on top. In a few minutes, Jim had a crackling fire going, and the warmth felt good. Winter was ending, but the cold north wind still pushed in off the lake, making the fire necessary.

Jim unloaded his gear, and secured the van before settling in. He checked the fridge, and found it well-stocked with beverages. The cupboards, filled with nonperishable foods, were evidence this summer getaway could accommodate a much longer stay.

"Frank," he thought to himself, "is always thinking ahead. But I wonder if he truly believes they're going to let him continue broadcasting after my series. He might need this hideout himself should things go sideways."

Jim settled in with a bowl of chili and some hot coffee. The overstuffed couch set in front of the rock fireplace was the perfect place to relax and enjoy a good meal. Jim thought it might make a nice backdrop for his next broadcast. The wind picked up, causing low-hanging branches to scrape and bang against the cabin.

Going through his notes and research, he rehearsed exactly what he wanted to say.

"This broadcast needs to be concise and to the point." Jim said, taking another sip of coffee. "I won't get but one, maybe two, more broadcasts in before things go south."

The first broadcast was pointed at the East facility only. But, since then, information had poured in from people in other areas who suspected something going on in the others as well. It hadn't taken him long to fill in the blanks. But he needed more than public support. He needed someone important, someone who had power, and wasn't afraid of Management. He hoped that over the years, Management had become complacent. Ten years was a long time, and much had changed.

He set up the cameras, and put the lighting in place before crashing on the couch. Sleep was hard to come by as ideas for his next ground-breaking broadcast kept rolling around in his head. After several hours, he finally managed to fall asleep.

The fire was just a pile of hot ashes when his alarm rang.

Sliding his feet out from under the warm wool blanket into his slippers, he grabbed some dry kindling from the box next to the fireplace. In a few minutes, the crackle and pop of cedar was welcoming larger pieces of fir. The firelight danced across the ceiling while Jim folded the blanket, putting it away in the cedar chest behind the couch.

He had turned on the water heater before turning in, and was being rewarded with a hot shower. The old water pipes complained as he shaved in the chipped porcelain sink set before the cracked mirror. The water changed from orange to clear just as he finished.

"Nothing like roughing it," Jim said, scraping the night's growth off his face.

The single bare bulb hanging from an open rafter made shaving an adventure, but he was careful not to nick himself. He needed to be sharp and look sharp.

"I must be crazy. Three months ago, I was the toast of the town. Women were chasing me, and I was making good money. Now here I am, avoiding being captured by people who would like to toast me for real."

In spite of his concern, however, he was back in the game--a true reporter again, hunting down a story. Only his current story could end up more about survival than anything else.

Checking the settings and adjustments, Jim satisfied himself that everything was ready. The cabin was better suited for a broadcast than he had first thought. Dark wooden walls made a good background for the bright lights. Knowing he would be without help, he set a large chalk board primer behind the camera to keep his thoughts organized. The broadcast would be taped so he could edit it before sending, but he wouldn't have time for a second take. He had to be perfect the first time.

Sitting on the couch in front of the flickering fire, he began the final review. He had a 6 AM broadcast prearranged with Frank. HOT News would pick up his signal, and resend it by cable and satellite.

He was excited, to say the least. This was going to be his signature broadcast. The fame of Jim the Weatherman was about to be eclipsed by Jim the Reporter.

The taping went well, but when he powered the transmission system, the lights on the panel wouldn't change from yellow to green. He checked every connection twice, and then three times, yet nothing helped. There was power, and an outgoing signal, but no connection. The sweat rolled down his forehead as he considered his options. He had little choice at this point. He would have to pack up, and take a copy of the tape directly to the studio, since there was no way for him to know what was causing the problem.

"I'm not a geek," he yelled in frustration, kicking an empty reel across the room. "I am a reporter. This is why I have a team of guys who know this stuff."

But the choice was clear. Without his team, he was stuck. He would have to risk being seen and, maybe, arrested if he wanted to get his message out.

It was still dark as he pulled out onto the main road from the lengthy dirt and gravel drive. He took the back roads and side streets through the city, and was only two miles out when a pair of headlights dropped in behind.

Jim's pulse raced as he sped up, hoping it was just a local.

But the lights closed tight, confirming Jim's fears. His van was not the most agile vehicle, even though it was powered by a big motor. Making several tight turns, it became apparent he couldn't lose the tail. The black car pulled up alongside and rammed him, trying to force him off the road. From the van's side mirror, he saw the car's window lower and the distinctive glow from a Nullifier. He was about to be blasted into oblivion.

He slammed on his brakes just as the man in the car discharged the weapon. The bright flash crossed inches in front of his windshield, vaporizing the middle of a large oak tree. The top of the tree crashed onto a parked car as he dropped in behind his pursuer. Knowing he wouldn't get a second chance, he floored it, driving the heavy front bumper into the car's rear, causing it to swerve wildly as the driver lost control. Jim continued pushing it sideways, sending it careening into a light pole. It dropped down a steep ditch, and flipped over.

Jim's hands were welded to the steering wheel as he skidded safely to a stop. There was nothing he could do to help them even if he wanted to.

"This van isn't even marked, so how did they know it was me?" he thought as he started off again. "The only way they could know is if there is an insider feeding information to Management. But who would do that…"

His thoughts trailed off as he made his way along, carefully checking for more tails, but there were none. The thought of betrayal was too heavy for him to bear. He had to stay on course. Jim rolled up to the backside of HOT News with the lights off. Pulling down a dark driveway barely visible from the road, he parked in a grove of trees on a slight bluff overlooking the station. From there, he could see several black SUVs in the parking lot. They were not trying to hide their presence, so it wasn't a trap.

"This isn't good," he said to himself, considering his options. "Without HOT News, there is no story; there is no me! The only thing we have going is we haven't announced another broadcast yet. Frank may have run some ticklers suggesting there could be another broadcast, but nothing definite; no timeline or dates. Maybe they're trying a preemptive strike, and got lucky. I'll have to trust Frank can hold out. If he cracks under the pressure, it's over."

He waited a while longer before pulling out, and heading back to the cabin. They had an emergency procedure in place if anything went wrong, so now he would have to wait for Frank.

Meanwhile, Harry was working his plan. He had guessed correctly that another broadcast was coming. Now he was hoping to get a lead, or some information out of Frank that could blow the deal wide open. However, even though coming down on Frank was ordered, he still needed to be careful. Management couldn't come off like they were trying to cover things up. That would damage their carefully crafted positive, benevolent image, and then they would have to deal with an outbreak of resistance.

"Frank will toe the line, considering the alternatives," he thought to himself. "He knows better than to go against me."

The only thing not going according to plan was Harry's hand. He didn't sleep well that night, and his doctor visit provided little help. His heart was fine, and the tests negative, but his pain was real. The ache in his hand stretched all the way to his shoulder, and it wasn't getting any better. In fact, it seemed to be getting progressively worse.

"I haven't seen Jim all week," Frank insisted, the sweat glistening off his forehead. "He came by to pick up his check, and then left."

"Don't screw with me!" Barron growled, leaning forward in his seat, and pounding his fist on Frank's desk.

Frank was seated behind the desk with two large men standing over him, one on either side, with Barron staring hard into his eyes.

"You don't think we know what's going on here?" Barron continued, a sinister smile covering his face. "You're playing with fire, and you're about to get burned."

"Look, I know you're upset," Frank replied, without blinking or looking away, "but I don't have control over everything here. We have a lot of topics approved at lower levels. It can put me in an awkward position sometimes, but I need my team to be creative. I can't micromanage them if I want them to grow."

"So, you want me to believe your leading broadcaster, "Jim the Weatherman," suddenly decided to become a reporter, produce a controversial broadcast, and you didn't know about it?"

Barron drilled his glare into Frank.

"Don't take me for a fool."

"Look, he had some vacation time coming." Frank responded without flinching, "He told me he needed some time off to work on a project, but he wouldn't tell me what it was. I guess now we know why."

Barron leaned back into the chair, and sized him up.

Glancing at the two men beside Frank, Barron motioned towards the door as he got up. He then leaned over the desk, putting his nose inches from Frank's.

"Ok, we're going, for now. But Harry will want to see you personally. I suggest you decide very quickly where you want to go in this world. There's a happy ending to this story, or an unhappy ending. Don't make me come back."

He pushed Frank in the chest with his fist, shoving him into the wall, and then slammed the door as they left.

Frank took a deep breath, his heart pounding in his ears as he watched them drive off. He had expected a response, but was surprised they bought his answers. It could have been much worse.

"Jim's really got them going," he thought as he leaned into his seat, wiping his forehead on his sleeve. "Now I must make sure things go in the right direction."

Frank knew Harry wasn't going to take this much longer. And, that thug of his, Barron was somebody not to be messed with. If there was another visit, he knew it wouldn't be healthy for him.

"Well," Frank said out loud as an idea flashed through his mind, "maybe it's all in how you look at it. Play my cards right, and things could be different."

Frank smiled. He still loved being in the middle.

CHAPTER 31

Jim made it safely back to the cabin, taking every side road he could think of, and parked the van deep in some thick evergreens, covering it with branches. He positioned it for a quick getaway before heading into the cabin. Settling in front of the fireplace, he stoked it absentmindedly with a poker, watching embers swirl before they went up the chimney. Reaching over, he grabbed another log, and tossed it on. It had been a stressful morning, and the heat pushed him onto the couch. He flopped his feet on the end of the couch, staring at the open beam ceiling, trying hard not to think of what might have happened with Frank. In a moment, he was snoring.

He was trapped; trapped in a cell, and pounding against a block wall as he struggled to escape. He pounded harder and harder, louder and louder.

The pounding was coming from the front door.

Jim jumped awake, heart pounding. Moving to the window, he lifted the curtain slightly.

It was Rita, Frank's assistant.

Relieved, Jim quickly unbolted the door.

"Rita! What's going on? What are you doing way out here? I drove over this morning, and saw some unfamiliar rigs at the studio. Is everything ok?"

Rita was tall, with dark hair. Frank hired her because even though she was attractive, she never used it to gain advantage. She liked being in the middle of the action, but not the center of attraction. It made her the perfect private secretary, especially for Frank, who was brilliant in leadership, but modest in appearance. She added that extra classy element, making him believable to his high-powered staff.

"No, things are not good," she replied as she stepped inside. "I recognized one of them as Barron from the Citadel. I listened from the outer office, and heard him threatening Frank. But you know Frank. That's like putting a red flag in front of a bull."

Jim motioned her over to the couch.

"So what did Frank say? I tried to make connection this morning, but they must have shut down the receiver."

"That was the first thing they did when they barged in," she said, squeezing Jim's hand. "They knew just where to go to shut off the broadcasting equipment. We went dark for about two hours."

"I realize you don't know all the details," Jim replied, putting his hand on her shoulder, "but you have to trust me. We aren't the only ones in danger."

Rita was shaking slightly. She was not easy to upset, but Management could make things really bad for everybody, and she knew it.

"Is Frank going to follow our plan?"

"He told me you would have a tape of the new broadcast," she replied, wringing her hands in her lap. "I'm to return with it, but he wants you to stay put until tonight. He'll meet you then."

Jim retrieved the leather bag sitting on the cabin floor. Opening one of the flaps, he handed a sealed envelope to Rita as she got up off the couch.

"You be careful," he said. "These are difficult times, and you need to stay safe. Are you sure nobody followed you?"

"Nobody followed me," she replied, putting the envelope into her purse, "and I will be careful. Frank gave me the keys to his sports car. Nobody can keep up with me at the wheel." Jim laughed.

She smiled slightly and gave him a warm squeeze before turning towards the door. Jim appreciated the courage she showed, coming all the way out to deliver this vital message, and returned the smile.

The morning light was giving way to afternoon sun as he walked her to the car. She stepped in as he held the door for her.

"Thanks, Rita," he said closing the door, and kneeling down. "You're a brave girl."

She smiled, and started the car. He patted her on the arm before she pulled away. Standing up, he suddenly noticed her. She had been at HOT News nearly as long as he had, but he had never even approached her for a date. Yet here she was, risking it all for him. He watched the taillights disappear up the narrow gravel drive that followed the lake back to the main road and stood in the doorway until they were out of sight. When they had gone, he went back inside, and fixed a bowl of soup and some toast.

The die was cast, and nothing more to do now but wait. The cabin was outfitted with a satellite system that allowed him to follow the local channels. HOT News was back on, doing normal broadcasting, with no more ticklers suggesting there could be more reports coming. It was several hours before dark as Jim settled in with the channel changer and his meal.

The hours dragged on as Jim's mind played and replayed the recent events. He was just starting to feel better when the wind began to blow, pelting the front window with rain. Then it thundered loudly, shaking the small cabin. Jim went to the window, and peered through the curtain. A dark cloud was forming in the middle of the lake.

Jim went outside without his coat, his weatherman curiosity rising, He walked through the tall grass to the edge of the lake for a better view.

"That's a weather pattern I've never seen before," Jim thought, shielding his face from the gusting wind and biting rain.

The small dark cloud appeared to be following the shoreline as it moved across the lake. It dipped near the surface, and then floated about fifty feet or so above the water. It continued its bobbing action as he stepped back from the water's edge, climbed up the bank.

He could see a glowing red object under the cloud.

Jim suddenly felt alone and afraid as he peeked around a large fir tree.

A red light lit up the shoreline as it approached, continuing its unusual action. In a few moments, it was at the edge nearest to Frank's cabin. The cloud was unusually dark, as if light could enter, but not escape. It stopped its bobbing action, hovering just above the tree line, and to Jim's dismay, moved in towards the cabin. The cabin sat nearly a hundred yards from the water's edge, and this object now stood half way between the lake and the cabin. The chimney had stopped smoking, so it gave the cabin a vacant look from the outside.

Suddenly, a wide beam of red light shone out of the cloud and onto the cabin for several minutes. After a moment, it narrowed into a thin beam, and focused on the ground directly below the cloud. Jim watched in disbelief as two red figures appeared from the light. Instantly, he recognized them.

They were Testers.

Jim hunkered down behind the tree, peering through some low-lying branches as they approached the cabin. The woods near the lake were thick, filled with brush and debris washed up from winter storms, and getting through them to the van would be nearly impossible. He had little choice but to sit there quietly and watch, hoping not to be spotted.

One of the Testers walked around behind the cabin while the other went to the door, pulled the handle, and went in. He could hear it crashing around in the dark as it moved through. Jim's equipment was still set up, so he could only imagine what damage was being done. Several minutes passed before it emerged, and was joined by its partner returning from the rear. The red light received the two Testers, and the cloud returned to its flight along the lake edge. He waited until it had moved around a bend before breaking into a sprint to the cabin.

Locking the door tightly, he checked out the window to make sure they were gone for good. Then he closed the storm shutters before turning on the lights. The room was a mess, with lights knocked over, and furniture overturned, but other than that, there appeared to be no real damage.

"What's this all about?" he asked himself as he finished putting the room back together. "I always wondered where those things came from, and now I know they're not from here. This isn't just about Management anymore; this is about something from beyond the wilderness, or worse, another planet. Unbelievable! This story is getting stranger by the second. I've got to tell Parks--we're going to need a better plan."

He checked out the window every five minutes or so, ready to make a break for it if they came back. The woods behind the cabin could serve as a good place to hide or get lost if needed, but he had to be ready. His packed bags sat next to the back door, ready to be grabbed.

He shut off all the lights, and finally collapsed over the couch pillows. He was exhausted, and drifted in and out of consciousness. He woke to the sound of an approaching vehicle.

Leaping from the couch, positioned himself behind the curtains. Lifting one corner slightly, he could see lights shining through the trees as the newcomer bumped along the rough drive. His heart raced. It could be anybody.

Jim let out a long exhale as Frank's little red sports car appeared under the light of a half moon.

He opened the cabin door as it pulled to a stop.

"Frank!" He exclaimed, taking several steps outside. "What took you so long, man? Are you ever a sight for sore eyes!"

Frank grabbed him by the arm as they met.

"Hey, had things to do," he said with that lighthearted, easy attitude he was known for. "Let's get out of this chilly air, and I'll tell you."

Jim closed and bolted the cabin door behind them as Frank took off his coat, and hung it on the deer antler rack.

"I'm dying to hear everything. I've been watching the news all day, but no mention of my broadcast from any station, including ours. What's going on out there?"

"Lots," Frank replied as he headed to the kitchen.

Popping a can of soda, Frank sat at the small table in the kitchenette as Jim joined him on one of the hard wooden chairs. A small brass light hung low over the round table. The spot had been home to many games and conversations over the years. It was one of Frank's favorite places to relax amid a warm summer evening with the windows open, just enjoying life.

Frank took a couple of sips from the can before setting it down. Leaning back, he scanned Jim's face.

"What? What?" Jim asked. "You're killing me here, man!"

Frank loved drama, even with the gravity of the situation. He was not going to give without a little "gamesmanship."

"You've got choices," he said, pushing the soda can with his index finger. "Rita told me you saw Management at the station this morning, and were chased by someone, so you know the stakes are high. I got a call from the Citadel later this morning. They wanted me to come up right away. It's tough to say no to those guys."

Jim leaned forward, pushing Frank's soda can back a few inches as he folded his hands.

"Harry met me," Frank continued, "and man, was he upset, and that's an understatement. But once he was done threatening and fuming, he came at me with a plan."

Jim leaned even further forward, unable to hide his interest.

"What kind of plan?"

"Not a plan you'll like. He wants me to let the story die. Basically, not replay it or reference it in any way. He believes the controversy created by your allegations and assertions will die down and go away if left alone."

"That sounds like him alright, mitigating the damage to protect the status quo."

"Well, that's just part of what he wants. After considerable browbeating and lecturing on how Management has allowed HOT News freedom to broadcast without accountability or *peer* review, Harry indicated there would need to be some changes. We must join the fold, so to speak, in order to preserve our continued existence."

"In other words, HOT News is to become LUKEWARM News."

"Yeah, and that's not all," Frank continued, picking up his soda again. "Then there's you. They can't have someone running loose with information that could hurt them, especially someone with your influence. So Harry made some "suggestions." One, convince you to leave the city like the resistors have been doing, or two, turn you in. I'm sure he believed I would be speaking with you eventually."

"So those are my choices," Jim said quietly, leaning back from the table. "I have to either run or be taken to wherever it is they take people like me. Not very attractive options."

"I didn't think you would like them. He did mention a third option, but I really didn't think you would take that one either."

"What's that?"

"Harry said if you wouldn't cooperate, I was to turn you in myself. He even suggested if you were to somehow die in the process, he would ask no questions, and HOT News could continue as is. He likes our new weather woman."

"How nice of him," Jim said, leaning back and putting his hands behind his head. "Were you considering that option?"

Frank looked hard at Jim for a moment, and then they both started laughing.

"I have to say, though," he replied, still chuckling, "it sounded like a good idea for a moment since you've been such a pain in my ass."

Jim laughed hard. It felt good to break the tension, but he still wanted to know what Frank really had in mind.

Frank drank the remaining soda from his can, and banked it off the kitchen wall into the waste basket.

"They think they have all the cards, and that's their weakness," Frank continued. "They don't know it yet, but I have a deck of my own. Rita brought me your tape this morning. I reviewed it, and added some additional commentary. When I got back from my "meeting," I packed our essential broadcasting equipment into several vans. A couple of trusted men have taken them to a discreet location. Then I met with the staff, and told them they would need to head home and look for new opportunities. I didn't give them all the reasons, only enough to know we were going out of business for a while. I think they expected it anyway."

He leaned over to the fridge, and grabbed another soda.

"I sent them off, and put the station on autopilot. Rita and I stayed to answer phones, so as to not raise suspicions. Then I told her to take a bag, and head home until she heard from me. The last thing I did before coming down here was to rig the broadcast. Tomorrow morning at six, your tape will be played throughout this area continuously on a loop. Oh, and just in case someone wants to power us down, I hooked the generators in direct. The only way to stop this broadcast now is to bomb the place, and even then I don't think it'll work. Nothing stops until the generators run out of fuel."

"That place is built like a bomb shelter," Jim replied, stroking his chin with his left hand. "In fact, I believe it once was."

"HOT News was built on top of an old concrete bomb shelter," Frank confirmed.

"So what are you going to do after tomorrow's broadcast?"

"Not 'what am I going to do,' but 'what are we going to do,'" Frank replied, popping his second soda. "We're leaving for the country to start a new career. I have some friends who will set us up. We're going underground, and starting a new broadcasting company."

"That's an awesome idea! But aren't you worried they'll find us."

"Yeah, they'll try, I'm sure," Frank responded, standing up to guzzle his soda. "But it has to happen. You may have started this, but we're going to finish it. Rumors have been flying for years. You just brought proof. We can't live life with intimidation and murders. It seems like time for a revolt or revolution or something."

"What if I told you there may be more going on than any of us can imagine?"

"What do you mean more? I thought you had the full scope on this?"

"It's not about my report. I saw something highly unusual this evening. Remember the Testers?"

"Those short, vicious, red guys who attacked the city?"

"The very same. We haven't seen them since then, but today, I witnessed them coming down from the sky out of what looked like a black cloud."

Frank looked Jim over carefully, not sure what to think.

"You're really serious, aren't you?"

"It sounds weird, I know, but they were here, and they were looking for something. Fortunately, it wasn't me."

"I don't know what to say."

"Is there something here they would be interested in?"

"I can't even imagine what those things would be looking for. This is just an old cabin. What would anyone want with it?"

"I have no idea, but I thought you should know. Something is definitely going on, even beyond our reality."

"We'd better get some shuteye," Frank said as he changed the subject. "We'll need to pick up the vans, and get out of town early. Once HOT News goes live, things are going to get crazy, and I want to be long gone before then."

Jim took the couch, and Frank stretched out on the thick rug in front of the fireplace. The night would pass quickly, and tomorrow would be the dawning of a new day. But there were no doubt more dark clouds were looming on the horizon.

CHAPTER 32

Parks could hear the sirens approaching. He knew Harry would have dispatched security by now, and they would be busy searching his apartment. It wouldn't take them long to figure out he was gone. But he needed to see Della one more time before leaving. He went around behind her apartment, and jumped over the fence into the small yard, being careful not to be seen. Pulling the spare key from the flowerbox, he let himself in through the sliding glass door. She had just come home for lunch, and was busy in the kitchen.

"Della," Parks said in a low voice. "We need to talk."

"Henry!" she answered, nearly dropping her plate. "What are you doing here?"

"I don't have much time to explain," Parks replied. "But things have happened. I can't stay in the city any longer, and I can't be seen here with you. It's too dangerous."

"What's wrong?" She asked, her voice filled with worry as she took him by the arm.

"Harry has a warrant out for my arrest. Jim and I exposed some pretty horrible things, and now they're out to get us. Even worse, I'm being set up."

"I saw the broadcast. You were involved with Jim on that? They won't just arrest you, Parks; they'll kill you!"

"You'll need to leave too. Make up an excuse or something, and drive out to your mother's. I'll meet up with you later."

"I can't leave now. There are people at the hospital counting on me. Bruce is better, and David got him out, but there are a lot more people needing similar care."

"You have to go," Parks said, taking her by the shoulders, and looking hard into her big brown eyes. "Management has turned against us. Pack your things, and call work. Tell them something has happened to your mother, and you'll be in touch. I have to go now before they find me here. Promise me you will get out."

"I'll try, but not before I know things are settled."

Parks left reluctantly. He knew how stubborn Della could be, especially when it involved other people's well-being. He wasn't worried for himself. Management would have a hard time following him through the canyon, and into the wilderness. He figured Barron was the likely candidate to track him, since they had worked together for years, and he possessed some specialized skills. But Parks also knew he wouldn't be alone. They wouldn't send just one man to do the job. Parks was too dangerous for that.

He worked his way through the brush, over large boulders, and up the side of the river to a wooded section just below the ridge. From there, he could see if anyone was on his trail. He heard the distinctive snapping of twigs and branches near the river, which was still raging due to the early spring runoff. Making his way up the hill several hundred yards below was Barron with one of the new Cadets in tow.

Parks laughed while watching the two men struggling through the rough terrain. Barron followed the Cadet, who was the better tracker. Barron always tried to stay back anyway, letting someone else take the point. That way, he had less of a chance of being hit, especially when following someone as powerful as Parks.

Glancing around, Parks suddenly realized his error. The hard winter had left large trees and debris on the patch, blocking his escape. What should have been an easy exit was now a steep, slippery bank full of twisted branches, stumps, and rocks. Spotting a large boulder caught by an upturned fir tree, he made his way along the steep slope. Then, using the stump as support against the slimy bank, he lifted the edge just enough for it to continue its journey to the bottom of the ravine, bouncing and crashing through the brush as it went, with Parks sliding down behind it.

The boulder sent Barron and the Cadet flying in different directions, just as he hoped. They managed to escape harm, but at least Parks had time to change his route. Barron took a shot just as Parks leapt over a fallen log, and grazed his left ankle. Before Parks could get moving again, the Cadet crossed the river, climbed to the ridge, and blocked his way out. He had little choice but to jump the river himself. He couldn't risk being in the open and giving Barron another shot.

He quickly scrambled up the washed out river bank, sending more rocks cascading into the water below. It took only seconds to reach the top, and then he would be in the safety of the wilderness.

Just as Parks made the ridge, the cadet jumped from behind a tree, Nullifier already humming. Parks managed to duck under the blast of energy. Then leaping up, he grabbed the Cadet by the shoulders, and smashed him to the ground. The impact dislodged the Nullifier, and sent it spinning away. The Cadet was outmatched, and unable to defend himself. It should have been over quickly, but suddenly, pain blossomed in his shoulder. Barron. Normally, even a glancing blow from Barron's powerful Equalizer would knock a man down, or even kill him.

But Parks was no ordinary man.

Barron's third shot ended the struggle as Parks swung the Cadet into its deadly path, the impact sending the man sailing over the ledge. The weapon had done its work, only the work was intended for Parks, not the young cadet. The echo from the canyon below confirmed the cadet's permanent removal from the Citadel's security forces.

Barron dropped his weapon to his side as he watched in shock. Then leaping off the side of the canyon, he slid feet-first down the steep slope, hitting the bottom so hard, his feet were buried in the gravelly sand. Pulling loose, Barron jumped between rocks and logs, and crossed the river in a single bound as he made for the other side. Scrambling up the rocky incline, he shot over the ridge.

The Equalizer glistened in the late afternoon light, buzzing with energy as he quickly glanced around.

"Parks!" he screamed at the top of his lungs., "You miserable bastard!"

Barron's voice echoed through the hills, but Parks was gone. He blended into the surroundings like the very rocks themselves.

Barron peered over the edge, hoping to see something that wasn't there. Focusing for a moment, he identified the cadet's path through the trail of broken limbs, and saw the dark outline of a crumpled figure on the rocks below, partially submerged along the river bank. It was sure to be dicey, explaining both the death of his new partner, and Parks' escape.

His instructions were clear: kill or capture Parks. He had done neither, and it would never do to come back empty handed. He would have to rally the Testers to his aid. Management had suspected something like this would happen, and had given him the go-ahead if he needed it.

Baron definitely needed it.

Parks moved quickly through the damp air towards the cave, gathering some dry kindling and a few logs as he went. Before long, the fire began to glow brightly. Hanging the leather strap that held his crystal weapons over a rocky outcropping, he settled in. His mind quickly turned to the one crystal blade that had been confiscated by General Olliver, and placed in lockup at the Citadel. Parks's protests, explaining the dangers of using the blades, had been ignored. Olliver thought it was silly to think the blades were more sophisticated or powerful than *their* weapons.

But the general belonged to Management. He was one of the main leaders of the force that had taken the city, and he, more than any of the invaders, had wanted to kill everybody, even as the City Fathers came to beg terms of surrender. But Parks had more to think about than a dead loser like General Olliver. He was planning for the right moment to break into the heart of the city, back into the very place where just a few days, before he was leading the cadets.

He poked the fire a bit, and threw another log on, the thoughts in his head burning as hot as the red embers swirling up the flue.

"I hope Della left for her mother's like we agreed," he said to himself as he stared into the fire. "But she doesn't always listen to what I say. And what about Jim? Did he finish the broadcast, or get caught? Then there was the situation with Kevin Knobbs. He found that strange magnifying glass, and it got him killed and nearly Bruce and George too."

His thoughts trailed off as he felt the book snuggled in the pouch against his chest.

"What a change a week can make. One minute, we're just living, and the next our lives are upside down."

The darkness was settling in as he stoked the fire one more time before lying back. He enjoyed the thick animal hides, which made for a comfortable bed. Soon, the warmth from the flickering fire was radiating on his face, and his eyes grew heavy. In a moment, all was at rest.

Parks climbed down the dark shaft, feeling for places to put his hands and feet. The rocks were slippery, and suddenly he lost his grip. He was freefalling into the blackness.

"Grab the cord, Henry!" Kirsten screamed as she tossed the silver cord down the shaft.

He reached out, grabbing it right before he hit the bottom. The next instant, he was standing safely in a cave illumined by phosphorescent rocks.

"Kirsten!" Parks yelled. "Look out behind you!"

A large dark shadow with glowing red eyes loomed behind his sister. Pulling the crystal blade from his belt, he threw it at the dark being.

Parks bolted upright, drenched in sweat. It was only a dream. But it had been years since he had even thought of the weekend they spent hunting the Zender. Relighting the lamp, he pulled the old book from his coat. It slipped from his hand, and landed open on the rocky floor. Picking it up, he began reading from where it had opened.

"Gifted is the man who walks in the light," the book read. "Six he holds; the seventh is hidden until the silver cord is broken."

"The silver cord? Is that the one Kirsten found? It's mentioned here in the book just like the crystal and the parchment, but what does it mean? The book is still such a mystery. I need to find Sterling. I don't think he was telling me everything when we were talking at the Island. He seemed to be holding something back."

Suddenly, the cave began to vibrate, and small rocks and sand pelted his head. Jumping to his feet, he pushed back the thick covering of moss and branches that hung across the entrance. It wasn't an earthquake. The vibrations were coming from a humming noise that grew louder by the second. He gathered up his belongings, and exited at the crest of the hill through a shaft that led up from his cave.

Slipping behind a rock outcropping, he positioned himself for a full view of the valley floor below. Now the humming was becoming deeper, and more pronounced. It sounded more like steady chanting.

Suddenly, he realized what it really was.

Testers. Lots of them, judging by the sound.

Management must be very concerned indeed to send the Testers.

He repositioned himself to get a better view.

But why bring them out now? He couldn't be that great a threat. Unless perhaps they were after more than just Parks.

Suddenly they came into view, a red tide spilling into the valley, like a giant wave pushing on shore. The valley floor below began to blow spurts of dust from vents scattered about in response to the heavy steps of the approaching horde. Everything shook, and a cloud of dust could be seen rising in the distance, just over the low-lying hills hung loosely around the edges of the valley.

Parks moved upwards along the edge of the ridge. From there he could see more Testers flooding in. He estimated there were at least several thousand of them. The Testers continued chanting their song. It was in a language only they knew, and he remembered its effect. It struck fear into the hearts of the listeners. It was a unique sound which vibrated within your head.

Taking some cotton from his bag, he rolled up several wads, and squeezed them into his ears. It was just enough to keep his head from banging off his shoulders as the chanting increased. They spread out across the valley floor like a tsunami. Things were becoming more dangerous by the second. Testers were not known for their visual acuity; they relied more on their sense of smell than eyesight. It was rumored they could smell fear itself. This made them extremely effective, as most people feared their presence. They fanned out, taking up positions like markers on a checker board, making it difficult to pass without being detected.

"The sea of red. That's the description in the book. Could it be it was talking about these?"

He slid along the narrow ledge, some two hundred feet above, amazed at the thought. But the revelation would have to wait until he solved a more pressing problem.

"Maybe Barron's not as dumb as I thought, or he just got lucky. He was correct if he guessed I would head across the valley away from the city, and then double back."

The gathering horde below turned their attention towards the mountain where Parks was hidden, and even though he was concealed from view, he felt they sensed his presence somehow.

"He's clever, alright," Parks thought as he moved away from the ledge.

But he knew it was about more than just capturing Parks. Management probably suspected the resistance was evolving. First, Jim and the broadcast; and then the death of General Olliver. Management needed to maintain control at all times, and capturing or killing Parks would act as a great diversion to their real plans.

"A most curious thing," Parks thought to himself, considering his options from the perch above. "These beings are quite the sight, standing in formation, hoping to block my exit."

Parks moved off the ledge, and down the canyon shaft to his cave. There were many ways to the desert floor below, and Parks would need to choose the safest one.

They obviously thought he was trapped, he thought, taking a few more items, and placing them in the leather belt around his waist.

But Parks was no easy prey.

He entered into a narrow opening in the back of his cave. It descended through the mountain, and exited behind some large boulders. The Testers were only a few feet away as he squeezed through into the morning light. Spaced little more than ten feet apart, he began to weave his way through them. Though they could barely "see", they used sounds and smells effectively. Fortunately, he smelled more like the wilderness than anything. He was nearly halfway across when the ground rumbled, and cracked in front of him.

He froze.

A large black scorpion emerged from one of the desert holes, quickly followed by several more. Black scorpions were the most deadly of all wilderness creatures. One sting would send a man into convulsions, and they always ended in a horrible death. The Testers paid no attention as their armor protected them, but Parks had no such advantage.

Sweat began to form on his forehead as they scurried around the legs of the Testers, heading towards his feet. He dealt with black scorpions in the past by simply kicking them away, or killing them with a rock or stick. Now, his only hope was that they would turn and go in another direction.

No such luck.

He could wait no longer. The first black scorpion was mere inches from his foot when he kicked, sending it flying over several Testers, and into the face of another. He took off, darting through the ranks, and heading for the safety of the tree line, but they were on him. Like ants attacking an intruder, they swarmed over him with their sharp instruments of death. He quickly pulled his longest crystal blade from the sheath that hung around his waist. It shone brighter than the sun as he carved a path through their ranks. Testers fell around, him their bodies and weapons cut in pieces by his blade.

But as good as Parks and his blade were, there were just too many Testers. He knew he wouldn't last long.

Suddenly, the ground erupted, tossing Parks and the Testers into the air as the distinctive shape of a zyklone burst from the sands. Zyklones were huge creatures covered with reptilian scales and sharp knife-like protrusions covering their bodies. They spun like giant drills, allowing them to burrow deep underground, even through rock. Its wide head had a hooked beak which snapped Testers in two as it rose above the earth, then dove back into the ground, drawing more with it, like flushing a toilet. It reemerged several hundred feet away in the middle of their ranks before diving down again.

Zyklones had been considered fictional, and were seen only in folklore books until the Testers came. For some reason, their chanting and vibrations penetrated through the ground, and drew them to the surface. The first one was only the beginning. More zyklones emerged across the valley floor, sending Testers scurrying in every direction. They managed to kill one of the zyklones, and wound a second.

The distraction gave Parks the opportunity he needed to shed his few remaining attackers, and race to the safety of the woods. Any hope they had of taking him now was long gone.

Barron was positioned on a nearby ridge, watching the carnage below.

"Parks is one lucky guy," he thought to himself, lowering his binoculars. "Or he has help."

"They've shown their hand," Park thought as he jogged along the overgrown path and away from the destruction. "I should have seen this coming. These people want chaos, not peace. The City Fathers were so wrong about them. What was their real plan anyway?"

He picked up the pace, jumping over fallen logs and scattered rocks as he made his way up the mountainside.

"And that's all they've brought us," his thoughts blackening as memories flashed through his mind. "The City Fathers promised things would be alright, but all we have gotten so far is misery. It's hard to figure out their true motive. It's like they want us to become evil or something. They keep working to stir up dissent and anger."

He tucked his chin tight to his chest, and quickened his pace. He went harder, faster; spurred on by anger.

Suddenly, he went flying head over heels through the underbrush, snapping off small alder trees before sliding to a stop against a large oak tree. Pain shot through his chest and exploded in his brain.

"Getting careless are you now, Parks?" a familiar voice boomed through the woods.

Barron had intended to hit him in the head, but shot just as he leapt over a log, hitting his midsection instead.

Parks quickly rolled around, flattening himself behind a tree.

"Barron!" he yelled back, still feeling the pain from where he took the shot. "I should've guessed you were around. It figures you'd need to ambush me. You never were one for a fair fight."

This was the second time in three days he'd been shot by Barron, who had succeeded this time in bruising or maybe even breaking some ribs.

"Hey," Barron yelled back, trying to make out where he was hiding, "whatever it takes to get the job done. You know how I am, always looking for the easy catch."

"Yeah, I know how you are," Parks said under his breath, keeping low.

He peered carefully around the base of the tree. The good news was it took a little time for Barron's weapon to recharge. He had maybe another fifteen to twenty seconds to make a move before Barron could fire again.

The area was open and exposed except along the lower edges of the path which had some skimpy cover. Making his way silently through the dry brush, he kept low to avoid being spotted. He figured Barron would choose a spot above where he could survey the area without risking exposure.

Sweat poured off Barron's forehead as he scanned the area. He wheeled around as a glint from something in the brush below caught his eye.

"So there you are," he said to himself, looking through his scope.

The brush was thick, but he was sure he saw what looked like a dark shape. It could be a shadow, or Parks hunkering down. Then the glistening object moved slightly.

"It can only be Parks' beloved crystals betraying his location." Barron said, taking steady aim. "I told him those things would be the death of him some day. Now it's coming true!"

The devastating weapon headed for its target. Its flight and path were exactly where aimed, and once over the target area, Barron detonated the device.

A combination of dust, shattered tree limbs, and rocks flew into the air. He quickly ducked behind a boulder protecting himself from broken rocks and steel which ricocheted off the cliff behind him. Dirt and rocks were still falling through branches as he rushed down the steep slope, through the brush, and over the path to the blast zone. Smoke rising from the area hid the full effect, but he knew the job was complete.

"It's going to be ugly," Barron said to himself with a laugh as he stepped through soft dirt churned by the blast. "I just hope there's enough left to identify."

He reached into his bag, pulling out a camera as he hopped up on the circular ridge created by the explosion to get a good picture. The dust was clearing as he steadied himself.

Suddenly, his back exploded in pain and he shot into the air, landing face first, his chin plowing a short furrow in the soft dirt.

"You're the one getting careless, Barron," Parks said in a chiding voice.

Parks was standing, hands on hips, at the edge of the crater. He had hit Barron square in the back with a forearm smash, and crushed several ribs, even through Barron's armored vest.

Barron wobbled as he stumbled to his feet, wiping the dirt from his eyes.

"You bastard," he said dropping to one knee. "I think you broke my back."

"That's too bad. But I'm going to break a lot more than that if you don't do exactly what I say."

He looked up to see Parks holding a sharp crystal blade in his hand. Barron didn't need to be told what that weapon could do if he made any quick moves.

"Ok, so you got me." Barron replied, coughing up some blood. "But you have to admit I nearly got you. How did you manage your escape anyway? I was dead on with my shot."

Parks reached into his pocket, pulled out a string with one of his crystals attached, and dangled it in front of him.

"I imagine this is what you thought was me. I figured you would be anxious, too anxious as usual. So I gave you something to focus on, something shiny. So here's the deal. I can take you out now, or you can climb up here and surrender."

Barron stumbled forward a bit, briefly considering his options. The bag containing his weapons still hung around his shoulder, but in the excitement, he hadn't recharged a second time. There would be no second chance now, not with Parks standing over him.

"Well, you don't give me much of a choice. I guess I have to take your offer. But what exactly do you intend to do with me? You're a wanted man, and everybody's after you. What do you think you can do about that? You'd be better off surrendering to me."

"Don't you worry; just get your butt up here."

Barron shook himself, and spit out some more dirt and blood before climbing out of the hole. He was just about out when he slipped at the edge, and tumbled back in.

He struggled to one knee, and then meekly put out his hand for help.

"I guess I am weaker than I thought. Can you get me out of here?"

Parks instinctively grabbed his hand, but that was a mistake.

Using Parks' hand as leverage, he swung his right leg around, and swept him off his feet. Kicking Parks in the chest, he sent him flying hard into a large tree as Barron pulled a long curved blade from under his coat. He was on his feet in an instant, lunging for his opponent.

Parks caught his wrist, the point of the blade nearly touching his throat. Barron pressed hard against the handle with his full weight on the weapon, intending to drive it into his neck. The two men grimaced, locked in struggle. Barron dipped his blades in poison, so even a scratch would mean certain death. The knife blade hovered close to its deadly mark as Parks repositioned his body, raised his abdomen, arched his back, and knocked Barron off balance. Barron struggled to maintain his position, but it was too late. Parks lifted him up, and shoved him into a pile of smoldering twisted limbs and roots.

Parks spun to his feet, crystal blade in hand.

Barron was up just as fast, slashing the air with his knife. There was little chance he could take Parks, but he might buy some time to pull the Nullifer he had stashed in his bag. He circled, making several lunges, which Parks easily avoided. Then, grabbing a broken limb, he swung it into Parks ribs.

Parks stumbled back as Barron broke for the bag. Grabbing it, Barron rolled down into the crater, and pulled the Nullifier out in one smooth motion. A bright flash exploded from the end of his weapon.

Barron shielded his face from the searing heat emanating from the blast. But instead of destroying Parks, the deadly beam split in two, blasting a boulder into dust on one side and cutting a large tree in half on the other. The tree stood for an awkward moment before crashing onto the ground.

The crystal blade Parks held in front of his body glowed bright orange, having absorbed some energy from the blast. It slowly returned to its clear state as he jumped onto Barron's chest, slicing the end of his Nullifier off before he could take another shot.

"I should kill you right now!" Parks growled, grabbing Barron by the neck, and holding the blade tight to his throat.

"You'll never see her again if you do," Barron gasped, his face turning red as Parks tightened his grip.

"Never see who again?" Parks asked, his eyes turning a shade of dark red and nearly popping out of his head.

"Della," Barron squeezed out.

Parks couldn't conceal his shock. His anger subsided as he tried to process the new information.

"What are you saying?" he yelled, yanking Barron to his feet.

"I said you'll never see her again," Barron sputtered between clenched teeth. "She's safe for now, but if I don't return, she dies."

He shoved Barron backwards, slamming him against what was left of a tree. Barron coughed, grabbing his throat.

"I needed her," he squeaked hoarsely. "She was my insurance if things went wrong."

"If you've hurt her," Parks threatened, his blade moving menacingly towards Barron's chest. "What have you done with her?"

"I said she's safe, for now. But I've arranged a little surprise only I know about. Without me, she'll be dead by morning."

Parks eyed Barron, realizing his most carefully guarded secret was out, and it could cost Della her life. The situation appeared hopeless. Fear of losing the one he cared about most overwhelmed him.

Taking his blade in both hands, he snapped off the sharp end, leaving a piece just big enough to fit in the palm of his hand. Grabbing Barron by the collar, he shoved it into his chest.

"What have you done?" Barron screamed as the heat from the crystal burned inside. "By killing me, you've killed her."

"Relax," he replied, holding him from falling. "You're not dead. I learned this little trick from someone who tried to kill a friend of mine. The crystal I put in you will kill you if you don't do as I say. You might think you know something about these crystals, but you don't. Let me tell you a little secret; they respond to intent. If you have negative or evil thoughts, it'll release an energy that will turn your insides solid. But as long as you think good thoughts, you'll be fine. So I suggest you tell me everything you planned to do to Della."

Barron rubbed his chest, feeling it burn inside as he looked angrily into Parks eyes.

"You think I am going to be different just because of your blasted crystal?"

"It's your choice. Either tell me or die. I'm going to save her no matter what you decide."

"She's ok for now. But, I have set up certain "events" that will happen if I don't return safely."

"Then we have a bargain. You return safely, change the events, and forget all about us, and the crystal will not kill you. Just report to Management that you've killed me."

Barron could feel a pulsing coming from his chest that wasn't his heart. He had seen enough of Parks' wizardry with his crystals to know anything was possible.

"It's a deal. But don't think I won't find a way to get this thing out, and when I do, I'm coming for you!"

"Be careful what you wish for," Parks said as he threw Barron's weapons into a ravine.

Parks watched Barron stagger off, and hoped that Della would be okay. Meanwhile, Parks needed more information. It was time to talk to Sterling again.

CHAPTER 34

Back at the corporate office, Harry was pacing when Birgit's voice came over the speaker.

"Sir, I have a call waiting for you from the Head Office."

"I'll take it," Harry replied, dropping into his chair, and grabbing the receiver.

He hesitated for a moment, thinking of ways to spin the conversation. He hadn't heard from Barron yet, and Jim's exposé was playing in a loop on TV. The team he had sent to shut it down was having difficulty getting into the underground broadcast area. The place was built with layers of military grade steel over several feet of hardened concrete. The door itself was several feet thick, with bomb-resistant material throughout. After several hours, they had only managed to cut in a few inches. Their best estimate for entry would be sometime tomorrow afternoon. In the meantime, HOT News would continue to broadcast unabated unless someone came up with a solution soon.

"Good morning," he said in his most upbeat voice.

"Harry!" came the sharp reply.

It was Dave, and he was looking for answers.

"What's going on out there?" Dave continued. "The phones are lighting up all over the place, with people asking hard questions. I thought we agreed this thing was going away. Why is it building like a mushroom cloud instead?"

"We're working on it as fast as possible," he replied calmly. "It shouldn't be much longer before we have things buttoned up and under control."

"Don't lie to me Harry; you need to end this right now," Dave responded in a growling tone. "My sources are telling me something different."

Dave was furious, and Harry knew it.

"Right," Harry replied confidently. "But I have another option. There's a large natural gas line running through that area. In fact, one of the main valve stations sits next door to HOT News. I suggest we feign a major gas leak incident, and blame the whole thing on that. The destruction could easily be explained, and the broadcast would be over permanently."

"What kind of kill zone are we talking about?"

"There's an elementary school and three blocks of homes and businesses that would likely be destroyed. We could affect an evacuation if you think that would be important."

The other end of the line was quiet for a moment.

"Evacuations are costly and slow. We don't have time to waste."

"You're right, of course, sir."

"How soon could you have this done? I don't have time for delays."

"Two hours, tops."

"Ok, get it done."

The phone went dead as Dave slammed it down.

Harry knew the consequences of failure, but he was taking a huge risk. If anyone discovered who was behind the coming events, things would turn ugly.

He went to a safe on the wall behind a picture, and took out a black case. Sitting down, he entered a code into the panel on the front. A low humming sounded as the top of the case slid back and a screen rose from the center. It locked into place while a keyboard extended from inside.

A flashing icon appeared on the screen, indicating the need for a password.

Harry typed in the required information, and pressed enter.

In a moment, another window opened with a line requesting additional clearance before continuing. It included a cryptic warning:

"AUTHORIZED ACCESS REQUIRED."

He typed in: "Atom one."

"ACCESS CONFIRMED"

After a few seconds, a map of the area came on the screen, and he quickly set the coordinates to the studio's location.

He looked at his watch, Ten minutes to nine. Setting the timer for nine, he pressed enter, and a digital clock on the screen began the countdown.

Pushing his chair back from the desk, Harry put his hands behind his head, and relaxed.

In a few minutes, the last few days would all be a distant memory. HOT News would be gone, and everyone else would be moving on.

Harry had discovered the case several years before, hidden behind a secret panel in his house. A long, thin black book explained its purpose, and the code to get into it. Mr. Watters, Iris's father, must have been involved in a secret security force. Harry wasn't sure how it all worked, but he kept it as his ace in the hole, for occasions just like this one.

He was feeling fine now. Just a few more minutes before going into rescue mode, even though there would likely be few left to be saved, including the several hundred children at school this morning.

"Collateral damage," he said out loud. "Not my problem."

Just then, someone knocked on his door.

"Just a minute," he said partially closing the case before getting up.

"Birgit must have stepped out. She knows I need people to be announced first."

He walked across the room, and flipped the lock.

The door flew open into his chest, sending him sprawling to the floor.

"Parks," he exclaimed in shock. "How did you get in here?"

"I thought you might be surprised to see me again," Parks replied coolly, stepping into the room, and shutting the door behind him. "You've been rather busy, haven't you, sending a full squad of Testers and Barron after me. I thought you understood me the last time I was here. I told you to leave me and my family alone."

Harry struggled to his feet, gaining as much distance as possible from him.

"Look, you're the one who killed General Olliver. You committed murder. You became a criminal, and I couldn't let justice be thwarted by anybody, even you."

"Justice? Justice? Who are you trying to kid?" Parks asked, moving closer. "You and Management have been stealing and hurting people in this city for years. You know nothing about justice. I'm sick of it, and I'm sick of you."

Harry glanced quickly at his watch as he slid behind his desk. Two minutes to nine.

"I don't know how you got in here, but you are not getting out unless we can work out an arrangement. Hundreds of my special forces are surrounding this place under instruction to shoot you on sight. I wasn't convinced the Testers or Barron could stop you, so I didn't take any chances. All I need to do is press this button, and you're done. They'll flow in here like raging water and take you out."

Harry reached into his pocket, retrieving a small signaling device with his finger on the button.

"It's not going to matter anyway, Parks," he continued, glancing again at his watch. "Your cousin and his friends at HOT News are about to disappear. In less than one minute, the whole lot of them are going to be blown away, and there's nothing you can do about it. It's over. Just give it up."

To his surprise, Parks seemed to relax a bit.

"I noticed you checking your watch. It wouldn't be because you're waiting for something, would it? It couldn't be a certain missile system operated from this office, could it?"

"What do you know of that? You're just guessing."

"No guess, I assure you, Mr. Allison," he said firmly, leaning over the desk. "I know about the missile system you activated. But you have just one of the controls, and yours is linked to a master console manned by a certain friend of mine with a speech impediment. He may stutter, but he knows his technology, and there's no way you're launching missiles at HOT News or anywhere for that matter."

"How, hhhow do you know all this?" Harry asked.

"It doesn't matter how I know, I just do. This can play out a lot of ways. One way is you can press that button and get your men up here, but I doubt they'll make it before I reach across and cut out your heart. Another way would be to surrender and come clean publicly. Jim is waiting to broadcast again from a new location since your workers are busy trying to break into the old one. One final way is for you to pull the gun you're reaching for under the desk in hopes of shooting me before I can finish you. I've had an interesting couple of days, so why don't you make up your mind, and we can get this done."

Harry swallowed hard as he glanced away from Parks' stare. It was five minutes after nine, and no explosion. He knew Parks was right, and now was not the time to make a challenge.

"It seems you have this all worked out. So where do we go from here? Even if you are able to get me out of the building, there's no way I am going to confess to anything; you know that. It seems we are at a bit of a stalemate. You can't force me to say anything, and I can't get rid of you."

"Wrong!" Parks said pulling Harry out of his seat by his button-down vest, and throwing him across the room.

He tumbled into his bookcase, sending a cascade of books down on his head. Struggling to his feet, he turned as Parks grabbed him again.

"You've hurt enough people long enough," Parks yelled as he threw him to the other end of the room like a rag doll. "Yeah, I may not be able to make you sing, but I can make you wish you had."

Harry hit hard into the side of his desk, cutting his forehead open on the leg. Parks was nearly on him again when he reached under the desk for his gun. Parks lifted Harry by the back of his coat, and tossed him into his bullet-proof window. It was the only thing that saved him from falling to his death. His mind was reeling, but he had his weapon, and turned to shoot, but was too late. Parks had him by the throat again, and easily knocked the gun from his hand.

"You think I'm easy?" Parks growled, pulling Harry close to his face.

His grip tightened around Harry's neck, turning his face red as a tint of blue appeared on his lips. Parks enjoyed squeezing the worthless life from his body as he pinned him tight against the window. In a few moments he would be dead, and Parks felt certain satisfaction by destroying this killer.

By chance, he glanced into the window and saw his own reflection. His eyes were glowing a dark red. Bewildered for a moment, he suddenly recognized the presence of the Zender, the beast. He released his grip instantly, and Harry dropped in an unconscious heap on the floor.

"This isn't me!" he said, stepping away from the window. "Harry may deserve death, but I'm not a killer."

Standing there for a moment, he pulled his mind and emotions back from the darkness. A power had risen inside, trying to dictate his thoughts and actions. Parks disciplined himself to control his emotions in times of stress so he could be rational when others were out of control, but he had nearly lost himself just now in the same way he warned others about. He was stunned by the power of the energy inside.

Checking for a pulse, he made sure Harry was alive before picking him up, and throwing him over his shoulder. He grabbed the case from his desk, and headed for the elevator. The escape from the Citadel went easier than expected as he drove Harry's car through the gate with Harry in the trunk. The blackened windows made it impossible for the guard to know who was at the wheel.

"What are you doing?" Harry said, his arms flailing about. "Put me down. We can still make a deal."

"This is your new home," Parks said, dropping him on the ground in the middle of nowhere.

"It wasn't me," he said, struggling to his feet. "Oh, sure, I knew about the scam going on at the Retraining Facilities, but it was mainly Bert. He set it up, and kept it going. I only covered his tracks if people got too nosy. But if you really want to know the leader of this little play, it was Dave Castle. He's behind everything."

"And why would the President involve himself in something like this?" Parks questioned sarcastically.

"It made money, lots of money, and Dave likes money just like we do. I can get you the evidence, and you can play it anyway you want. What do you say, Parks? Is it a deal?"

"A few hours ago, you were willing to kill hundreds of innocent people, including children, in order to protect yourself, and now you want me to believe some bogus story? I don't think so. The solution is not removing one of you worthless guys, but all of you."

Suddenly, Harry's arm cramped, causing him to double over as pain shot into his chest.

"I noticed your hand looked a little pale. You didn't try to use a certain blade General Olliver took from me and put in Locker 66 did you?"

"So what if I did," he grimaced, holding his limp arm.

"There's a price to pay for using the blades. I tried to warn all of you to be careful with them, and not to use them with malice. I guess you weren't listening."

He slumped to the ground as Parks got back into his car.

"You're not leaving me out here alone, are you?"

"Here you go!" Parks said, tossing a bag with water and some food at his feet. "It's more than you did for those you sent out here, and more than you deserve."

He roared away, watching Harry disappear in the dust. The beast hadn't won that time, but he could still feel an anger burning deep inside. The battle wasn't over.

CHAPTER 35

Jim and Frank cruised through the city in the early morning hours, heading for the country. Jim didn't like leaving his truck behind, but he knew that it was too recognizable. Frank was in the first van, forging on ahead, while he followed in a second one. Jim made a quick detour to pick up Rita, who lived on the South side of the city in one of the many upscale apartment complexes.

"Maybe this is all a big mistake," he said as she settled into the van. "Look at what we have to do. We're running from the city we love to hide out somewhere. It just seems crazy."

Rita's dark eyes flashed in the city lights as they drove along.

"We can't think like that," she replied. "I don't like this anymore than you, but it's not our city anymore, and it hasn't been for a long time. I remember the days when I lived with my parents just outside the limits. We had a beautiful home and acreage. Dad always kept the lawn mowed, and Mom loved to tend the garden and her flowers. It was such a wonderful time."

"Yeah, I suppose you're right," Jim said thoughtfully. "And it's kind of nice to hear you say it."

Jim felt responsible for the recent events. After all, it was his drive to be a news reporter that had had made it necessary for them to run, and he couldn't help feeling bad about it, seeing how others were affected.

"Why did you move to the city, anyway?" He asked. "If you loved country living so much, I mean?"

"Not by choice-that's for sure. My parents owned a peculiar piece of property that fell just outside the city, bordering a sizable stretch of Johnson's river. Back then, there were rumors flying around, claiming my parents were helping resisters by hiding them, and then sending them off on rafts built on the farm."

"Did your parents help resisters escape?"

"Maybe, I don't know. Dad was never one to turn someone in need away, so he could have, but I never saw him do it. Anyway, one day a man showed up with some papers, saying our farm was being impounded. Eminent domain or something they said. Dad told him they had no right, and to get off his land, but the man said they had one week to pack up and leave. We had a family meeting that night, and Dad said I needed to go to my aunt's while they sorted the whole thing out. I protested, but my mother finally convinced me it was for the best. They were to contact me as soon as things were settled."

"Did they call for you?"

"I stayed at my aunt's for three weeks before going home to check on them. I knew something was wrong the minute I pulled in the driveway. The lawn hadn't been mowed, and dad was very particular about his grass. I knocked on the door, and peeked in the windows, but nobody answered. The front door was locked, so I went around back, and let myself in from the porch. The house was cool and quiet, and Dad's shoes were by the door where he always kept them. Mom's "go to meeting" coat was hanging on the rack where she always kept it. Nothing in the house was disturbed. I checked their bedroom. The bed was made, and all their clothes neatly put away. I looked in every room, including the garage and the barn. I looked everywhere, but they were nowhere to be found. It was like they just disappeared."

"Maybe they went into town or something."

"I thought that too, except their car was in the garage, and the keys in the house. I felt sick, but kept thinking they must have gone to a neighbors or something. So I checked with every neighbor and friend they had. No one had seen or heard from them in over two weeks. It just wasn't normal or natural. Dad and Mom were homebodies. They liked hanging out and working on the farm. There's no way they would have just up and left without telling me. I spent the next six months checking every lead or idea I could come up with, but there was no sign of them. I checked the city records, and found ownership of my parent's property had shifted, but the new owner's name was not recorded. Somebody took my parent's land, and I believe they took them too."

Jim kept to the side streets as they made their way along. He was sure they wouldn't be noticed, but he didn't feel comfortable either. They were making good time cruising along through the empty streets, and they were nearly to the east side bridge. Frank had said he would meet them after they crossed on the other side. A large roundabout intersection was the last obstacle, and stood just before the bridge to keep traffic moving into the nearby residential neighborhoods during rush hour.

As he drove into the open, Jim noticed a large truck several hundred yards away on the far side of the roundabout. It appeared to be stopped at first which is unusual for a roundabout, since the whole point is to keep traffic moving. The truck entered the roundabout just as he was arriving. It lumbered around, apparently heading for the bridge, and Jim had little choice but to slow nearly to a stop since the truck had the right of way. The driver made a wide turn because of the trailer he was pulling.

Suddenly, the truck straightened out, and creamed the van broadside.

Shifting down, the driver drove the van sideways through a barbed wire fence, and toward a concrete barrier built to hold back the river at high tide. The roar of the motor blew through the broken window and into Jim's face. Headlights brightly lit the cab, allowing him to see Rita's limp body crushed against the side door post by a large camera box which had broken loose, and slid forward from the impact.

There were mere seconds between them and certain death as the truck continued bulldozing them across the blacktopped parking lot. He released his seat belt, but his left foot was trapped at the ankle between the crushed door and the brake pedal. Pushing with his free leg against the dash, he screamed in pain as the bent pedal dug through his ankle bone. His foot finally came free, and he yanked the box back, releasing Rita.

She had a gash across her scalp, and blood ran down her face, soaking her jet-black hair. He glanced out the side window at the fast approaching concrete wall. The wall was only fifty feet away when Jim pulled her limp body into the rear of the van. Using both feet, in spite of the shooting pain from his ankle, he managed to get Rita positioned by the rear doors the instant before they were smashed into the concrete.

Like a grape squished between two fingers, they shot out the doors onto the blacktop followed by boxes, tapes, speakers, electronic gear, and clothing. Jim held her tight to his chest, cushioning her fall, as he landed on his back, and skidded to a stop nearly sixty feet from the crash site. Jim was conscious and surrounded by debris, but amazingly, not further injured. He knew he wouldn't be able to run on what felt like a broken ankle, and Rita wasn't moving.

His only hope was the river.

The semi backed off the wreckage, and the air brakes sounded as two dark figures climbed down with flashlights. Fortunately, they were thrown far enough not to be immediately spotted.

Pulling his thoughts together, Jim got on one knee, and tested his foot.

A sharp pain shot up his leg, and he crumpled to the pavement in agony.

He felt helpless, but a few choices remained. Face their attackers? In his current condition, he was sure to lose. Then he remembered the river was high from the early spring runoff. Normally, there would be a twenty foot fall to a rocky bank, but instead the fast-moving water was only ten feet below.

Getting to his knees, he pulled Rita's limp body to his chest, and leaned against the three foot wall. Using everything he had, he stood on his good leg just enough to make the top edge. Holding Rita tight in his arms, gravity took over, sending them both tumbling into the frigid water below.

Dark waters engulfed them, and submersed him completely for a few seconds before he pushed to the surface. Jim wasn't a great swimmer, but the adrenaline rush gave him new strength. Fortunately, he still had a grip on Rita's arm, and was able to get her head above water. They were both wearing winter coats zipped tightly around the waist with elastic at the wrists. The jackets provided some buoyancy, and helped momentarily block the chilling effect of the water. He could hear shouting coming from above.

Two flashlights scanned the water, looking for them.

Fortunately, a large log floated by, allowing Jim cover and flotation. He grabbed onto a branch with one hand while holding Rita with the other.

The two men took several shots from guns with silencers at floating debris on the water. Some of them even hit the log Jim was holding, but the swift current moved them out of range, and took them under the bridge. A large, wide, concrete area used as a boat launch stood on the other side of the bridge. The river nearly covered it, but Jim was just able to pull Rita onto the concrete, and out of the water.

The pain in his ankle was gone due to the cold. Even though they had been in less than five minutes, the water had sucked most of their body heat out. Exhausted, he lay back, listening to the semi that had attacked them roar as it crossed over the bridge to the other side. There were other vehicles coming now, and he guessed they didn't want to be seen at the crash site. Even if their attackers thought they survived, he knew the only way down to this dock was from a narrow dirt road several miles away. It would take some time to get there, and it didn't seem like they were that interested. They must have assumed they were dead.

Picking up Rita's hand, he checked her wrist for a pulse. Faint, but there, and he could see her chest rising and falling slightly. The bleeding had stopped, but her hand had a slight tint of blue. He realized he needed to get her out of the cold morning, air and to some medical help as quickly as possible. Taking off his coat, he covered her with it. It wasn't much, but it was something at least.

His ankle throbbed as he stripped off his sweater and undershirt. The cold breeze coming down the river sent shivers up his spine while he ripped his t-shirt into strips. Tightly wrapping his ankle, he hobbled to his feet. He wrung the water from his sweater as best as he could before putting it back on. The sun was beginning to peek over the hill when he spotted a branch large enough to work as a makeshift crutch. He worked his way up the bank through twisted limbs and tangled vines, and managed to make it over a barbed wire fence, and into the ditch along the edge of the road above. From his vantage point, he could see the van in the distance. It was a mess, and would be of no help, even if he could get across the four lanes to the other side.

Crawling through the ditch and up the steep graveled bank to the road, he positioned himself where the morning commuters could see him. Lights were cascading over the bridge as he waved his arms, signaling for help.

Several cars shot by without stopping, but finally a large black SUV with blackened windows slowed, and pulled onto the wide shoulder. He hobbled up to the passenger window, where a slightly built blonde lowered the window.

"Are you alright, sir?" she asked with genuine concern.

"My wife and I were out on our boat early this morning when it overturned." he replied, grabbing the door to steady himself. "She needs medical help. Can you call for me? She's down on the boat dock, unconscious."

The rear door on the SUV opened, and a large man exited, grabbing Jim by the arm, and twisting it behind him.

Jim reacted instinctively, and managed to break away just enough to punch the man in the face with his free hand.

His attacker released his grip, stumbling backward as Jim broke the branch he was using for a crutch over his head. The man hit the ground hard.

"You have beautiful eyes," Jim said, looking into Rita's glowing face.

The moonlight danced across her cheeks as she smiled warmly. He had never felt this way before. He had always known she was pretty, but he had never noticed just how beautiful she was. Like a goddess, with her olive colored skin, big dark eyes, and wonderful smile.

He leaned in to kiss her, but she stepped back suddenly, slapping him hard across the face. Then she slapped him again and again and again.

"Give him a break!" a familiar voice said. "You knocked him out. Give him a moment to come back."

Jim blinked his eyes open. It took a moment to adjust to the brightly-lit room. The woman from the SUV was about to smack him again when Parks spoke.

"You're back," she said with a snarl. "Good, now we can get started."

Jim's head was pounding like a drum. Apparently, she had come around from the driver's side, and hit him with something hard, knocking him unconscious. Then they loaded him in the back, and transported him to—wherever they were. It looked like an interrogation room. His hands and feet were tightly bound to a hard, wooden chair, and he was seated in only his boxers. Looking around in the direction of the familiar voice, he saw Parks in a similar condition.

"Hi, cousin," he said in his normal, unflappable voice. "Having a bad day?"

"Where are we?" Jim replied, shaking his head, and still trying to clear his mind. "And where's Rita? What have you done with Rita?"

Jim shouted, pulling against his bindings.

"Shut up!" the woman said coldly, kicking his broken ankle with her sharp boot.

Pain shot through his leg. Someone had bandaged his ankle, but it was far from better.

"Where's Rita?" He screamed again as he strained against the rope tied around his neck.

She glanced up at a large, dark glass panel on one end of the cinder block room as she leaned back against the metal desk.

"We didn't find her or anyone else where you said," she answered, reaching up to adjust her ear piece. "There was no one there, just your coat. Maybe she slid back into the river and drowned."

He leaned back into the chair, his head dropping slightly.

"You bastards, you killed her. She did nothing to deserve this."

The woman laughed cruelly.

"Ok, enough of this foolishness," the tall young woman continued, stepping behind the desk, and sitting down. "You're going to give us names, addresses, phone numbers--anything we want to know about these resistors."

Jim looked at Parks, who just shrugged his shoulders as she placed a worn, black leather satchel on the desk.

CHAPTER 36

The cell was cold and dark as Parks checked Jim's ankle. It wasn't looking good, and had swollen to the size of a soccer ball. He moaned as Parks elevated his leg. Jim desperately needed medical care, but all Parks could do was try to keep him comfortable. Parks took off his shirt, and covered Jim, as he was shivering from the dankness of the cold cell. The filthy cot provided little comfort, but it was all they had for now.

The woman had shot both of the men full of drugs from her little black bag, hoping to gain quick answers,. but Jim had passed out while Parks pretended to be cooperative. Parks figured they had about four hours before his "leads" were found to be bogus. Drugs were ineffective on him, but they had no way of knowing that. They dumped them both into the cell, thinking they were unconscious. Chances were they would be less "gentle" the next time.

Parks carefully examined his cage. Cinder block walls with a single steel door. A narrow, barred window near the top of the wall allowed a sliver of light through. He could tell by the sounds outside they were in the Citadel's high security area, and he knew this place well. It often held the resisters and other troublemakers. Parks had never realized how dismal this place really was.

"I was doing my duty," he said to himself. "Trying to save the majority, as the City Fathers said. I see now what a mistake that was."

His thoughts trailed off as Jim moaned again. He was finally gaining consciousness.

"Where, where am I?" he asked, not yet fully awake.

"You're with me," Parks answered gently.

Jim winced as he carefully raised himself onto his elbows.

"Where are we?" Jim asked again as he looked in dismay at the swollen appendage on the end of his leg.

"The Citadel," Parks replied, kneeling next to him.

"Wonderful," he moaned, lying back down. "I get how I got here, but what are you doing here? I thought you would be long gone by now."

"I was. I even took Harry with me."

"You kidnapped Harry? That was a ballsy move!"

"It kind of was, wasn't it?" Parks said with a smile. "I even took him out in his own car. He has those guards so well trained, I was able to fly past them wearing one of his coats and hat. They were so busy rushing to get the gate opened, they didn't even look. Little did they know he was in the trunk."

"Then what are you doing here?"

"Harry's car is equipped with a two-way radio. That way, he can communicate with his troops, and monitor them. I heard his daughter, Ivy calling in your capture, so I left him in a safe place, and came back to save you again. Unfortunately, Harry had troops stationed everywhere, and one of them saw me get out of his car once I drove back inside. I guess I'm a little too big to pass for him, and they noticed me. Anyway, I let them capture me. I figured if they had you, they might put us together. It was my only option."

Parks paused for a moment as he adjusted the makeshift pad under Jim's foot.

"Then they dragged me down here, where I found you. I guess that part of my plan worked anyway."

"What about Harry? Did they ask you about him?"

"Funny you should mention that. I get the impression they're not too worried about him. Maybe they think I've killed him, or they're relieved he's gone. His daughter didn't ask a single question about her father. Kind of weird, but they say an apple doesn't fall far from the tree."

Parks got up, and listened at the door. There wasn't anyone on the other side, or he would have heard them breathing. They must have felt comfortable, leaving their cell unguarded. After all, who would expect an escape from the Citadel? Even if they could get out of their cell, they would still need to pass through barred checkpoints with armed guards. Not a good prospect.

"What are we going to do?" Jim asked. "They're never going to let us out of here alive."

"You could be right," Parks replied, still listening at the door. "But who's to say they have a choice?"

"What are you saying?" Jim asked. "You have a plan, don't you?"

Parks stepped away from the door, and turned towards the outside wall. A low hum could be heard coming through the solid block wall. Suddenly, the wall began to change from a dull, concrete grey to a translucent orange. Light flowed into their tiny cell, and a shadowy figure appeared. A tall, red-haired man in his early twenties stepped through the wall into their cell.

"Hi, Mr. Parks," the young man said brightly. "I thought you might need some help."

"Good to see you, Normand," Parks replied as the wall closed behind him. "I see you've discovered one of the unique qualities of that ring I gave you."

"Normand? Who's Normand?" Jim said numbly as he rose up on his elbows.

"Normand is an old friend," Parks said calmly. "We go back quite a few years."

"We'd best be going," Normand said anxiously. "I passed some folks in black SUV's leaving as I was coming this way. They didn't look too happy. You probably had something to do with that."

Parks reached down, and helped Jim sit up.

"Here, you'll be needing this," Normand said handing Parks his coat and leather belt, complete with all his weapons.

"Where did you find these?" Parks asked as he strapped it on.

"Oh, let's just say we have some mutual friends in high places around here."

"Lead the way," Parks said as he picked Jim up in his arms.

Jim couldn't stand, let alone walk. If they didn't get him help soon, he might lose his foot, or worse. Time was of the essence.

Normand pointed the ring on his finger towards the wall. It turned translucent again, and gave off a low hum. Grabbing Parks by the arm, he led their exit into the main courtyard behind a large laundry truck. He carefully checked the area before opening the back, and motioning the men inside.

"I wondered why you were dressed in white," Jim said to Normand as Parks laid him in the back and began to cover him with bags of dirty laundry. "For a minute there, I thought you were an angel or something."

"Not an angel," Normand said humbly, "but hopefully a rescuer, if I can get us out of here before they discover you're gone."

They settled in, and Normand threw the remaining laundry bags over them. He headed across the yard towards the main gate, doing his best to drive nonchalantly.

"Looks like some of those SUVs are heading back in," Normand said through the small opening to the back. "Hey, that looks like your boss, Harry, riding in one of the trucks."

"I can't believe it!" Parks replied. "I should have searched him. He must have had a signaling device hidden somewhere. Well, I doubt he'll be having a good day anyway. He has a lot of explaining to do, and will need to get his arm looked at soon. Without my help, it'll likely need to be amputated."

Normand rolled up, and stopped at the main gate as the guard came out, clipboard in hand.

"Hi, Jason," Normand said, rolling down his window.

"On time as usual, I see," the guard, replied handing him the clipboard and a pen.

The guard walked around the truck, glancing halfheartedly underneath a few times before returning to retrieve his clipboard. "See you tomorrow," he said, waving Normand through.

They were only half a mile away when the sirens sounded behind them.

"That was close," Parks said, breathing a sigh of relief. "They should be putting a lock down in effect about now."

"Our next stop is the hospital," Normand said as they headed across town. "When we pull in the service entrance, you will need to get Jim into one of the laundry carts. There are some clothes in the bag hanging over the door for you. Just keep your hat pulled down, and I'll pass you off as my new helper."

They breezed through the hospital halls, stopping only to pick up laundry along the way. Jim was uncomfortable, and struggled to breathe under bags of dirty laundry, but it was better than the alternative. Normand opened the hall closet, making sure no one was paying attention as Parks lifted Jim out, and into the secret elevator.

"Thanks, Normand," Parks said as the elevator door opened. "I guess this makes us even."

"Even? I don't think so," Normand said with a smile. "I'm only making a down payment."

"Young man," Parks said, with a sense of pride, "you've done well with what I gave you. I trust your seven friends have followed a similar path."

"More than you could know," Normand replied confidently. "We won't let you down."

"I believe that," Parks replied as the door closed.

The doors opened into Dr. Larson's private care facility where she was waiting with a gurney.

"Hi, fellas," Dr. Larson said encouragingly as she wheeled Jim around to the examination room. "What have you been doing? It looks like you tried to pull your foot off."

"Is it going to be ok?" Jim asked nervously.

"You'll be just fine," she said comfortingly, "unless you were thinking of playing golf today. It might take a little longer than that."

She could tell his injury was serious, but she had seen worse.

"How did this all happen?" Jim asked as she set up his IV. "One minute we're escaping town, the next we're in prison, and now here. This is one crazy roller coaster ride."

"You have someone special to thank for it," Dr. Larson replied.

Just then, the door from Dr. Larson's office opened, and in walked Rita.

"Rita!" Jim exclaimed, nearly pulling out his IV as he tried to get off the gurney. "You're alive! Am I ever glad to see you!"

She walked over to help him back into bed. But he hugged her tight when she got close, and kissed her cheek impetuously. She returned the embrace as she eased him down.

"How did you get here?" he asked holding her hand tightly. "They told me you drowned."

"I woke up along the river, and heard you talking to someone above on the road." Rita explained. "I got up just in time to see them stuffing you into their rig. Fortunately, I'm very familiar with that area. My dad used to take me fishing down there when I was a kid. I managed to make it to a friend's house about a half mile away. I hadn't seen her for a long time, and I thought if anyone could help, I knew it would be her."

Dr. Larson medicated Jim, and he began to feel better as the drugs kicked in.

"How did you get her here?" Jim asked, looking at Dr. Larson as the tension slowly drained from his body.

"There are people who aren't sympathetic with the way Management is running things," Dr. Larson said as she adjusted the pillow under his head. "I made a few phone calls, and got things moving. Rita's friends brought her in, and I was able to fix that nasty gash on her forehead. It shouldn't even leave a scar."

258

"Very nice," Parks interrupted. "But there will be plenty of time for explanations later. Right now, we need a plan in case things get ugly."

Parks knew the city would be on lock down, searching every home and business looking for them.

"Della," Parks said gently, pulling her aside while Rita stayed next to Jim, "I thought you were going to your mother's."

"I told you I couldn't leave just yet," Della replied firmly.

"Barron has found out about us," Parks continued. "He knows we're together, and has planned some things that could hurt you. I don't know what they are, but you need to be more careful than ever. I believe I have it under control, but I'm not sure for how long. We need to leave right now. I know where there's a secret escape route that can get us out of the city."

"I'll be extra careful," she replied softly. "But I can't leave now. There are too many people counting on me, and you just brought one more. It's really up to you, Henry, how things go. I'm counting on you."

He knew Della was telling the truth, but he hated the thought of leaving her to deal with Management. Even worse, if Barron knew about their relationship, it could be that he wasn't the only one. It plagued his mind.

"How did Bruce make out?" Parks asked, remembering the last time he had been in this room.

"Recovered faster than expected," Della responded, "and then Bruce and Mary both left with David."

"I'm glad to hear he's doing ok," Parks said. "So there's no way you would consider leaving with me?"

Parks already knew the answer as he gave Della a loving hug and kiss before leaving. He had to get back to the Island, and talk with Sterling to see if he could understand more of what all this was about. He got a ride from Normand, and picked up Jim's truck, which was hidden behind Rita's apartment building. It was a mess, and the door nearly fell off as he opened it, but it started without hesitation. He hated leaving Della alone, but she promised to be extra careful, and remain in her special, hidden office as much as possible. When she wasn't there, she agreed to stay with her best friend Darla, and wasn't to return to her apartment for any reason. It was the best he could do.

Meanwhile, on the other side of the city, Kirsten was meeting with Normand and the rest of the young resisters in their barn hideout. They discussed recent developments, and tried to understand why people were searching for objects that seemed linked to an ancient, possibly mythical world. She had also been training them, teaching them now to use the blades she had made from the meteorite. She was determined they would win the coming battle.

Management, on the other hand, had suffered a serious blow. Jim's broadcast had the city in turmoil, and people were angry, to say the least. But there was more to do if they were to reclaim their city-- much more. The battle for the future was beginning, and the next generation was preparing.

They would need the ancient teachings, special understanding, and unique information from Parks's book if they were going to save themselves, let alone their city, from Management's clutches. But that wasn't even the half of it. Behind the unfolding events lurked a dark power, and the energy of the Zender…